Courting Anna

By Cate Simon

Courting Anna

Cover Design Livia Reasoner

Prairie Rose Publications

www.prairierosepublications.com

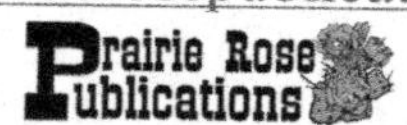

ISBN: 9781081299880

This is a work of fiction. The characters, incidents, and dialogues are products of the author's imagination and are not to be construed as real.

Acknowledgements

There are three people without whom this book would not exist: Wilkie Collins, Arabella Mansfield, and C. A. Asbrey.

Wilkie Collins, because when I was delving into his 1875 novel *The Law and the Lady* in grad school, I started wondering when women could become lawyers – not until the early 20th century in Great Britain, where his book takes place, but much earlier in the United States.

Arabella (Belle) Mansfield, for becoming that first "lady lawyer" when she was admitted to the bar in Iowa in 1869. The Equity Club, the corresponding society of women lawyers that Jonathan mentions in the book, was real. There were 100 members in 1880, which grew to 200 by 1890.

C. A. Asbrey, for introducing me to Prairie Rose and the Women of Destiny series, and for support and encouragement above and beyond. If you haven't read her *The Innocents* mystery series, featuring a female Pinkerton, you should rectify that immediately.

Gill Adams came up with the tagline; Livia Reasoner created a cover so striking that I haven't been able to stop showing it to people ever since she sent the file.

And always, Marty, who likes the idea of being married to a writer, and therefore puts up with a lot.

Chapter 1

It was the middle of the afternoon, that dry, sunny day in Carter's Creek, Montana, when Nicholas Powell, Anna's esteemed opponent in just about everything, stopped by her office to offer her a case.

When Nick did that, she was fully aware that meant it was a case he didn't want himself. After all, they were the only lawyers in town.

"Two boys locked up down at the sheriff's office, name of Jeremiah Brown and Edward Marcus," he said. "Bounty hunter brought 'em in, claims they're actually a notorious pair of outlaws called Tommy Slade and Johnny Nevada, worth five thousand dollars apiece. They deny it, and they're demandin' to see an attorney."

"Why aren't you representing them?" she asked, suspicious about the reasons behind this sudden generosity. She'd heard of Nevada and Slade, but not a thing about them, recently.

"Didn't really see eye to eye with 'em. Besides," he grinned complacently, "I think there's a good chance that they really are worth the ten grand, and I thought I might like to represent the bounty hunter, instead." That smile on his broad, red face showed just how pleased he was with the prospect. Nick was an honest man—honest about his greed, anyway. And he knew that he was attorney of choice for a certain type of client. The kind that paid the best. The type of folks that Anna preferred to represent tended to gravitate towards her, anyway. Unfortunately, sometimes two money hungry cattle barons came to blows, but their generous fees made up for some of the folks she was eager to represent who couldn't afford to pay her regular rates.

And then there was Sheriff Delevan. Even though he'd respected her father, he somehow just couldn't see her in the old man's shoes.

"So you told them I was coming?"

"I told 'em Lawyer Harrison would be in to see 'em, that's all."

She gave him one of her patented *"Now, Nick, really"* looks, but then they both smiled. So, with a few words to her clerk, she slipped on her coat and hat, and headed on down to the sheriff's.

• ❤ •

There were two of them, like he said, one Mister Jeremiah Brown and one Mister Edward Marcus, a dark-haired man and a blond, both about thirty, both lean and handsome, and both with that look that spoke of having ridden many miles and seen a lot. That could make them outlaws, or it could just mean they were restless drifters, like they'd claimed to Nick they were.

"Someone here to see you boys," said the deputy, clearly relishing the fact that he was in on something.

The men both smiled, through the bars of the sheriff's lockup. The blond one had an open, friendly look, and a classically handsome face, but the dark-haired one, Jeremiah Brown, lit up the room with that broad smile of his. "Well, hello, ma'am," he said. "It's nice of you to come and call. But we were expecting..."

"You were expecting a lawyer named Harrison, weren't

you? Well, that's me, Anna Harrison."

Their smiles faded quickly. They thought it was a joke on them. She was used to it—most everyone who wasn't from around those parts thought the same. That was the other reason the sheriff always called Nick in first.

"No rule against it in this territory. My father was a lawyer before me, and he didn't have any sons to clerk for him, so I'm carrying on the family profession." She crossed her arms and looked squarely at them, the way she'd learned to do when anybody expected her to simper and blush. "Ask anyone around here...right, Deke?" She glanced at the deputy, who winked at her.

"Right," he said. "And she's a fine lawyer, too." Deke was young, and none too clever, but he always took her side.

"Besides," she added, "Nick Powell doesn't want the case, so it's me or no one. Your pick."

The two men glanced at each other for a moment, and then Mr. Brown spoke. "You'll do for us just fine, ma'am. We apologize, it's just that—"

She waved her hand so he'd know he didn't have to say the rest. It got pretty tedious hearing it, she thought. Lady lawyer, indeed. When was the last time anyone said anything about a "man lawyer"? To mark her professional status, she wore a neat-fitting black jacket over her shirtwaist, and sometimes a little silk tie. Of course, that was hardly unusual day dress for the ladies in town. It was mostly her big leather satchel full of legal papers which set her apart. "So, tell me about your situation."

Brown looked a little uncomfortable.

"Shall I come in and sit down?" She signaled to Deke, who unlocked the door and let her inside the cage. "You gentlemen aren't going to bolt on me, are you?"

"Why, no, ma'am," said Mr. Marcus, who was clearly very polite. Whether he was an outlaw was, of course, another story.

"All right, then, why don't you begin?" She seated herself and took out her notebook.

Brown began the story. "Well, you see, ma'am, we bear this unfortunate resemblance to a pair of notorious outlaws—superficial resemblance, of course."

"Of course," she nodded, keeping her tone of voice deliberately non-commital.

He went on. "Tommy Slade and Johnny Nevada. Why, we saw 'em once, and we don't look anything like them. But if you take a look at those wanted posters over there, you can see the reason for the confusion."

She nodded to Deke, who took down the two posters and brought them over to her. "Hmm, Tommy Slade, age 30, dark brown hair, I guess that one would be you. Six feet tall...surely a shade under that." She was tall for a woman, and as she'd walked into the cell, she'd noticed that the man standing in front of her wasn't more than an inch or so taller than she was. Though he was handsome and still youthful-looking, there was something in his eyes that suggested he'd seen a great deal more than most folks would have in thirty years. Maybe in a hundred. It was almost unsettling, so she looked away and continued to read. "But the rest of this sounds about right, though the description is a little vague. No sketch, no photo. And Mr. Marcus does fit the description of Johnny Nevada to perfection—what there is of it. So that's what you're claiming? A case of mistaken identity? We should be able to clear that up easily enough, if there's anyone local who can vouch for you."

Jeremiah Brown shook his head ruefully. "No, ma'am,

there's not. We were coming through town on the way back from a courier run." He looked thoughtful for a moment. "Like you pointed out, those descriptions are pretty vague. Why is everyone so anxious to believe a bounty hunter, anyway? It's not exactly the most honorable profession, is it?"

"No," she said, "but Nick Powell is convinced that Mr. Larkin is telling the truth."

"Larkin?" asked Brown. "Fred Larkin?"

She nodded.

"No wonder he wouldn't tell us his name. He said just to call him John." He shot Marcus a look she'd have almost described as triumphant. "Deadeye Fred Larkin, huh? He's a notorious liar. Even me and my friend have heard about him, honest citizens that we are. Well, ma'am, like I was saying, we're not known locally, but if you wire Sheriff Leon Anderson in Simpson Pass, why, he'd be happy to tell you who we are. He's known us for a long time, and he arranged this courier job for us."

"Don't know if that'll be enough for the judge. How would we know this Sheriff Anderson is for real?"

"Well, you could check him out first, if you like. We're not going anywhere," said Brown.

"Guess we could, at that." She turned to the blond man. "Don't you ever talk?"

"When I've a mind to," Marcus replied. "But Jeremiah, here, is better at lawyers and stuff than me."

"Ah. More the litigious sort." She noticed that Brown smiled at that, but Marcus looked puzzled. Perhaps he didn't know what the word meant. Maybe that was one of the reasons that Brown did most of the talking. "We'll see about getting bail set. How much money do you two have?"

They conferred for a moment, and Marcus spoke up,

clearly nettled by her earlier comment. "About sixty-five dollars between us."

"Well, that doesn't look too good, set up against a ten thousand-dollar reward, but let me see Judge Clayton and I'll see what I can do."

And with that she rose, shook both their hands, and signaled for Deke to let her out of the cell.

It was evening by the time she returned, and Deke had been replaced as deputy on duty by Karl Rasmussen, a taciturn Swede who was so big and so quiet that many around town found him intimidating. She knew him as a gentle soul who sang in the choir at church on Sundays. Most men would take a lot of grief about something like that, but not Karl. He scared too many folks. He had a beautiful deep voice, though, and brought tears to nearly everybody's eyes when he sang "Amazing Grace."

"Hello, Karl," she said. "I'd like to see my clients."

He nodded. This time, she just walked up to the bars, since she wasn't staying long.

"You on a first-name basis with every deputy in town, Miss Harrison?" asked Marcus, by way of greeting.

"It's a small town and there aren't too many deputies," she responded.

"Lots of towns we been through are even smaller. Only one lawyer instead of two."

"One lawyer will starve. Two lawyers make work for each other. It's the logic of the business." She mentally filed away the fact that they'd done an attorney count on small towns, for whatever that was worth. "I'll give you the bad news first. Judge Clayton just doesn't see his way clear to that bail. I'm afraid Nick Powell was a little too persuasive about protecting his client's property rights to the bounty on you two, if you should really turn out to be who he says you are."

"And there's good news?" asked Brown, with just the slightest undertone of sarcasm.

"He's wired the U.S. Marshal's Office, and they've confirmed that Leon Anderson is indeed the sheriff of a town called Simpson Pass."

"Did you say why?" Brown looked worried, which showed in his dark eyes, and in a certain tension between his eyebrows. Another fact she filed away.

"Not at all. Just that we thought we might have a transaction with him soon, and we wanted to be extra cautious. Judge Clayton isn't known for his trusting nature." She thought that she'd like it just a little bit better if he didn't trust Nick Powell so readily. "We've got a wire in to Simpson Pass, so it's pretty much a matter of hearing back from Sheriff Anderson."

"So all we have to do is wait for the telegram, and this Fred Larkin can't do anything with us until the judge says so?"

"That's about the size of it. Have a pleasant night. I'm sorry you have to spend it here."

"So am I, Miss Harrison," said Brown, and there was something in his eyes that she wished she hadn't seen, especially not in a client, and an alleged outlaw at that. Nonsense, Anna Harrison, she thought to herself, there's no one so unsusceptible to men as you. Not since David died.

She'd have preferred it if it was her brilliant legal mind that got Brown and Marcus sprung from jail the next day, but it wasn't. Not on this occasion, anyway, although it was just one chapter in her ongoing battle with Nick. What happened was that Sheriff Anderson got back to them, and confirmed the identity of Mr. Jeremiah Brown and Mr. Edward Marcus, and the bounty hunter rode out of town muttering things not fit for a lady to hear. He didn't even pay Nick's bill.

"I don't feel right charging for such easy work," she said to her clients, when she went to give them the good news. "I'm quite busy at the moment, and from the look of you two, I'm afraid you may be finding times a little bit lean."

"Ma'am," began Marcus, but Brown interrupted him.

"We wouldn't feel right not paying you. Admittedly, we're not especially flush at the moment, but," he looked back at his partner, "maybe we could take you out to dinner tonight?"

"Only if it's in place of my fee."

The two men looked at each other, then back at her. "If you insist," said Brown.

"If you're sure that's all right by you, Miss Harrison," added Marcus.

"Call for me at my office, at about seven this evening. Anyone in town can tell you where that is."

She hurried home to clean up and put on her nicest dress, laughing at herself all the while. The dress showed off her slender, graceful figure to its best advantage, and she did her hair up the softer, more flattering way that she saved for holidays and special occasions. She wasn't much used to worrying about whether she looked pretty, anymore, but when she looked in the mirror, she was pleased. The blue dress brought out the blue in her eyes, and made a nice contrast with her light blonde hair. She examined her features critically, trying to pretend she was a stranger, and she decided they'd do. People still called her pretty, although usually in sentences that had a "but" in them, as in, "Anna Harrison is still an attractive woman, but—"

How absurd, she thought, making such a fuss over a pair of drifters, but after all, she had the reputation of lady lawyers to uphold. Especially since there weren't that many of them to begin with. Regretfully, she considered those aristocratic English ladies in books, with their lady's maids who specialized in taking care of their clothes and hair. She lived alone except for her ward Sarah, an orphan she'd taken in. Sarah had an eye for that sort of thing, but she was spending the night with a friend who was celebrating her eighteenth birthday, at her home on a ranch some ways outside of town.

When the drifters finally arrived, she was pleased to see that they had cleaned up nicely. They must have had room for suits somewhere in their saddlebags, as they wouldn't have had time to get Burt, the only tailor in town, to fit them up. The bounty hunter had already ridden off on his way, disgruntled, so nobody much except the parties directly involved even knew who they were. They looked like perfectly respectable gentleman dinner companions, and certainly handsomer than most of the men in town. Besides, everyone in town knew all about Anna Harrison, and how she'd turned down every man who'd come courting since her fiancé died, some years ago, now. How, when she was seen out in public with a man, it was inevitably on business. She couldn't create a scandal if she'd wanted to. She and young Jonathan, her law clerk, spent hours in the office alone together, and nobody thought a thing of it, even though her rooms were right upstairs.

The dining room at the Grand Central Hotel not only served the best food in town, but was also the only place in Carter's Creek where a respectable lady could dine in public. The cook there was quite good—he called himself a chef—and his idea of fancy food ran to more things than just steak and potatoes. There was even some good wine in stock—sometimes they ran out, since supplies like that didn't come through town too often—and they shared a bottle between them.

As for the company, it had been a long time since she'd enjoyed herself so much. They told her tales about their wandering through the West, and she told them courtroom stories, and the evening passed more quickly than she'd thought time could out there in Carter's Creek.

"Don't forget the time when we agreed to transport that load of dynamite up to that mine in the mountains." Marcus's blue eyes twinkled.

"*You* agreed. That one wasn't on me..." Brown turned to her, with that easy smile, the one she couldn't help returning. "If I'd been involved in the decision-making, I'd have reminded you how rough the roads were."

"Well, we didn't blow ourselves up, anyway."

"Not that time," his companion agreed.

At first, it seemed like they were competing for her attention; Marcus was no longer the silent one, as he'd been in the sheriff's lockup, but joked and laughed easily with his friend. But as the evening wore on, he seemed to ease back, letting Brown take the lead.

The dark-eyed drifter, on the other hand, was quite possibly the most charming man she'd ever met. *So this was flirtation done correctly,* she thought. She and David had never needed to flirt—they'd both just known, very soon after they'd met, that they'd be spending the rest of their lives together. What they hadn't known was how short his life would be. A number of men since then had attempted to court her, but none of them had captured her interest. Certainly not enough for her to want to give up what they expected of her.

They'd all thought, every one of them, that she was just waiting for a man to come along to rescue her, and that she'd give up her independence and her hard-won profession. And that would never do. David had been her first and only true love, with all the heart-flutterings that a nineteen-year-old girl could expect to feel, but David had also genuinely delighted in the idea that she'd be practicing law at his side. The two most important men in her life, her fiancé and her father, had understood her completely. One had been gone for eight years, and the other, the elder, for almost three. Now, here she was, all on her own, but for her ward and her law clerk.

While Marcus seemed happy with the give-and-take of the conversation, Brown actively tried to draw her out about her professional life. "You said you joined your father in his practice, so that must have eased the way for you, but still there have to have been a lot of clients who reacted the way that we did at first." If she wasn't mistaken, that was a look of sympathy he was giving her. Maybe even understanding.

It felt a little awkward, discussing her personal and professional history with complete strangers. "The locals got used to the idea quickly—even as a little girl, I hung around my father's office rather than my mother's kitchen. After the third time I accidentally set something on fire, Mother and I agreed that it was safer that way." They all laughed. "But yes, when we've got outsiders coming in, railroad right-of-way cases, things like that, there's a certain surprise, even disbelief. Since Father's passed on, I'd have to say my business has declined a little." She took another sip of her wine. "Of course, what with there only being Nick and me, in the end, they tend to come around."

Brown smiled, that broad, easy smile. "You two have quite the rivalry going, don't you?"

"We have our version of a good time together. I enjoy the challenge, and we're pretty evenly matched." She launched into tales of a few of their most memorable battles. Most men, in her experience, weren't really all that interested in what women had to say, but that wasn't the case, here. Brown and Marcus both listened attentively, laughed genuinely, and asked questions that made her feel that her stories had actually interested them. But Brown's gaze on her remained the more intent.

There was one moment where Marcus slipped, and referred to his friend as Tom, then went on as if he'd meant to say, "...Tomorrow, Jeremiah, we need to get going early, if we're going to make it to Helena before nightfall." But she'd suspected it, and the answers she'd received from Sheriff Anderson had put her mind at ease. Whatever they'd been once, they were law-abiding citizens now.

Besides, if Nick had taken the case, she wouldn't have been sitting at dinner with two of the handsomest strangers to pass this way since the town was first settled.

They'd finished their meal, and the wine was gone, and she thought with surprising regret that this was no doubt the end of their acquaintance. As they rose from the table, Jeremiah Brown offered to see her home, while Edward Marcus excused himself by saying something about a poker game. Brown smiled that lopsided smile, which gave her a funny feeling that ran right down her insides—the way she hadn't felt since David used to smile at her.

Chapter 2

Jeremiah Brown gave her his arm as they strolled down the main street, for the all-too-regrettably short walk home. In her high-heeled boots, they were much of a height, and she found she liked that. The only man she walked around town with on a regular basis, these days, was her clerk Jonathan, who was considerably over six feet tall. She liked looking Jeremiah Brown straight in the eye, those large, liquid brown eyes.

"Here," she said. "Remember?" She wished her building to the far side of town, so the walk could continue, but disobligingly, it stayed right where it was.

"You live above your office?" He looked surprised.

"Not in a boarding house, or with a respectable old lady somewhere?" She winked at him. "It's just that I own the building, you see, and it would be silly not to take advantage of the rooms upstairs. Anyhow, my ward lives with me, so I'm not all alone, and it's right in the center of town, so we're perfectly safe."

"It's just not the usual thing," he said.

"*I'm* just not the usual thing, either," she shook her head. "As you might have noticed. My sister wants me to move out to her husband's ranch, but it's too far from town for me to get to the office when the roads get bad in winter. Besides, she'd keep wanting me to help her mind her children every time I turned around. Here, I'm not so far from the sheriff, or the hotel, or lots of other places where there are plenty of people." She found that she didn't want to tell him about the other reason, about her ironclad respectability, about how her mourning for David had carried on for years and years until everybody practically forgot Anna Harrison was still an attractive woman and figured no man would come near her anyhow because none of them had a chance.

She didn't want to tell him that because she found, absurdly, that she was hoping he would kiss her. And, suddenly, he did. Kissed her gently, and pulled away, looking at her to see if she wanted him to continue. She supposed that he could tell by the look in her eyes, and her suddenly heavy, shallow breathing, that she wanted it as much as he did, because he leaned in and kissed her again, harder this time. And this time, she kissed back.

But not for long. "Why don't you step in for a moment," she said. "It's chilly out here, and this isn't going to do my reputation any good."

"What about your ward?" he asked. "If she's just upstairs, won't we disturb her?"

She blushed a little, and wondered if he could tell, in the darkness. "She's staying with a school friend tonight. A birthday celebration, for a friend who lives a little way out of town, and we thought it would be safer for her to ride home in the daytime, tomorrow."

She unlocked the door and they stepped inside. They found themselves in a large, open room. The walls were lined with bookshelves, a filing cabinet, and a safe. Her desk and Jonathan's, as well as a large conference table, were covered in books and papers. There was a Turkish patterned rug that covered most of the floor, and a few photographs here and there—her late parents, David, Jonathan's sweetheart

Melanie. She felt like she should turn David's picture to face the wall before she kissed this man again, but she didn't.

Brown looked at her curiously, as though he weren't sure what to expect. She was a proper lady, despite her unusual profession, and she imagined that all he'd intended was a goodnight kiss. Even that was a bit forward, with a woman like her, but it had been such a pleasant evening, and perhaps that was the reason that he couldn't resist. And here they were, the two of them all alone in her home.

Taking his hand, she led him through the office, to the back staircase and up the stairs into her parlor. Her fingers were tingling all the while.

They'd barely entered the room when he kissed her again, more deeply than before. And now, the kisses were openmouthed, and they stood pressed close together, their tongues playing as well as their lips, and she felt as though that part of her was alive again, as though it hadn't been eight years since…

He pulled back—they both caught their breath—and they stood there, looking at each other. The dark suit fit him well, and she was intensely aware of the lean, powerful form underneath. The planes of his face were sharply defined, intriguing, framed by hair in sore need of a trim. The expression in his dark brown eyes was one of mingled delight and sadness. Whoever he was, she thought, he was a lot more complicated than he liked people to know.

"You've already told me how you got to be a lawyer," he said, "and a damned good one, at that. But I am going to ask what a beautiful woman like you is doing living here all alone?"

She took a deep breath. "I was engaged to be married, once. David Callaghan was his name, and he was my father's law clerk. Once he was admitted to the Bar, we were going to get married. I was twenty then. But when he went down to the capitol to get sworn in, he got caught in a snowstorm. He came down with a bad case of pneumonia, and he died, just two weeks before the wedding was supposed to be."

"So instead of marrying your father's law clerk, you took his role yourself?"

"That had always been our plan, once David joined Father as a partner. And after he died, well, I didn't want anyone else, and neither did Father, and as I told you, there's no law against it in this territory. But folks didn't need to know that."

"I see," he said. "You ended up with a romantic story, instead of a husband."

"I was sacrificing my youth, and what everyone saw as a young woman's only chance at happiness, to honoring David's memory. It was a lot easier for folks to understand than that I'd been planning to grow up and do what Daddy did ever since I was a little girl."

"And since then?"

"Folks around here see me as carrying on for David's sake. And for Father's, too, since he's been gone. No man in these parts has thought he could compete with that. Or, honestly, some did, but I let them down gently–or otherwise, if they were too persistent. I've found that I like it on my own." She smiled, and this time she did blush. "But you're the most interesting man I've met in a long time."

Jeremiah took a deep breath. "I'm going to be leaving town tomorrow."

"I know. If you weren't, we wouldn't be here right now."

He raised an eyebrow.

She looked away in embarrassment. "I like you. I've enjoyed spending time with you over these past few days, more than you can imagine. But you're not the kind to settle down, and that makes you perfect. Because it's been eight years since David's been gone, and I've come to like it on my own, but I very much want to feel something again. Just for one night." She met his eyes, finally. "I gave Sarah permission to stay at her friend's house tonight a week ago, before you and I had ever met, long before I knew this would be your last night in town. It feels as though the Fates are telling me to take this chance. If you feel the same way, of course."

"And you're not a—"

"Maiden lady? Not quite." She looked away again. "A few months before the wedding was to be, we were working late one night, and Father'd gone home. We were young and in love, and it hardly seemed to matter. After that, we came up with excuses to work late as often as we could. But then, unexpectedly, he was gone. There hasn't been anyone else, since–I haven't wanted anyone. But you won't expect anything from me that I can't promise."

"I understand," he said softly, and he looked at her for a moment with those sad, joyful eyes, and then he took her in his arms again, and kissed her, deeply. And she kissed him back, with all the fervor that went along with the fact that she knew he was going away tomorrow and she'd never see him again.

After awhile, his mouth uncovered hers, and he began showering kisses on her forehead, her temple, her cheekbone, her jawline, her neck. The pretty blue dress she was wearing had an open neckline, and she felt his kisses trailing down her neck, to her collarbone, while one of his hands had come up to cup her breast. As his mouth went lower, she reached back to unfasten the bodice of her dress, and soon he was assisting her, unbuttoning it and pulling it down, helping her slip her arms out so that as the top of her dress fell down to her waist, she was clad above in only her camisole and her corset.

"You're so lovely," he said softly, his mouth moving to her bare shoulder for a kiss before she took his hand again and led him into the bedroom.

He reached up and unloosed her fair hair, and it tumbled down around her shoulders and down her back, as he stroked it gently. "You are certainly the prettiest lawyer it has ever been my privilege to meet," he said, his deep voice husky.

"I'm going to guess that I'm the only pretty lawyer it has ever been your privilege to meet," she pointed out. "I'm glad. It means you'll remember me."

He pulled away for a moment. "I would remember you no matter what. I've said to women before, if only things were different, if only I could stay, because I knew it's what they wanted to hear. But you, I've never met anyone like you, Anna. When I say that wish I could stay and get to know you, I mean it." He pulled her to him, tightly, and they held each other for a moment, feeling each other's breathing.

"I would have liked that," she said softly. "And that's not something I thought I'd ever want again."

And then, they undressed one another. The feel of flesh against flesh was a luxury she'd never known. David and she had had to be so quick and careful, and those final delights had been reserved for the wedding night that never came. She and Jeremiah kissed again, pressed close together, and then they toppled together onto what was usually her cold, lonely bed.

"Jeremiah," she whispered, when they'd exhausted themselves with their lovemaking. "Stay tonight. You can leave just before dawn." In answer, he kissed her again, gently this time, and drew her close to him, so that she lay with her head on his chest. She fell asleep for a little while, but woke up again, suddenly, frightened by the thought that she was wasting any of this precious night.

She felt his fingers stroking her hair, and she looked up to see that his eyes were wide open. He smiled when he saw that she was awake, and she pulled herself up even to his face. "What are you thinking?" he asked.

"How happy I am at this moment. How I wish time could just stop here, now."

He smiled in answer, that smile that could light up a whole town the size of Carter's Creek. "Maybe it's because it's just this night that it's so perfect. But I can't help but feel it, too." He ran his hand against her shoulder, her arm, her breasts.

Whatever he'd slicked his dark hair back with had worn off by now, because it was soft and fell forward again and she touched it and it felt as good as she'd imagined back there as she talked to him through the bars. "I have to ask you this, Jeremiah. What's your real name? Mr. Marcus started to call you by another name in the restaurant tonight. He covered it pretty well, but—"

He stiffened and pulled away from her. He'd been seduced and betrayed in the past, clearly, and he thought that's what she was doing. "There's a little thing called attorney-client privilege," she said. "I couldn't tell, even if I wanted to."

He laughed, then, long and hard and loud enough that she began to wonder if maybe the neighbors would hear and scandal could touch her, after all. Finally, when he was completely winded, he stopped and he said, "Anna, you really are one of a kind. I never thought I'd have a woman talk about attorney-client privilege in bed with me. Jeremiah Brown is my real name, and always has been. But when Edward and me crossed over to the wrong side of the law, we were still in our teens. We thought it might be a good idea to call ourselves something else, just in case we ever wanted to slip back into anonymity. And we were so young and naïve, we chose outlaw names straight out of dime novels. Yes, I was known as Tommy Slade. Ed's so used to calling me that, sometimes he forgets it's not my real name."

He told her the story of how he and his partner had been trying to get themselves right with the law for the past three years, staying honest and riding out the statute of limitations on the crimes they'd committed in several territories. The only problem was, though neither had broken the law in all that time, there was still a sizable reward on their heads. For the first couple of years, they'd worked on a friend's ranch in Texas. But he'd died suddenly, in his sleep, and his heirs, a couple of nephews back East, had sold the place. So for the past year, they'd kept on the move, hoping to keep their identities secret and bounty hunters off their trail. They normally stayed south of these parts, sticking to areas where they'd never committed a crime. But personal business had brought them north for a time.

"And this sheriff, Leon Anderson, has been helping you?"

"As much as he can. He has a past on the other side of the law, too, but long enough ago that these things were easier then. He sympathizes with us, helps us find jobs that keep us moving around, and he's got the ear of the governor of Dakota Territory, who's been willing to look leniently on us in exchange for some favors. We used to ride in the Black Hills, for awhile."

"I hope one of those jurisdictions wasn't Wyoming. You know there's no statute of limitations there, right?"

He winked at her. "No statute, and enough outlaws of its own. We read enough dime novels, as kids, to know to steer clear of Wyoming."

"So they do have some educational value, after all." She laughed. "Just one more question, then. Why did it make such a difference when you found out who it was who'd brought you in?"

"Lying for us was never part of the deal with Leon; he has to tread a very fine line where we're concerned. But I knew he'd had some troubles of his own in times past with Fred Larkin. I knew, under those circumstances, he'd want to take our part." He reached over and touched the side of her face. "You can't tell anyone about that. We don't want to get Leon in trouble for helping us out."

"My lips are sealed."

"Your lips are…wonderful," he said, and then he was kissing her again and it seemed as though time did stop because they touched each other a thousand different ways in a thousand different places, until finally dawn began to break, and it was time for him to go.

"I know we said just this night," he said, as she sat there in her dressing gown and watched him pull on his boots. "But I find myself wishing. If I was still an outlaw, I could rob a bank and take you away with me to South America. And if my record was clear, I could stay here with you. But as things stand, I've got to be moving along."

"We both knew that when I asked you in," she said. "Anyway, I studied French and Latin, not Spanish, so I wouldn't be much use in South America. Maybe someday you'll be back this way, and maybe I'll never see you again. But tonight, I got back a part of me that I thought was long gone." She looked at him, fearing that she'd already said too much. "Thank you for that."

His brown eyes were serious. "I'm sorry that I have to go."

It was dawn already, lighter than they'd anticipated. "Now, is there a back way out of this place?"

And she showed him, and he held her close one last time, and then, he was gone.

Chapter 3

It was supposed to be an easy job—they'd agreed on that. All they had to do was to haul some old furniture from a New Mexico ranch that was still a three-hour ride from the nearest railway spur that would take them to Albuquerque, load it onto the train, and ride with it, changing trains several times in Colorado and Utah. The final leg of the trip ran from Salt Lake City, Utah to Townsend, Montana, in the general direction of Billings.

Then, they had to buy themselves another horse cart, load the furniture on it again, and take it to a small town called Greenville, about four hours away. The railroad was supposed to be making its way toward Greenville from the nearest town in the other direction, and a telegraph line had already been laid, but for purposes of the current delivery, Greenville might as well be a wilderness. Still, what could be easier than delivering a wagonload of what amounted to fancy household goods?

"Jeremiah, I'm beginning to think that nothing we do is ever gonna be easy." Ed Marcus couldn't quite repress a sigh. "First, we lose the shipping papers, and the railroad doesn't want to give us the furniture. Then, we telegraph down to New Mexico, clear things up, and it's a whole two days before we can find a cart to hire. And now, we're driving through country that looks just like outlaw country to me. The only bright side I can see is that nobody's gonna want a bunch of old furniture, and we don't have any money left for anyone to steal."

"But when we make the delivery, we'll be paid a thousand dollars each, plus expenses," Jeremiah Brown reminded him, his grin lighting up his face. "And they call them *antiques*." He quickly returned his gaze to the road in front of them, as he tightened the reins on the team of horses.

"Call what?"

"The old furniture. Mr. Roberts that hired us told us this furniture is older than the United States itself, remember? Apparently, it has some considerable value—he said that when Mr. Fitzgerald was down there in the New Mexico Territory last winter, he made him an offer that was too good to pass up. "

The two men rode in silence for awhile, along the plain that was shadowed by mountain ranges on either side.

"You're right about one thing, though," Brown said, suddenly. "This sure looks like outlaw country. Were we ever here when we were outlawing?"

"Nah," said Ed. "I think I'd remember mountains like these." He turned his gaze on the towering bare peaks that surrounded them, squinting a little against the brightness of the day. And those were only the foothills. The mountains themselves were blue in the distance, on both sides. "Thought we were trying to steer clear of Montana, anyway, 'til the statute's run, at least. When was the last time we were up this way? Must've been eight, nine months ago. Remember? That bounty hunter tried to turn us in, and the lady lawyer got us off. She sure was a nice lady, wasn't she?"

Jeremiah was silent, and when Ed turned to look at him, his dark eyes were fixed on the horizon.

"Jer? Didn't you think so?"

"Oh...yeah...real nice. Good at her job, too." He fell silent again, tugging the reins slightly.

Ed waited for a moment, and began again. "You know, you never did tell me if anything happened between you and her that night. I left you to walk her home, and you never showed up at the saloon. And I got back pretty late, and you still weren't there. But when I woke up that morning, there you were, all tucked in and sound asleep." Seeing there was still no response, he tried again, in his best wheedling tone. "Come on, you always tell me about that stuff."

"Yeah, Ed, but you don't always tell me."

"Not about the ones that are special—" Marcus broke off. "You really liked her, didn't you? That doesn't have anything to do with us accepting this job, does it?"

Brown laughed. "Maybe just a little. Then again, the fact that it pays pretty good for honest work had something to do with it, too. I don't recall you raising any objections to a couple of thousand dollars between us. Anyway, this is a completely different part of the territory. Let's make the delivery first, and we can think about where we head next afterwards."

"I don't want to stand in your way or anything, Jer, but I don't know if showing up in Carter's Creek would be the smartest thing. I don't think that other lawyer really believed we weren't us, and Montana's not the healthiest place for us at the moment."

"Maybe not, but the judge was willing to believe we weren't Tommy Slade and Johnny Nevada, and what he says goes. Right now, let's worry about getting out of these mountains before sundown. It looks like it's going to be pretty close." They both reflexively looked at the sun, which was closer to the horizon than either of them was comfortable with. Despite the sky's current brightness, the mountains were close enough on either side of the valley that it would get dark early.

They drove on, Marcus mounting guard with a shotgun and Brown pushing the team of horses as much as he dared, and the wagon with its heavy load trundled on. It looked like they just might make it into town on time, when suddenly, they heard the sounds of hoofs in the near distance. Brown began to pull on the team harder, to try to get the wagon to outrun them, but the horses were tired and the load was heavy, and the pursuing horsemen gained on them every moment. With rapid and steady progress, a gang of nine men was heading toward them, and then surrounding them.

"I sure liked it better when we were on the pursuing end of this deal," Marcus muttered, his blue eyes narrowed.

"Hold up there!" called the leader of the mounted outlaws, a large man with grizzled hair under his brown hat, and a bandana covering the lower half of his face. "Whatcha got in that wagon, boys?"

Marcus looked at Brown, hoping his quick mind wouldn't fail him this time.

Brown shifted the reins to one hand, and tipped his hat back in a casual, almost arrogant, manner. "Just a bunch of old furniture. Nothing of interest to you."

"Oh, but it is," said the leader. "We hear there's a real market for old furniture hereabouts."

"Antiques, they call 'em, boss," said a redheaded outlaw with a weak chin.

"I don't care what they call them. I know that this is the load we want. Now, there's nine of us with rifles, and only two of you, and one of you's got his gun hand occupied with driving the cart. So I suggest you give us what we want."

"And if we don't?" asked Marcus.

"Now, that'd be downright stupid."

"Hey, Boss," said a weathered-looking outlaw, "I think I know these two." He rode up closer to them. "Well, tie me down to a cactus, if it ain't...Johnny Nevada and Tommy Slade. What are you two doing delivering furniture? Or have you beaten us to it, and stolen it already?"

Brown tried his most charming smile on the man. "Hello, Dusty. Different bunch than you used to ride with." He surveyed the group, just the slightest expression of disdain crossing his features. "No, we're currently in retirement. Giving honest work a try for a change."

"Honest work? You two?" Dusty guffawed, and several of the other outlaws joined him.

Marcus bristled with indignation. "Well, it's different for a guy like you, Dusty. Guys like us, who have major reward money on them—" He stopped suddenly, and turned to meet Brown's glare.

The redhead spoke up, his voice breaking high with excitement. "Reward money? I bet there's a lot on Johnny Nevada and Tommy Slade! Why don't we just turn them in, and forget the antiques?"

The grizzled leader gave him a silencing look. "'Cause that ain't what the job is. The furniture's what we're after, and the furniture's what we're taking. 'Sides, there's enough of a reward out on a couple of you that I think you'd have a little more sympathy for these boys."

Brown turned his smile on the leader. "Well, since there are nine of you, and two of us, as you point out, I don't see that there's any use in our starting a disagreement over this. But maybe as a sort of professional courtesy, you'd let us have a couple of horses, seein' as we were so recently in the same line of work, and all. We were kind of counting on making it into town tonight, and we're not really prepared for camping out."

"Sorry, Brown, no can do," said the boss. "How'd we know you wouldn't ride right into town and get a posse after us first thing? It's not real likely the sheriff'd recognize you as quick as Dusty, here, did. If you have to camp out tonight that gives us enough of a head start to get away with this load. But, as a professional courtesy and all, we will let you keep those saddlebags I see tossed back there, if it's only your own stuff in 'em, and we'll leave you some water and supplies. You'll have to give us your guns, though."

Brown and Marcus looked at one another, and then Brown spoke. "Well, I guess it's better than nothing." They unholstered their six-guns, and placed them on the floor of the cart. Marcus set down his rifle, and they jumped down off the wagon's front seat, while an outlaw on horseback reached for their saddlebags and tossed them after them. The redheaded outlaw took Brown's place at the reins, and his horse was tied to another man's saddle. Then they rode off, back in the direction from which the wagon had come.

Brown and Marcus watched them disappear. "Damn!" exclaimed Marcus, as soon as the party was out of sight. "Now we're out of luck."

"I was hoping we wouldn't have to spend the night out here. Let's get going. The closer to town we are when we bunk down tonight, the happier I'll be. It's too bad we don't know the country around here. I'm afraid we'll have to stop when it gets dark." Brown tossed his saddlebags over his shoulder and began trudging forward, and in a moment, Ed had joined him.

Shortly after dark, they realized that they couldn't see the path anymore, and that they'd just get lost if they kept going, so they broke to set up camp. Once they'd lit the fire and set out their bedrolls, Brown looked into the sack of provisions the gang had left them with. "Beans and jerky? Well, what did I expect?" he asked. "Tomorrow night a big steak dinner, if I have to play poker all day to earn it." He didn't bother to mention where he was planning on getting a stake to get into the game with, and Marcus didn't ask. He always trusted his partner to come up with something.

"Poker. Sounds rough. And a nice long bath at the hotel?"

"Cigars."

"And real beds—nice soft ones."

"We should've stayed at the better hotel in Townsend."

"If I'd have known the wagon was going to get stolen from us I'd have suggested it."

"Watch it, Ed, you're getting sarcastic in your old age."

"Long as I *reach* my old age, I'm happy."

And with visions of small luxuries in their heads, they drifted off to sleep.

• ♥ •

It was midmorning when Brown and Marcus reached town, the sun not yet near the meridian, and they agreed that a bath and a meal were in order, first thing.

"Only thing is, how we gonna pay for it?" asked Marcus.

"Well, I'd think Mr. Fitzgerald's got to pay us something for all our trouble, seeing as how we laid out some of our own money for the train fare and the cart hire and all. At least we should break even," Brown reasoned. He knew his chances of paying a call in Carter's Creek were down to next to nothing, with the way things had turned out, but maybe that was just as well. He was probably crazy to think that Anna Harrison would want someone like Jeremiah Brown complicating her life, anyway. Best to leave things alone.

They swung open the door of the hotel, only to find a choleric-looking man, short, stout, and white-haired, awaiting them in the lobby. "Mr. Brown? Mr. Marcus? Where's my delivery? I got your wire about the earlier delay, which was bad enough. You should have been here yesterday!"

"Mr. Fitzgerald?" asked Brown, extending his hand. "I'm Jeremiah Brown, and this is my partner Edward Marcus, and I'm afraid we have some bad news for you."

Fitzgerald ignored the proffered hand. "Bad news? You weren't hired to bring me bad news! Where's my furniture?"

"Well, sir, the honest truth is—we don't know. There was a band of outlaws who were real interested in your antiques—nine of them, actually. They surrounded us, and they took your furniture, cart and all. We had to spend last night out in the pass, and we walked all the way into town this morning to tell you."

"Mr. Brown, this is unacceptable! It was a simple delivery, and you couldn't even manage that."

Brown patiently assumed his best conciliatory tone. "Mr. Fitzgerald, my partner and I are truly sorry. We're not any happier than you are about what happened, and we'd be glad to lead a search party out to see if there's anything we can do. But the men who stopped us were heavily armed, and there were nine of them, and even though my partner, here, is a crack shot, we didn't have a chance. So, if you'll just pay us our expenses, we'll call it even."

"Even? *Even!* What do you mean, *even*? You owe me for those antiques, and you're going to pay every penny of it!" The old man was red-faced and shouting by now, completely indifferent to the disturbance he was causing.

The outer door opened, and a tall, mustached man, wearing a star on his vest, crossed the threshold into the lobby. "What's going on here?"

"Well, you see, sheriff—" Brown began, relieved to see that

the long arm of the law in Greenville, Montana was personified by a complete stranger.

"Arrest these men, Sheriff Marley," said Fitzgerald. "They stole my antiques."

"We were delivering his antiques. They were stolen from us. We're victims in this, too," protested Brown.

The sheriff looked at Fitzgerald, and then at the two tired-looking strangers. He sighed, as if to say that when Fitzgerald got this way, he didn't stop until he got what he wanted, so there was no point in arguing about it. Not even if you were the sheriff. "I'll have to ask you men to come with me," he said, and ushered them out through the lobby.

"Well, at least we'll have a place to sleep tonight that won't cost us anything," said Brown, flashing a wry smile in Ed's direction.

"That's what I like about you, Jeremiah. Always looking on the bright side." Marcus rolled his eyes in response.

• ❤ •

"So, you see," Sheriff Marley explained, as he returned back to the lockup where Brown was pacing and Ed was sitting on his bunk. "Fitzgerald will be satisfied with a civil trial. He just wants the value of the shipment back."

"But isn't that the business of Mr. Roberts down in New Mexico?" asked Brown.

"Well, I just heard over the telegraph about that. You see, he's already been paid. He says that he was just the agent in arranging a delivery agreement on Fitzgerald's behalf. He won't return the money unless he gets the furniture back. Fitzgerald, on the other hand, wants the money back if he doesn't have the furniture. And as he sees it, you two are the ones that lost it."

"So, how much money?" asked Brown. "Maybe we can

borrow it from somewhere."

"Fitzgerald says all that old stuff is worth about $15,000, if you can believe it."

"I can't," said Marcus, shaking his head.

"Neither can I," said Brown. "It sounds suspicious. Don't you think so, Sheriff?"

"Maybe so, boys, but apparently there were some papers tucked into a desk that more than double the value of the shipment. Fitzgerald wants to sue you for restitution. He'll most likely drop the criminal charges, but he doesn't want you two skipping town on him."

"How can we be responsible for those papers if we didn't know about them?" asked Brown.

"I think you'd want to talk to a lawyer about that. Only problem is, we only got one around here, and that's Ebenezer Hicks, and he's in Sam Fitzgerald's hip pocket. Could probably get you one down in Townsend, but I don't know much about 'em."

"Can I talk to my friend privately?" asked Brown.

"Sure thing," said Sheriff Marley, affably. "I'll send a deputy in to check on you in, say, twenty minutes."

When he'd gone, Brown turned to Marcus, a worried expression in his dark eyes. "So, if we lose this lawsuit, we may have to pay this Fitzgerald $15,000. How can we possibly raise that much money?"

"You know how, Jer. We'd have to pull a job—a big one. Maybe more than one."

"And start the statute of limitations clock all over again, when we've come this far? No way, Ed. But we can't stand trial, either. What if we're recognized as Tommy Slade and Johnny Nevada? I don't think telling the jury that they never really existed and that we're law-abiding citizens these days is gonna help." He paused for a moment. "Of course, if we turned ourselves in, we'd only be $5,000 short." He looked at Marcus's horrified expression and said, "Take it easy, Ed, I'm only joking."

Ed Marcus shook his head. "Figures we'd end up in another one-lawyer town. Remember what Miss Harrison said to us? No sense in only one lawyer in a town, because who do they fight with? Two lawyers make work for each other."

"Miss Harrison—you're a genius, Ed! Anna Harrison would help us out. And remember all those courtroom stories she told us? Sounds like she's real good at her job."

"Jeremiah, you said yourself it was a completely different part of the territory. I'm sure she can't just drop everything and come running to our rescue. And anyway, that doesn't solve our problem of taking the stand."

"She'd find a way around it."

"Why'd she do that?"

Jeremiah Brown gave him a look. "Because she knows who we are."

"She what?"

"She guessed. And I wasn't exactly in a situation where I would have felt right about lying to her."

"Guess that answers my question. About you and her, I mean." Trust Jeremiah to pick 'em. Edward couldn't keep from grinning despite the grimness of their situation. "You don't make a habit of telling every girl that you—"

"Shut up, Ed. We got a telegram to write."

When the deputy entered the room, Brown asked him if they could trouble him to send a telegram to their attorney, and handed him a scrap of paper directed to A. Harrison, Esq., Carter's Creek, Montana.

Chapter 4

When the stage from Townsend arrived several days later, the deputy was there to meet it. Two passengers got out. One was a very tall, very lanky young man, with an aquiline nose, pale green eyes, and curly dark hair. The other was a woman, attractive and a few years older than her companion. She was quietly dressed, and her light blonde hair was swept into a neat knot at the nape of her neck. They appeared to be traveling together.

"Mr. Harrison? I'm Deputy Sheriff Dickens." The deputy looked at the man, and thought he was a little young to be an experienced lawyer. He couldn't be too far into his twenties. The woman could be his sister, or even conceivably his wife—she didn't seem to be that much older, and despite her rather serious expression, she was pretty, with small, regular features and large blue eyes. The firm, square set of her jawline had a certain charm of its own.

The couple gave a polite, awkward laugh, and the young man said, "My name is Jonathan Cranbrook." He extended his hand to the deputy, who shook it, and then continued, "This is Anna Harrison."

"Where you want this?" the driver interrupted them, pointing to a large steamer trunk. It was the woman who turned to respond.

"Have it sent to the hotel," she said, with a surprisingly

authoritative manner, and turned to face the deputy. "Hello, Mr. Dickens. Any relation?" As he shook his head she smiled. "I expect you get asked that all the time. Well, then, you can imagine the things I get asked, but yes, I am an attorney. I take it Mr. Brown didn't bother to tell you my first name? You were expecting an Arthur or an Allan, I suppose."

"Yes'm, I expect I was," admitted Dickens.

"Well, I'm at an equal disadvantage, because Mr. Brown didn't give me many details on exactly why we're here. That trunk is filled with law books, so we can prepare our case, once we know what it is."

The deputy took another moment to swallow his surprise, and held out his arm gallantly to the lady. "Well, Miss Harrison, Mr. Cranbrook, if you'll accompany me to the sheriff's office, you'll find Mr. Brown and Mr. Marcus waiting for you."

• ♥ •

When the telegram arrived, Anna Harrison was more than a little surprised. When Jeremiah Brown left her that morning in Carter's Creek, eight months back, she didn't think she'd ever see him again. That kind of thing only happened to a woman like her once in her life…well, strictly speaking, that kind of thing *never* happened to a woman like her at all. A night spent in passionate lovemaking with a stranger, a client, and an outlaw, no matter how handsome and charming, simply wasn't a possibility, especially not for a woman as well known for her propriety and rectitude as Anna Harrison, Esq.

But it *had* happened. Something about Jeremiah Brown had touched her in a place she had thought couldn't be reached anymore. They'd only had the one night together between the time he was released and the time he and his partner were to leave town, but she still recalled his kisses, and the way it felt when he touched her, as she drifted off to sleep, nearly every night since. But she hadn't expected to see him again, and any lingering daydreams otherwise had evaporated over the last eight months. She told herself she didn't even want him to be real, since real things had a way of disappointing, and outlaws and lawyers didn't mix too well even under the best of circumstances. Leave that one perfect experience as a memory, and go on with life as it is.

And here was a wire, addressed to A. Harrison, Esq. and signed Jeremiah Brown. It read, "In a one lawyer town, and need your services. Come to Greenville Montana soonest. Inquire with sheriff. Reply."

After her hand stopped shaking, she penned a response. "Need to wind up business here. Arrive Thursday afternoon. A. Harrison, Esq." No need to provide any more information than necessary. But it would have been nice of him to have told her what was the matter, so that she and her clerk could have begun plotting their legal strategy beforehand. Instead, she had Jonathan pack up an old steamer trunk of her mother's with as many law books as it held. She didn't want to count on the professional courtesy of opposing counsel to have access to a law library.

Then, she called on her esteemed and eternal opponent, Nick Powell, the only other lawyer in town, and they agreed that the people of Carter's Creek could live without their disputes being resolved for a week or so. Both their practices had been booming lately, between a couple of serious land disputes and that business with the railroad. He could take the time she was out of town to catch up on his paperwork and relax a little, with the added extra advantage of knowing she'd arrive back from her journey tired from traveling.

"Well, Anna," he said, a smile creasing his broad, red face, "you're going to appear before a judge who's not Clayton, and against opposing counsel who's not me. You know they'll likely give you a hard time about being a woman. Are you sure you wouldn't rather just hand this case over to me, instead?"

She batted her eyelashes and said, mock-flirtatiously, "Why, Mister Powell, I am sure that my esteem for you will only grow when I have another worthy opponent with whom to compare you. And besides," she resumed her normal tone, "I'm bringing Jonathan with me. If for some reason anyone's incapable of speaking directly to a woman, he can translate."

"Won't you need a chaperone, then?" His eyes sparkled with mischief.

"To protect me from a man I already spend ten or twelve hours a day with? You might as well suggest I have my office chaperoned."

"Well, now that you mention it, folks have been talking..." Nick grinned at her, and then ducked as she crumpled a piece of paper from the top of his desk and threw it at him. "Hey, that was a page of the Chambers will. I'm going to have to have it recopied now."

"Serves you right," she said, but she blushed her apology at the same time. She knew how long it took the elderly man who did Nick's copying for him to get through a page. The fact that he kept him in his employ suggested there was a bit more to Nick than what appeared on the surface.

And soon, she'd taken her leave of both Nick and of Carter's Creek, and they were on their way to Greenville. It was an eight-hour train ride, and then another four by stage from the depot, so they'd have to spend the night in Townsend, in between.

That night in the hotel, she could barely sleep. Between her worries about whether she'd be taken seriously in a place where nobody knew her, and her apprehensions about what it would be like to see Jeremiah Brown again, she spent most of the night tossing and turning in the uncomfortable hotel bed. They'd treat themselves to the town's fancier hotel on the way home, she decided.

On the way home. She hadn't even seen Jeremiah Brown yet, and already she was thinking about how it would be afterwards. The one thing she couldn't allow herself to think about was during. She kept telling herself that he'd only wired her because he needed a lawyer.

It was a good thing that her father had trained her to present a calm exterior in all situations, she thought. It had often served her well in the past, and this time it was going to keep her from making a lovesick fool of herself.

Of course, the deputy sheriff thought that Jonathan was A. Harrison, Esq. She had no idea what, if anything, he thought of her at first glimpse. She'd worn a dark, plain coat and skirt, with a neat white shirtwaist, and done up her hair simply. She hoped Brown wouldn't be too disappointed when he caught sight of her, and then she remembered she'd been dressed like that when she'd met him the first time. In any case, what was more important was that the sheriff and her new esteemed opponent saw that she meant business.

But what she was thinking of when the deputy took her arm to escort her to the sheriff's office was that it was a pretty safe assumption that Jeremiah Brown was in custody. Surely, he'd have been at the stage to meet them, otherwise. She hoped this wasn't going to be another one of those cases of mistaken identity. It would be a little trickier to handle one of those now that she knew who he and his partner really were.

When they entered the sheriff's office, and they were led to the back where the cells were, she knew she'd been right. She wondered, for the seven hundredth time or so since she'd received the wire, what kind of trouble Brown and Marcus had managed to get themselves into this time. Her heart was pounding, and her throat was dry. If she could keep herself from blushing and stammering when she saw him, it would be a miracle.

She entered the room, to find the sheriff sitting at a table and her clients standing behind bars, looking a little worse for wear. In fact, they looked as though they'd spent a night or two sleeping rough and then had ended up in jail before they'd had a chance to really clean up. They were still two of the most beautiful men she'd ever seen, Ed Marcus with his even features and crisp blond hair, and Jeremiah Brown... well, he was just the way she remembered him, lean and comfortable in his own skin, with his expressive features and those brown eyes which were happy and sad all at once.

"Well, gentlemen," she said in her most formal manner, and not meeting their eyes. "I believe you've requested my presence." She turned to the sheriff, who looked from her to Jonathan and back again. "If my clerk and I could have a few moments with our clients?"

Brown and Marcus were clearly enjoying the sheriff's confusion, and as for Jonathan, if his smile got any broader, she thought it might get stuck permanently. "I beg your pardon, sheriff. I'm Anna Harrison. I'm Mr. Brown's and Mr. Marcus's attorney." She waited for the two men to nod their assent. "This is Jonathan Cranbrook, my law clerk. He should be sworn into the Bar in about six months." Make it perfectly clear to all involved that she was the attorney, and they'd have to deal with her. A couple of those railroad officials back home had tried to transact all their business with Jonathan, though he had been loyally uncooperative.

The sheriff finally closed his hanging jaw, and offered her his hand. "Sheriff Robert Marley, ma'am, and pardon me for my..." He clearly didn't know how to end his sentence. Pardon him for his surprise?

Anna turned to the matter at hand. "Now, what are these men being held for?"

The sheriff looked at her uncomfortably, so uncomfortably that she knew whatever he was about to say was not the whole truth. "Suspicion of robbery."

"What are they supposed to have stolen?"

"Well, they were delivering a load of furniture, ma'am, and they ended up in town without it. Sam Fitzgerald insists they have to pay him the value of the furniture, and they claim he's got to pay their expenses."

"Doesn't sound much like robbery to me," she said. "Now does it, Jonathan?"

"Not one bit, Miss Anna." He never called her "Miss" under ordinary circumstances, but he was clearly enjoying himself a little too much.

"So exactly why are you holding these men, Sheriff Marley?"

He sighed, and his moustache drooped. "Sam was afraid they might skip town. Now that you're here, it looks like they're planning to stay. I think it'd be all right if we released them."

"Well, that all sounds more than a little questionable, sheriff," she said. "Cooking up a charge just to detain them?" It was downright illegal, but it was common practice, and in any case, she couldn't exactly ask Sheriff Marley to arrest himself for doing it.

He motioned to the deputy, who unlocked their cage.

Marcus stretched and picked up his bag, and Brown followed, passing close by her and flashing her one of his smiles. She got that funny feeling in her stomach, and thought she might melt into a puddle on the floor right there and then, but instead she said, somewhat stiffly, "I'll need a place where I can meet with my clients. Does the hotel have a sitting room we can hire?" She didn't particularly want to meet with them at the sheriff's office, but it wouldn't be proper to receive them in her hotel room, either.

Sheriff Marley offered to escort Anna and Jonathan back to the hotel, and to fill them in on the rest of Sam Fitzgerald's charges. She suggested to her clients they get themselves some lunch or a drink or something, and meet them there in an hour.

They just looked at each other and away, and then they stood there for a minute, not moving and neither of them quite meeting her eyes.

"Um..." Brown began. She'd never imagined him at a loss for words.

"We—uh..." Marcus continued.

"Don't have any..." Brown went on. "That is, we were expecting to get paid when we got here, and—"

She grabbed a small embroidered purse and pulled out a couple of bills, which she placed in their outstretched hands. They still couldn't quite meet her eyes. "Jonathan," she said, "make a note that we've just advanced our clients twenty dollars. And gentlemen," she added, as they turned to go, "this is going on your bill." She didn't actually expect to get paid for this case, but she wasn't going to let Jonathan know that. She didn't want to set a bad example, after all.

The hotel had just the thing: a small, private sitting room on the ground floor that they were willing to let the out-of-town lawyers have exclusive use of for quite a low fee. Anna suspected that management was so relieved not to have to haul her steamer trunk up a flight of stairs that they would have let them have it for free, if they'd shown any hesitation. Jonathan went up to see to his room, but she didn't want to lose any of their limited time, so she settled herself in at a small writing table, with a pen and ink and an American annotation of Blackstone's *Commentaries*. She got so absorbed in what she was reading, that when she felt a pair of hands on her shoulders, she started, and the person behind her stepped back quickly.

She turned around in her chair and saw that it was Jeremiah Brown, unaccompanied and all cleaned up. Clearly, he'd spent his time productively. She couldn't help noticing the way his dark hair fell softly around his face, until he shook it back, or the way his clean trousers clung close to his thighs.

"Oh, Mr. Brown," she said, "you frightened me." She stood up and faced him, allowing herself to look into his dark eyes for the first time. Her expression was carefully neutral, but her heart was pounding so hard she was sure he must have heard it. It was pounding so hard that she was fairly sure that Jonathan, two flights away, must have heard it.

"You don't have to call me that when we're alone," he said, taking a step closer to her.

"I'm afraid I do," she said. Suddenly, the whole world had shrunk to this man standing before her, and she found it hard to speak, to say anything. "Otherwise, I'll get to concentrating on some point of the case, and someone will distract me, and next thing you know, I'll refer to you as Jeremiah right in the middle of court."

She took a step or two backward, and resumed her seat, even though it was the last thing in the world she wanted to do. "Which would send entirely the wrong message. But right now, we need to focus on the matter at hand. Exactly what did happen?"

He sat down on a settee across the small room from her and began to tell her about Mr. Roberts, and the agreement made in New Mexico. She wondered if she was just imagining it, or if he looked a little wounded. "It would be better if we didn't have to testify. I'm a little concerned about being recognized as Tommy Slade and Johnny Nevada."

"We'll do our best to avoid either of you taking the stand," she agreed.

He nodded. "So, what was it you needed to know?"

She asked him questions, taking careful notes on his responses, for some time, until the door opened, and Jonathan entered, followed by Ed Marcus. Marcus sat down on the settee next to his partner, while Jonathan crossed the room to stand near Anna. "All right. Mr. Brown was telling me about the agreement, and I think we may have a problem. You two never got anything in writing, right?"

The outlaws looked at each other. "Should we have?" asked Brown.

"Well, it would be a lot easier to prove a breach of contract if there was an actual document. Some courts don't like to enforce verbal agreements. Did you wire Fitzgerald?"

"Roberts did that. Sheriff Marley said that he claimed he was only an agent in making the arrangements between Fitzgerald and us, if that means anything."

"Oh, it does," she said. "It means he's not willing to take any responsibility in the matter. And it means you're dealing with as slippery a pair as you could have found. Well, we may not be able to get you two paid, but we should be able to keep you out of jail and free from any liability. Now, Mr. Brown, you were saying that Fitzgerald's trying to hold you liable for the value of some papers that you didn't know about?"

And so it went.

The circuit judge happened to be in the area already, and he didn't have a crowded trial calendar, so he set the date for as quickly as she was willing to allow. They had exactly three days to prepare for the trial, so they put the time to use, questioning Brown and Marcus over and over again about the events of that day, their agreement with the man who had hired them back in New Mexico, and their understanding of what Fitzgerald was expecting from them.

When the lawyers didn't need their clients, when they were busy researching the case law or working out their strategies, Brown and Marcus wandered about the town. Anna thought they played a lot of poker at the saloon. She knew they did, actually, because they had to borrow their first stake from her, and she knew they won, because Brown paid her back for both of them the next day and they kept on playing.

The former outlaws certainly saw a lot more of the town than their attorneys did, even if it was mostly the inside of the saloon. Anna and Jonathan had meals delivered to them in the sitting room that had become their office, in order to save the time that it would have taken them to go to the dining room. She never saw Jeremiah Brown alone again, after that first afternoon. There was an awkwardness between them and she avoided thinking about it too much by throwing herself into trial preparations. She was there to do a job, and she was going to do it right, without letting herself get distracted. Anything else they had to say to each other could wait until afterwards.

The day before the trial, her opponent called on them at the hotel for one final conference. Ebenezer Hicks was a tall, heavy-set man with dark whiskers, and throughout their discussion of the preliminaries of the case, he treated her in a matter-of-fact way, as though she was just any attorney of the more usual gender, as he had at their previous meetings. When he turned to go, though, he said the thing she'd been waiting for.

"I think you should know that most of the town is going to be there."

"Trials a great entertainment in this town?" she asked, knowing what was coming.

"Well, we don't get many of them, seeing as how we don't often have a second lawyer in town, Miss Harrison. There's that. But it's more...you." He looked right at her.

"Ah. They want to see the circus act."

"Excuse me, Miss Harrison?"

"That saying of Doctor Johnson's about women preaching and dogs walking on their hind legs. It isn't so much that it's done *well*, what's remarkable is that it's done *at all*. They want to see it done at all."

She doubted whether Hicks had the vaguest idea who Samuel Johnson was, but he understood what she was saying, all right. "I'm afraid that's about the size of it, Miss Harrison. If I might make a suggestion, it might be easier all around if you were comfortable permitting Mr. Cranbrook—"

Jonathan looked flushed and angry as he opened his mouth to speak, but she intervened, staying calm by sheer force of will. "Mister Cranbrook is not a member of the Bar of the Territory of Montana. I am. I'll thank you to remember that, Mr. Hicks. Good day." And she turned her back on him.

After he'd gone, she lost her temper entirely. "Jonathan, you're a bright young man, and you're going to be a distinguished lawyer one of these days, but you're twenty-two years old and you barely look it. I'm six years older than you, and just once in my life I'd like someone who doesn't already know us to make an initial presumption that I might just be a better, more experienced lawyer than you are!"

Jonathan sighed in that endearing kid brother way of his, and sat down right in front of her, taking her hands in his big ones. "Now, Anna, you knew it'd probably be like this. And you know that you can beat this man six ways to Sunday, even if the case isn't as strong as you might like it to be. You're smarter than he is, besides which, Nick keeps you on your toes in court on a regular basis. You'll have him all figured out before he's even got it straight whether it's Brown or Marcus who's named Edward."

She laughed a little at that. "Jonathan, how was I ever so lucky to get you working with me?"

"'Cause my parents knew your daddy and it was set I was going to clerk there long before you or I had any choice in the matter. Not that I'd change a thing if I could."

During that last, the door had opened quickly, and shut again. She caught a quick flash of dark hair and dark eyes. Jeremiah Brown had seen Jonathan holding her hands in his own, and their heads bent close together, and she knew just what he was thinking. Knew, and didn't know what she could do about it. She didn't know how she could bring the subject up, and she didn't even know if he'd believe her. Still, she needed to try.

By the time she'd made up her mind what to do, and made her excuses to Jonathan, Brown was already gone. She stepped off the hotel's front porch and saw his black hat and blue jacket disappearing down the street. She didn't want to call out his name and make a public spectacle, especially with the trial coming up and folks in town having heard both their names. It was easy to guess where he was headed, and when he turned in there, she bit her lip. Being a lady lawyer took her places a lot of ladies didn't ordinarily go, but she'd still never set foot inside a saloon in her entire life, and she was frankly more than a little uncomfortable with the idea. She debated with herself every step of the way, and if she'd hesitated at the door any longer, she thought, she probably would have gotten arrested for loitering and vagrancy.

Finally, she made up her mind to take the plunge through those swinging doors. It was dark inside, even though it was the middle of the afternoon. There were smells of beer and whiskey, and some unwashed cowboys, mixed with the scent of cheap perfume. She spotted Brown sitting with Marcus and a bunch of other men at a card table. A pretty girl with a feather in her hair was taking what she assumed must be his drink order. The girl was wearing something not so different from Anna's camisole and petticoat, but it was red satin, and she wore nothing over it.

Just then she heard the bartender calling to her. "Ma'am? Excuse me, ma'am? You want a drink, or are you looking for someone?" He had her figured, all right.

"Oh—" she began, but she lost her nerve and fled.

Chapter 5

She looked into the courtroom, and it was as packed as Ebenezer Hicks had said it would be. Every seat on the benches was taken, and people had brought their own chairs, besides. Folks were standing at the back and along the side walls, and there were even a few people sitting on blankets at odd places on the floor. There were ranchers, and cowboys, and most of the townspeople must have shut their businesses for the afternoon. Entire families had picnic baskets with them. It was a little frightening to understand that she was the main attraction. All she could hope was that a little girl or two might get some ideas in her head. Oh, and that they'd win the case, of course.

And then she had her horrible thought. Her clients and Jonathan were waiting for her in a little back room, behind the place where the judge sat. Brown and Marcus were all spit-polished clean and tidy for the occasion, in gray suits of darker and lighter shades. She'd decided that as long as her femininity was on display, she might as well play to it, and had set aside her black coat and skirt for a quiet but feminine Sunday go-to-meeting dress in a deep blue-green.

"You look pretty," said Brown.

"She sure does," said Jonathan, like a proud kid brother, but she was still certain Brown didn't quite hear it that way. She made some excuse why Jonathan needed to go and check with the judge on something right that minute. As soon as the door shut behind him, she turned back to her clients.

"I am so sorry," she said. "I should have realized this was going to happen, but as you know, I don't stray from home very often, and I'm old news there. Everybody in three counties has come to see the Amazing Amazonian Lady Lawyer, and I may have put you both in danger. What do you think the chances are of folks around here recognizing you?"

"We never rode in this area," said Brown, his expression thoughtful, "so it's not that likely. Of course, the gang that actually stole the stuff knew—one of them used to know us—but they're not going to show up today. I guess it's a risk we'll have to take."

She sat down and put her head in her hands. "How could I have been so stupid, not to know this would happen? I should have sent Nick Powell."

"Nick Powell?" asked Ed Marcus, suspiciously. "Isn't he the one who'd turn us in for the reward money as soon as look at us?"

"Guess that's why I didn't." She smiled at him.

Jeremiah Brown walked over to her and put a hand on her shoulder. "Anna, you know I'm a gambler, and I play the odds. And these odds look pretty good to me. This place is out of the way enough, and we've spent so little time in these parts, that the chances against us being spotted are about as good as we'd have anyplace this far north. And at least we know we have a good lawyer on our side." She reached up and squeezed his hand, but the door opened, and he pulled away quickly. Wonderful, she thought. He didn't want Jonathan catching him. Well, there were other things to think about now.

"We're ready to begin."

Despite the circus atmosphere, the circuit judge maintained a firm grip on the courtroom. Hicks made his opening arguments: namely, that there was no contract, that his client was under no obligation to pay for services rendered since the valuable antiques were not delivered, and that Mr. Brown and Mr. Marcus were fully liable for the value of the missing property, in the amount of $15,000.

"That's an awful lot of money for some old furniture, Mr. Hicks," she suggested. They were the first words of her opening statement, and they caused enough of a sensation that she was worried about the rest of the trial. Maybe the crowd thought this was some kind of ventriloquist act and they'd been expecting to hear Jonathan's voice issuing from her mouth. Well, wait 'til they heard what she *really* had to say.

"In fact, Your Honor, ladies and gentleman, I am going to prove today that the only reason that Mr. Fitzgerald values these old pieces of furniture so highly is that one of them contained something that Jeremiah Brown and Edward Marcus had no idea they were transporting, something that would have caused them to have conducted the transportation in a much different fashion, or possibly to have declined this employment altogether. I am further going to demonstrate that because of this deception, Mr. Brown and Mr. Marcus are not only entitled to payment in the full amount of the agreement, but it is this Court's duty to award them damages in the amount of a reasonable fee for transporting a valuable article of this nature." Well, no court had actually gone this far yet, but it was worth a try, she thought.

Having concluded her opening arguments, she returned to the table where she was seated with Jonathan and her clients. Ebenezer Hicks returned to the front of the courtroom.

"Your honor, this young lady's unreasonable demands --"

She was on her feet, "Objection. The fact that I'm a young lady has nothing to do with the case." It was the moment of truth.

"Sustained. Mr. Hicks, you will refer to your learned opposing counsel as such, or else the young lady has my permission to refer to you as the 'fat, pompous old windbag.'"

Hicks sputtered for a moment. "It was a term of deference to the young lady's...that is, to my learned opponent's status as a member of the gentler sex."

"I know just what it was, Hicks, and you're not to try it again."

The laughter of the assembled crowd spread throughout the courtroom. The crowd was hers to win now, if she could. Bless the judge's irascible old heart. He had a weakness for the underdog.

Hicks continued with his arguments, but even though he had the majority of the case law on his side for several of the counts, his performance was uninspired. His logic was not precisely crystalline, and he made each point as though he were lecturing a particularly dull group of schoolchildren. Clearly, he was not a local favorite. Of course, the popular perception that he was in Sam Fitzgerald's—what was it the sheriff had told Brown?—*hip pocket*, might have contributed to that.

But if this man had ever seen an itinerant troupe doing Shakespeare, he should have learned a little something about presentation, she reflected. He called Sam Fitzgerald to the stand, and essentially let him sputter on in the same fashion. They lost his property and they were going to recompense him for it, regardless of their ability to pay.

And then, it was her turn to cross-examine. She rose and approached the bench, and then turned and looked at her clerk and her clients. Jonathan's curly head was bent over his notepad, already, but Brown and Marcus were leaning back in their chairs, looking like they were ready to enjoy the show. *Don't get too relaxed,* she wanted to tell them. But she couldn't help but find their confidence encouraging. She took a deep breath, and began. A woman's voice wouldn't project as easily as a man's, but she'd learned how to compensate for that from Karl Rasmussen, the deputy sheriff in Carter's Creek, who doubled as a singing teacher to some of the ladies in town.

"Mister Fitzgerald," she began, "I'm still trying to determine upon what basis you are making this outrageous claim for recompense."

"Objection," came Hicks's monotone.

"Sustained. You will keep the questions factual, counselor." But he didn't look harsh, just businesslike. She looked over at her clients again. Ed Marcus looked a little nervous, but Jeremiah Brown gave her a broad smile. He'd noticed not only her discomfiture, but the speed with which she'd recovered from it.

"My apologies, Your Honor, Mr. Fitzgerald. However, I am curious on what basis you are valuing the goods transported by my clients. I've done some checking, by telegraph, with some of the auction houses in New York and San Francisco, and they estimate a shipment of this sort to be worth a good deal less than what you claim." She raised her hand to forestall the inevitable objection. "Your Honor, I will introduce this testimony at the appropriate time. Right now, I am simply trying to establish the basis of Mr. Fitzgerald's valuation."

The judge nodded. "Answer the question, Mr. Fitzgerald."

"Well," he said nervously, "the value isn't just contained in the antique furniture. There were some documents concealed in the desk which were also of some significant value."

"Were my clients made aware that they were transporting goods other than the furniture which they had contracted to transport?"

"Umm...I'm not aware of what Mr. Roberts might have told them."

"And yet, you claim that the agreement was made by Mr. Roberts as your agent? Who, then, was responsible for informing my clients?"

"Well, I guess I was—"

"Objection!"

"Overruled. Counselor?"

"I've finished with the witness, Your Honor. I simply wish to present my own case."

"Very well, Counselor."

Her clients looked pleased. If she'd kept her cross-examination that short, it would look less peculiar when she didn't call them to the stand. Jonathan made their private victory sign. She felt rather less satisfied than any of them.

However, she turned and addressed the court. "Your Honor, my clients are not sophisticated businessmen, like Mister Samuel Fitzgerald, nor wealthy ranchers like Mister Arthur Roberts. No, your honor, they are sons of the West, who love this fair land of ours, and who have chosen a way of life that some among us may not understand, and others may find enviable. They travel around, doing odd jobs, and exploring our frontier. It may be fair to refer to Mister Jeremiah Brown and Mister Edward Marcus as jacks of all trades, and masters of none," she saw Brown wince at this, "but in their world, a man's word is still his bond, and written agreements are not necessary. Mr. Brown and Mr. Marcus have traveled a long way in pursuit of this commission, and they should not be penalized because of an unfortunate mishap."

She went on to discuss the mysterious hidden document at more length. Most of Hicks's objections were overruled, except quite fairly, the one to her speculation on the nature of the document. She knew she'd gone too far there, but she'd been making such a dramatic statement. She brought Jonathan up, briefly, to introduce the subject of the valuation of the antiques in question. At the most extravagant estimate, they were worth just short of five thousand dollars. About the price on each of her clients' heads.

And then it was over, and she'd managed to get through it smoothly without the omission of her clients taking the stand being too glaringly obvious, or so she hoped. In a strange way, the focus on her performance as a woman lawyer had shifted the spotlight from anything she actually did. She just hoped it would be enough.

From the murmurs that she could hear, she knew the crowd, at least, was on their side. The judge made his way back to his chambers for deliberation. She sank into her chair at the defendant's table, while Jonathan poured her water. Jeremiah Brown leaned past him to whisper, "Worth every penny we're paying you."

"You're paying me? With what?" she asked. "Your luck at the poker table had better have been pretty good."

“Who said anything about luck?” He winked at her.

Very shortly, the judge had returned to his bench, and was ready to make his pronouncement. Jonathan reached over and gripped her wrist convulsively, to the point where it hurt. She was going to have to train him not to do that in court.

"Learned counsel," he began, "Mister Fitzgerald, Mister Brown, Mister Marcus, I find myself at an impasse."

"A what?" she heard Marcus whisper to Brown.

"He's stuck."

"Why didn't he just say so?"

"That's not how judges talk. Now, be quiet and listen."

"While the common law supports Mr. Fitzgerald's contentions, equity would have me favor the claims of Mr. Brown and Mr. Marcus. Therefore, I am reserving my decision pending a suggestion."

"Your Honor?" asked Hicks. "What kind of a suggestion?"

"That Mr. Brown and Mr. Marcus, in the company of Deputy Sheriff Dickens and Deputy Sheriff Lodge, be sent to try to recover the stolen property."

Brown jumped to his feet. "Your Honor, that's what we were trying to do when Sheriff Marley put us in jail in the first place. He's cost us days. It may be impossible to track the gang now."

Now, Fitzgerald was on his feet, as well. "How could I trust them not to just flee the jurisdiction?"

The judge banged his gavel several times. "Order in the court. Order! Now, Mr. Fitzgerald, your fears were understandable at the time, but as Mr. Brown points out, the delay that your actions have caused may have made the recovery of your property impossible. However, I order that Mr. Brown and Mr. Marcus be permitted to make a good faith effort to provide restitution of the stolen goods. They are bound over to this court, and if they do not reappear with either the property or an account of said good faith effort within a reasonable time, they will be liable to arrest. If they do make said effort, it will stand in place of the restitution you request, Mr. Fitzgerald."

Fitzgerald submitted, with less than good grace, while Brown and Marcus were so anxious to go that Anna had the impression that they would have left the courtroom and hit the trail that very moment, if they'd had horses and guns. But it was already late afternoon, and the rest of the day would have to be spent in provisioning them.

Then, Sheriff Marley offered an objection of his own. "I can't let both of my deputies go off for a week or more at a time."

There was a stirring at Anna's side. "Can I go?" asked a timid voice. "You could deputize me, temporarily, couldn't you?"

Brown looked closely at the eager young man. "Well, Cranbrook, we'd be glad to have you, except for one thing. How are you at riding and tracking?"

"I'm a pretty good rider," he said hopefully. "I won the local steeplechase last year."

Jonathan had spent most of his young life in schools and in offices. This was his chance to have an adventure, to be a man. Brown caught Anna's eye, and she nodded. "It's acceptable to us, Your Honor," he said.

"It's acceptable to me," said the sheriff.

"It sounds like I don't have much of a choice," grumbled Fitzgerald. "All right by me. But are we certain that these men are coming back, with or without my property?"

There was mischief in Brown's eyes when he spoke. "Why of course we'll come back. After all, we couldn't possibly run off on such a lovely young la— Excuse me, such a lovely *learned counsel* as Miss Harrison, now could we?" He winked at her, and gave her one of those smiles.

She took a deep breath. The judge was bending the law in their favor as far as he could go, and not one person had stood up in court and identified her clients as Tommy Slade and Johnny Nevada. No whispers, even, as far as she could tell. If her client chose to be exasperating, she would just have to live with it.

Chapter 6

Shortly after sunrise the morning after the trial, a party of four horsemen left Greenville, heading back into the mountains. They rode in silence until they reached the edge of the pass that lead through the mountains to Townsend.

"The trail is going to be cold," commented Brown. "Our best bet is probably the size of the gang."

"How do you mean?" asked Jim Dickens, the deputy. He was a strongly-built man of medium height, with a closely-trimmed black beard, gray eyes, and a straight nose.

"Well, if there was a gang of nine men riding those hills all the time, it's a fair bet you would have known about it, right?"

"Sure. But there's nobody regularly in the mountains. We'd be in a real fix around here, if there were, with the nearest train station on the other side, wouldn't we?"

Brown continued. "So, it's a reasonable assumption that the group of men was assembled for one purpose—to hijack that load we were hauling. The boss of the gang even said as much, remember, Edward?"

Marcus frowned. "Oh, yeah. We asked him what he'd want with a bunch of old furniture, and he kinda said it was the old furniture he'd been employed to get."

"So, if they were hired for a particular job, and they're not all a regular gang, they might have split up by now. And they wouldn't have the same kind of loyalty to each other that a real gang would have."

"Makes sense." Ed nodded.

"How do you know so much about how a gang of outlaws would think?" Jonathan Cranbrook asked. He had a bewildered look on his young face. He was a good horseman, but he seemed to regard the whole tracking process as a mystery too complex for his comprehension.

"Oh, Jeremiah is just real smart," Marcus quickly replied.

"Yeah, that's what Anna said."

"Did she?" Brown looked interested.

"She said you were one of the smartest men she'd ever met. I probably shouldn't tell you this, but she was pretty nervous coming here. She said she probably wouldn't be able to impress you in the courtroom, like she can with most clients. She said you'd probably have her strategy all figured out as soon as she opened her mouth, and she'd have to stand there and look at you, looking back at her, and thinking about how she could have done it better." Jonathan smiled sheepishly. "But you won't tell her I told you?"

"No, I won't," Brown reassured him. So, he made her nervous, did he? Well, she sure hadn't showed it. He wondered what else she didn't show. Jonathan seemed a lot younger and more vulnerable outside his own element, and he wondered if he'd been right in his assumptions about Anna and the boy. They'd seemed so close, but why had he jumped to the conclusion that there was something romantic between them? That was for thinking about later. "So, they were headed over the hills to the west, not back toward Townsend at all. We had plenty of time to watch them disappear. Jim, what's the nearest town in that direction?"

"Oh, Ford's Landing, over by the river. But that's a good three days' ride ahead."

"Three days on horseback, or three days with a heavy wagon and tired horses?" asked Brown, frowning thoughtfully.

"Three days on horseback. From the way you described that load, I'd say it'd take them closer to four."

"Well, it doesn't make up for the week we lost waiting around Greenville, but it's better than nothing. At least we ought to get word of whether they were there, and where they might have been going."

And they rode on in silence.

Near nightfall, they stopped and made camp. Brown and the deputy lit the fire and began to make dinner, while Marcus made a reconnaissance of the area. Jonathan was at Brown's elbow, as he'd been ever since they set out.

"Is there anything else I can do?" he asked in a helpless helpful sort of way.

Didn't lawyers learn anything about anything important, even how to make a fire? But Jonathan had consistently brought the wrong kind of wood, spilled the container of beans he was trying to open into the flames, and cut his thumb on his utility knife. Dickens helped him bind it up, while Brown restrained himself to a single suggestion. "Why don't you go see what Ed is doing?" Let his partner handle the kid for a while.

Jonathan saw the lean figure of Edward Marcus in the distance, and started off. He moved quietly, as he'd been taught by one of his favorite clients, a Native tribal leader whose land claims Anna had become interested in. It was the only wilderness skill he had, other than a good seat on a horse, and he wanted to impress Marcus after making such a fool of himself in front of Brown and the deputy. When he'd gotten within a few yards, he stepped on a piece of underbrush, and found himself face to face with a gun. Marcus was the quickest draw he'd ever seen.

The gun was lowered. "Don't ever do that again, Cranbrook! Sneak up on me like that and I could have had a bullet through you before I even knew it was you."

Jonathan sighed loudly. "I thought that was the one thing I could do right. I've made a complete idiot of myself trying to help out back at the campfire. I'm afraid your friend thinks I'm the next best thing to useless."

Marcus couldn't help but smile at that. "Jeremiah gets a little impatient sometimes. But I can tell you that he didn't think you were useless at all back when you and Miss Anna were planning for that trial."

"Well, yeah, I can do that. But it's about all I *can* do. Sometimes, I think I should've stayed back East when I got out of school, instead of coming home where I don't fit in anymore."

"You went to school back East?"

"Massachusetts. From the time I was fourteen until I started working for Anna. I could have gone to a law school out there, but my father thought training in an office would be better experience for me. And Anna's father was one of his oldest friends. They came out to Montana territory from Boston together, thirty years ago."

"Massachusetts...that's something. I was in Boston, once. Was your school near there?"

"Western Massachusetts, but I stayed with relatives in Boston over the holidays."

Marcus smiled, conspiratorially. "Jeremiah has never been back East. So, you've been all over."

Jonathan shrugged. "Anyone can get on a train and ride."

Ed was about to contradict him, thinking of all the trains he and Jeremiah had stopped when they were still riding the outlaw trail, but he thought better of it. "You know, that sneaking up might have its uses when we catch up with them. Just don't try it with me again. I'm kind of quick on the draw."

"I noticed. Could you...could you teach me? I mean, not how to draw as fast as you, but give me a few tips on how to improve my shooting? I've really only done a little target practice, and I don't get to use it much in my line of work."

"No, I imagine not. Words are your weapons. Jeremiah's that way, too, when he has his preference. I like action, myself. But sure, I'll give you a few pointers. We've got plenty of ammunition, and we're so many days behind the men we're chasing that they're not going to hear us." Marcus unholstered his gun, and demonstrated a few shots. "You, see, if you hold the gun like this, you get a clearer aim." He handed the gun to Jonathan. "Why don't you try?"

Jonathan took aim at the mark his instructor indicated. He did a lot better than Ed would have expected. But before he could take a second shot, there was a sound of men running toward them, and then Brown's voice crying out "What the hell was that?"

"Just showing Jonathan a few pointers."

"Well, next time can you do it silently? We thought you'd been ambushed." Brown and the deputy trudged back toward the fire.

Jonathan turned to follow them, but then looked at Marcus. "That was some impressive shooting. You don't see a man who can handle a gun like that every day." He had a peculiar expression.

"Yeah, well, you're not so bad yourself, for a lawyer," Marcus smiled after him. When he'd gone, the blond outlaw smacked his own forehead. *Idiot,* he thought. *Cranbrook may be naïve, but he's plenty smart, and he's got to realize that nobody who can shoot like I do is any mere drifter.* It might not be a complete disaster if he found out, because of his loyalty to Anna. Keeping it from Dickens, though, was another, more vital, manner entirely.

• ♥ •

The path over the mountains was a difficult one, but Dickens was sure it was the way they must have gone, and in fact, there was evidence of a cart having passed that way, in the form of tracks, and dislodged stones along the path. "Well," he said thoughtfully, "they certainly have gone out of their way to make things easy for us. They must have lost a lot of time bringing the load this way."

"Must have figured it was too dangerous to bring it back through Townsend," contributed Marcus.

"It makes me wonder if it was really the furniture the bandits were after, or the mysterious contents of that drawer," said Brown. "Chances of banging it up this way are pretty good, and that's not going to increase its value any."

"What if you were right and it was a commission job?" asked Dickens.

"So, the outlaws were only doing what they'd been asked to do, whether it was the easiest way, or the best way, or not."

"Then all we'd need to figure out is—"

"Who made the commission. Well, Dickens, you're the only one of us who knows the folk hereabouts. Can you think of anything?"

"No. Unless..."

"Well, does Fitzgerald have any enemies? He sure don't seem to be all that popular for a man who owns as much as he does."

"No one much likes him. But there was the land dispute a

ways back. He used to have a partner, a Dan Thomas, 'til he did him pretty dirty on a big deal. Thomas disappeared awhile ago, though. Last anyone around these parts heard, he was out in Nevada."

Brown looked thoughtful. "So there's the chance that he found out about the shipment from New Mexico, hired these outlaws, and had them steal the furniture."

"But why?" asked Dickens.

"Well, it could have to do with the documents that we know are concealed in the desk."

"Then why steal all the furniture?"

"He may not know which piece of the furniture the documents are hidden in. He may not know exactly what is hidden. And he may not even know about any documents, and just wants to keep Fitzgerald from having his heart's desire. But in any case, it's doubtful that Thomas, if it is Thomas, would have told the outlaws exactly why he wants the furniture. So, the shipment should stay intact. We're still two days out from Ford's Landing, right?"

"Afraid so," said Dickens. "Time to stop talking and start riding."

The mountain trails were difficult, and more than once, their horses balked. Jonathan Cranbrook, who was the least used to this type of riding, showed remarkable determination.

There hadn't been time to outfit him in the proper trail clothes. Since he was extremely tall, he'd been unable to borrow much from anyone, and so he cut an interesting figure on horseback, in the jacket and trousers from his second-best suit, his once-shiny shoes, a hat the sheriff had lent him, and a bandana belonging to Brown. He was a handsome young man, which compensated some, if not quite enough, for the incongruity of his appearance. The mountain nights were cold, and he wasn't dressed warmly enough, but he stoically refused to complain.

Brown, particularly, had gotten over his earlier annoyance, and seemed protective of the younger man. "We don't want to bring him back damaged any more than the furniture. Wouldn't do to annoy our lawyer," he mumbled to Marcus.

"He's tryin'. He's asked me for some more shooting pointers."

"Well, I hope you're being a little more careful about showing him what you can do."

"I ain't stupid, Jer. I just wasn't thinking, that first time. Speaking of stupid, though, how we gonna get around the fact that the outlaws know who we are?"

"I have no idea, Ed, and it's been worrying me plenty. Maybe we're best off if we search and search and don't find them."

"Are you sure we wouldn't still be liable for the money, then?"

"The judge said we had to make the effort. I had the feeling he knew there was no way we could come up with the money. Shame if we don't get paid, but right now, I'd settle for getting out of Montana free and in one piece."

"Sounds good to me."

The afternoon sun was low in the sky of the third day, when they saw the river in the distance, and the little town of Ford's Landing nestled on its banks. Brown and Marcus looked at each other with mixed emotions. Dickens and Cranbrook seemed excited, the latter in particular. Their adventure was about to begin. Jeremiah Brown just hoped his and his partner's wasn't about to end.

They arrived in town before dark, and looped their reins to a rail on the main street. Dickens and Cranbrook went to check in the sheriff's office, while Brown and Marcus headed into the saloon.

They'd barely ordered their drinks when they heard from behind them, "Well, if it ain't Johnny Nevada and Tommy Slade! You boys do know how to come lookin' for trouble, don't you?"

"Hello, Dusty," said Brown, turning around calmly. "I hope that's not a threat. 'Cause Johnny's pretty tired, and you know he don't react well to threats when he's tired."

"Why'd I threaten you? We got what we want, and me and my friends got paid." The outlaw gestured to a table behind him, where three of the other men who'd ambushed them that day were sitting, in various states of drunkenness. Dusty, who was weaving slightly, was the soberest of them all. "Paid real good, for the amount of work. 'Course, getting that stuff over the mountains was tough, but we managed okay."

Brown smiled his most charming smile. "Well, that's good, because you got us into real bad trouble. We need to get that furniture back in the worst way."

"I'm sorry, Tommy. If I'd've known it was you, I never would've taken the job. We were told some fellas named Brown and Marcus would be transporting the load... Oh. I get it. That's what you go by now, huh?"

"You don't think we can do honest work as Slade and Nevada, do you, Dusty?" *Not lying, just not explaining which were our real names,* Jeremiah thought.

"Guess not. Well, listen, I done my job and got paid and all, but it's not like I got any loyalty to the man that hired me. And you was always good to me, in the old days in the Black Hills. Tell ya what. I know them other five boys were headed down the river, towards a big spread a couple days' ride south of here. They were shippin' the anti—the old furniture—on a barge down the river, to a place owned by a feller called Thomas."

"Well, thanks Dusty, you've been a big help," said Brown, quickly, turning toward the saloon door, which had just opened.

"We'd buy you a drink, but we don't got any money, thanks to you," said Marcus, following him.

And Dusty's eyes widened, to see the two outlaws intercepting a lawman with a star on his vest, and a tall young slicker in a weatherbeaten dress suit. Maybe they really had reformed. He shrugged. What he needed was another drink.

• ♥ •

"There's a trail along the river we can ride. The man we met tells us Thomas's place is downriver a couple of days."

"How you get that much information that fast?" asked Dickens. "Sheriff barely remembers someone transferring a load of old furniture onto a barge. Can't even recall what day it was."

Brown grinned. "Saloon's always a better source of information than the sheriff's office, don't you agree, Edward?"

"Oh, absolutely, Jeremiah." Marcus looked at his partner, with relief visible in his frank blue eyes. The die was cast and they'd have to pursue the matter to its end, but their quick encounter with Dusty guaranteed them a few more days without their cover blown. Who knew between now and then what might not happen? Jeremiah had figured their way out of tighter spots.

"Aren't we going to sleep in town tonight?" asked Jonathan, hopefully.

"Well, we really should push on," said Brown quickly. It would be difficult to avoid running into Dusty and his boys again, in a town so small. He didn't relish the idea of doing any more explaining than was absolutely necessary. "Looks like the path is pretty clearly marked. We could ride for several hours of darkness, before we had to make camp."

"Agreed," said the deputy. "We don't want to lose any more time than we have to."

Marcus nodded his agreement, so Jonathan was overruled.

• ❤ •

Jonathan awoke at first light, and pushed himself up from the hard ground. He hated to admit it, even to himself, but this outdoor living had certain disadvantages. An unfamiliar blanket was covering him and his bedroll, and as he looked around to see how it had gotten there, he caught sight of Edward Marcus putting a coffeepot on the fire.

"This yours?" he asked Marcus, gesturing to the blanket.

"Yeah. I got up in the middle of the night, and I saw you there, shivering in your sleep. Your clothes aren't as warm as the rest of ours, so I figured you could use the blanket more than me."

"Well, thanks. If I'd have known about this little expedition in advance, maybe I'd have brought warmer clothing, but..." Jonathan smiled and shrugged. "Who knew? Sure is the most adventure I've had on a law case."

"Wait'll we actually get down to Thomas's place before you decide whether you're enjoying your adventure or not."

Jonathan looked around. The deputy was still asleep by the fire. "Where's Brown?"

"I think he's taking a bath down in the river."

"Sounds like a good idea."

"I wouldn't recommend it. Water's mighty cold until the sun's been on it for awhile, and you don't want to take a chill, since—"

Jonathan finished his sentence for him. "—my clothes aren't

warm enough." He looked around him and spotted something that gave him an odd feeling. "Hey, Marcus, what's that curled up by the deputy's side?"

Before he'd blinked, Marcus had drawn his gun and shot the rattlesnake. Dickens sat bolt upright.

"Wha—"

"You had a visitor while you were sleeping."

"What's going on here?" It was Brown, wet and wrapped in a drab-colored blanket, his clothes bundled underneath the arm that wasn't clutching the blanket closed. His eyes went to the gun in Marcus's hand. "Didn't I tell you not to—" He stopped at the sight of the still-twitching rattlesnake. "Oh."

"Weren't you taking an awful chance?" asked Jonathan. "That snake was only inches from his side."

"He wouldn't have made the shot if he hadn't have known he would hit that rattler and not me," said Dickens firmly. He looked Marcus right in the eyes. "I'm certain of that."

• ❤ •

It was early morning of the next day that they came upon the first signs of habitation.

"Think this is it?" Dickens asked Brown.

"Got to be. Wonder how far we are from the main house?"

"You know what I'm worryin' about," Marcus muttered under his breath to Brown. If only Dusty had kept their other identities to himself in the first place, they wouldn't be approaching their goal with such mixed feelings. That look Dickens had given him the other morning when he'd shot the rattlesnake made him wonder if he hadn't figured it out, anyway—maybe not that he was Johnny Nevada, but that he was a well-known gun. Not many would have even risked the shot, but Marcus had panicked when he saw the danger that the deputy was in. All he could hope was that Dickens's gratitude outweighed his sense of duty to his job.

They rode on, through much of the morning, across the vast land holdings that they were all assuming belonged to Dan Thomas.

The sun was still a bit short of its high noon position when they saw horsemen heading their way. There were six of them.

"Looks like we've found who we're looking for," Jeremiah said, giving Ed a particular look, as if to say, *well, freedom's been nice*. "The one on the good horse must be Thomas." And they continued to ride toward them, until both groups pulled up, within speaking distance.

The man on the gray dapple pulled out in front of the rest of the party. Brown and Marcus recognized the grizzled outlaw known as "Boss" and the redheaded one among the party. The man who spoke was in his late 40s, his hat tipped back to reveal a balding forehead.

"Hello, gentlemen. I was hoping it wouldn't come to this, but I can't say I'm surprised. Dan Thomas, at your service... Oh, and, by the way, my men are armed and all very good shots."

"We've just come for what you took from us," said Brown.

"Well, isn't that a coincidence? Because I was just taking back what Sam Fitzgerald stole from me—the deed to 20,000 acres around Greenville, Montana."

"We don't know about that. We know about some old furniture, and that we were supposed to deliver it to Mr. Fitzgerald, and that he's mighty displeased we didn't make the delivery. And we've been specifically instructed to bring it back."

"Don't it make some strange bedfellows? What do we have here, but Johnny Nevada and Tommy Slade, accompanied by a man wearing a star, and...who's the young guy? Your accountant, or something?"

Brown didn't bother to deny the identification, since Thomas's companions were all part of the gang that had been riding with Dusty that day, but he threw a quick glance over his shoulder to see how Dickens and Cranbrook were taking the information. Somehow, neither of them was showing any reaction at all. Dickens was staring straight ahead, apparently gauging the strength of the opposition. Jonathan had a cold fire in his eyes that Brown hadn't expected to see there.

"Look, Mr. Thomas, we don't know anything about a deed. All we want is the stuff we were supposed to deliver. We're willing to search through the drawers with you. And we got the law with us, so you might want to think twice before you refuse to cooperate." Should be easy enough to "miss" the secret drawer.

"Well, as it happens, I'm glad you came calling. You see, my men and I have searched and come up with nothing. But Tommy Slade, now… I hear tell he might just be able to find what we're looking for."

"And then you'll let us have the furniture?"

"I don't think so. You're trespassing on private property, and if that deputy don't have something better to do with two notorious outlaws than help 'em chase after some old junk, maybe our local sheriff ought to hear about it."

Brown opened his mouth to respond, but before he could, the sound of a shot had rung out from the other side.

• ❤ •

Jonathan Cranbrook followed the next several minutes in a bewildered haze of adrenaline, fear, and another emotion he had never experienced before and was puzzled by, since it left him feeling cold, clear, and eager.

One of Thomas's men, a small redheaded fellow, had

apparently fired the first shot by mistake. He was holding his rifle cocked, when his horse stumbled. However, Thomas's men took this as a signal, and began firing on the quartet that faced them.

Quick as lightning, the man Jonathan knew as Edward Marcus had drawn and returned fire on the redhead, shooting him square in the shoulder. Nobody could shoot that accurately from that distance, Jonathan thought to himself. Nobody but...his eyes widened as he realized that the man he had been trailing around the mountains really *was* Johnny Nevada, as Dan Thomas had claimed. As Nick Powell and the bounty hunter had claimed. And that meant that the other man must indeed be...

Jonathan turned his head quickly to watch as Tommy Slade aimed directly at Dan Thomas. No, not at Mr. Thomas, but at his—

And then he felt a searing pain in his arm as the impact of a bullet threw him backwards on his horse, and he managed to keep from falling only by the sheerest exertion of will and physical force.

Meanwhile, Ed had taken aim again, firing toward Dan Thomas and the outlaw leader, firing to frighten them, this time, not to hit them. He saw that the redheaded outlaw was down off his horse, and then that Thomas's gray horse had been shot out from under him, probably by Brown. Jonathan had been wounded, too, and Marcus was aiming again at the outlaw known as Boss, when the man began to shout, "Hold off, men. Hold off!"

Marcus, Brown, and Dickens held back, and Jonathan's gun had been knocked from his hand by the impact of the shot that grazed his arm. Boss's men quickly held up, too.

"Now, then," said Boss. "I didn't sign onto this job for any killing. There's plenty worth killing over, but old furniture ain't it, and neither is grudges I don't know anything about. Red started it first, so I can't lay the blame on our visitors, here. But it looks like we got a couple men need medical attention, Mister Thomas, and I aim to see they get it."

Thomas looked up from where his horse was pinning him to the ground by the leg, and said, "For chrissakes, get this thing off of me!"

Without his men backing him, Thomas was powerless to prevent Dickens from claiming the powers of the law to reclaim stolen property. Besides, he was somewhat preoccupied with the agony from his shattered leg.

• ❤ •

The furniture was discovered in an outbuilding. Jonathan, his arm in a sling, was examining it with amazement. "He was just gonna leave this stuff out here? You can't leave stuff like this in a barn. The wood'll get ruined!"

"You're lucky *you* didn't get ruined, Cranbrook," said Marcus. "That bullet just grazed your arm. Jeremiah was pretty scared, there. He wasn't exactly looking forward to going back and telling Miss Anna we'd lost her sidekick."

"Any luck finding the documents?" Marcus asked.

"Nothing in here but some old papers in Spanish that I found fastened to the underside of a drawer," Dickens answered. "My Spanish isn't very good, but I know enough that I can tell you it's a land deed, for sure. But it's a land deed for south of the Rio Grande. It's got nothing at all to do with Dan Thomas."

"All that trouble, men wounded, and that horse killed—not to mention me and my partner in jail for days—for something that had nothing to do with him?"

"It's worse than that. This deed is a hundred years old. That land's probably belonged to someone else for nearly a century."

They loaded the furniture onto the old cart, still sound although somewhat the worse for wear after its trip through the mountains. Deputy Sheriff Dickens rather ceremoniously paid Boss, as representative for the still mostly-unconscious Thomas, for the purchase of several fresh cart horses, to add to the original team. Jonathan insisted on writing out a little transfer document, although he had to do it with his left hand, and it looked like it had been executed by a small child. But, as he pointed out, Fitzgerald was going to be paying for this.

When they'd gotten off of Thomas's land, Brown called for the cart to pull up. He jumped up onto the back and lifted the canvas coverings. Searching the desk, he soon found what he was looking for—the secret drawer. "Don't feel bad, Cranbrook, it was well hidden." Jonathan's documents weren't the only secret contents, after all. Inside was an oblong black box, which he lifted out.

Marcus looked at him, with his raised eyebrows, and asked, "What is it?"

Jeremiah whistled in response. "What's in here is no land deed. And it's not worth $15,000, either. It's worth a whole lot more." He held out a box containing a large cache of jewelry: a magnificent diamond necklace in an old-fashioned setting, and likewise, one of sapphires, as well as a number of unset rubies and emeralds. He and Ed looked at each other, and then somewhat regretfully at the deputy. "I assume this is what we were really transporting?"

"Unless it really was those Mexican deeds, and Fitzgerald don't know about the jewels."

"Well, Ed, we'll never know that, will we?" Brown turned to the deputy. "I suppose you'll be notifying the sheriff when we get back to Greenville, now that you know all about who we are."

"I don't know what you're talking about, Mister Brown."

"Sure, you do."

"I'm sure I don't. Do you, Cranbrook?"

"Why, no, I have no idea what he's talking about."

"You're not going to turn us in for the reward? The $5,000 reward on each of us?"

"When I look at you, what I see is two men who saved my life. And just like those jewels, I think that's worth a little bit more than $10,000 or so."

Brown and Marcus broke into huge grins.

"You're a good man, Jim Dickens," said Brown.

"The best," said Marcus. "Now, if I'm not mistaken, we've got a load of high-priced old furniture to deliver, Jeremiah."

"Antiques, Edward. Antiques."

As the other two drove the cart along, Jeremiah and Ed rode ahead. They were bringing the load around by way of Townsend, retracing their earlier route and avoiding the strenuous mountain paths.

Marcus turned to Brown with a smile. "So, we're heading back to Greenville and that pretty lady lawyer. What you gonna do about it?"

Brown sighed. "Guess that depends on what the lady wants. And whether I have a rival or not." He glanced involuntarily backward at the cart. "He's around her all the time, and he's a lot steadier than I am. Who could blame her?"

Ed just shook his head. From what he could see, Anna treated Jonathan the same way Jeremiah treated him—like a younger brother. But he'd have to figure that out for himself. Funny how someone so smart could be so stupid sometimes.

Chapter 7

Anna found herself sitting on the veranda of the hotel, pretending to read *Middlemarch,* all that afternoon. She reflected that if she had to pretend to read her favorite book, that suggested how jangled her nerves were.

They'd been gone for well over a week, and not a word. Although she knew that Jeremiah Brown and Ed Marcus could take care of themselves, she found that she was worried about them, anyway. Maybe they'd been through a lot, but not with her sitting and waiting for them to finish it and get on back home. As for Jonathan, she'd already come up with about a dozen different ways of explaining to his parents how he had died, nobly, in the cause of duty. She had a very distinct mental picture of them telling her that the reason they'd sent him to become a lawyer in the first place was because lawyers don't die in the cause of duty, nobly or otherwise.

Finally, when she'd gotten absorbed in the part of the story where the protagonist, Dorothea, goes to see Rosamund Vincy, only to discover her in a *tête-à-tête* with her own, as yet unacknowledged, love interest Will Ladislaw, and immediately assumes the worst, she heard the rattle of cart wheels. She looked up to see that Jonathan and the deputy were driving a wagon, which looked like it was loaded with old furniture. Brown and Marcus were following them on horseback. She threw down her book, and ran after them, catching them because they'd pulled to a stop in front of the sheriff's office.

Without thinking, she found herself running right past Jonathan, whose arm was in a sling, past Ed Marcus and the deputy, and right to Jeremiah Brown, who had just tied up his horse. As he turned to face her, she ran to him and flung her arms around his neck, crying, "You're back! I was so worried about you all!"

He put his arms around her, and hugged her, a surprised look on his face. "We're just fine. We got everything back. We're good at this." He paused, pulled away, and looked at her, not having quite let go of her. "Anna, are you all right?"

"Well, I am now," she said, and stopped to collect herself. "After all, I would have had a hard time collecting my fees if my clients never came back to town…and how would I have gotten all those law books back to Carter's Creek without Jonathan?"

He laughed and released her. She went to check on Jonathan, but she saw from looking around that her actions had not gone unnoticed. Marcus was grinning and the deputy seemed amused by her sudden, obvious preference for Mr. Brown, whom she'd previously been treating in the most distant and professional manner.

Jonathan, however, remained oblivious, since he had climbed into the back of the wagon, and was fumbling with the canvas coverings and ropes that covered the furniture. "Anna!" he called, finally. "Come look." He waited patiently, until she reached his side, when he rather perfunctorily showed her some old Mexican legal documents and a flat, black box, which he opened and closed again rather quickly. She saw the flash of jewels, and if that brief glance was any indication, she knew she'd never doubt her clients' good faith again. They could have fled to South America with what was in that box, and lived comfortably for the rest of their lives. But Jonathan had already lost interest in that, and lowered his sling so she could fuss over his injuries. Sometimes, she reflected, he was more like a little brother than anyone not born a Harrison had any right to be.

Sam Fitzgerald was satisfied by the return of his furniture, and particularly of the desk, the contents of its secret drawer still intact. He even paid them what they claimed he owed them, with no more discussion of implied contracts or reliance.

As Jeremiah carefully tucked away his banknotes, she turned to scold him. "Now, you two be more careful about making agreements from now on. You get a signed piece of paper."

"Yeah?" asked Ed, who'd walked up while she was speaking. "You think we should hire you and Jonathan to ride around with us as our own personal lawyers? He's pretty good with a horse, too, and he wasn't half bad with a gun for someone who'd had so little practice."

"What do you think, Jonathan? We get that cart back, we could load it up with our law books and follow them all around the West, making sure they get their agreements notarized and negotiating escape clauses?"

Jonathan laughed. "And how many states and territories would we have to get called to the bar in, in order to keep up with them?"

"A few too many for my comfort," she acknowledged. "And some of them won't take women, either. Besides," she turned to Ed, "I think there's a pair of bright eyes at home, impatiently waiting for Mister Cranbrook's return. Not to mention a pair of beady eyes waiting for mine. Jonathan, I think Nick

Powell's going to press ahead with the Dowling matter as soon as we return. I got an impatient telegram a few days back. You have to admit, it takes a certain brilliance to make a telegram sound impatient."

"Well," said Jeremiah, "we've got about two hours until the next stage leaves for Townsend, and then we've all got trains to catch there the next day. We found a telegram waiting for us from Leon Anderson, and it looks like there's a job for us down in Colorado we need to get to."

Ed and Jonathan walked on ahead to the hotel, but Jeremiah detained Anna with a hand on her shoulder. She turned to face him, very aware of just how close he was standing. He spoke. "So, I guess I was wrong when I thought maybe you and Jonathan—"

"Jonathan?" she exclaimed. "He's practically a child...why, he's young enough to be my much younger brother! Which, by the way, is exactly how I think of him."

"I thought—he's about the same age that David must have been when he died. I thought maybe he reminded you of something you'd lost. And any man'd want you, if he thought he had a chance."

She laughed. "Me and Jonathan Cranbrook...my word! I've never heard such a silly thing. He's engaged to Melanie Norton, the prettiest girl in Carter's Creek. A lot of boys in town were all broken up when she picked Jonathan." But she couldn't help but be flattered by the fact that he'd spent so much energy thinking it through.

Jeremiah gave her one of those brilliant smiles of his, as his glance traveled from her soft blonde hair and delicate features to her slender, graceful figure. "I thought *you* were the prettiest girl in Carter's Creek."

She smiled ruefully. "Maybe once. But that time, if it ever

was, is long past."

But apparently, that wasn't what he wanted to hear about, because he pressed his lips to hers and then whispered in her ear, "I didn't know what to think when you pushed me away like that, the first day. I thought that maybe you'd really only come to do your job. Just think of all this time we've been wasting. We've only got this evening and…tonight."

Brown eyes met blue ones, and he found the confirmation he was looking for. *Tonight*. She thought about that night back in Carter's Creek, the one they'd had together. That there might be another was more than she'd ever really let herself hope. Maybe that was why she had backed away from him that first day in Greenville—sheer disbelief that their first meeting hadn't all been a dream. She took his hand, and held it tight for a moment. "I'd better go see to my bags," she said, because there were no words for what she really wanted to say. "I'll see you on the stage."

Townsend was a much bigger place than Greenville had been. Brown and Marcus went in to help with the room reservations while Anna and Jonathan saw to the baggage—they, of course, had the steamer trunk and a couple of valises, as compared to the saddlebags the others so casually slung over their shoulders. She went right up to her room to have a nice long bath, and then she dressed in a new silk dress she had brought along, thinking…thinking what? *Hoping*, rather, that she'd have occasion to wear it, and to look pretty for Jeremiah Brown.

There was a good restaurant in town, and the quartet had an excellent dinner. Anna was just beginning to feel that time was passing too quickly, and more particularly, to feel the constraints forced on her by Jonathan's presence, when

Marcus spoke up. *Bless him,* she thought.

"Well, this has been a fine meal, but I would really like to go celebrate in the way I'm used to celebratin', begging your pardon, Miss Anna. I'd like to go to the saloon and throw back a few drinks, play some cards, maybe. You comin', Jer? Cranbrook?" From the glance the two outlaws gave each other, it was apparent to Anna that this had been prearranged.

"Drinks sound real good," said Jeremiah, and from the sparkle in his eyes she knew he was doing it to torment her. "Cranbrook, here, has been working real hard on our behalf, and I think we should show him the kind of time he don't get at home, under the watchful eye of Miss Anna, here. But I don't like the idea of making her spend the evening in her hotel room with a good book, even that *Middle*-whatever it is she likes so much, when she's got a winning case to celebrate, too. Tell you what, Ed, why don't you take Cranbrook with you? Have a wild time. I'll stay here and keep Anna company. Maybe I'll catch up with you later." He said it with just enough of an air of martyrdom that she half-believed him herself, even though he had taken hold of her hand under the table almost as soon as he opened his mouth, and pressed it tightly at those final words.

And so, it was arranged, Jonathan looking at her dubiously as though to say he'd stay if she wanted him to. Needless to say, she encouraged him to go and have a good time.

As soon as they were gone, Jeremiah ordered himself a whiskey, and a sherry for his companion, and settled into a position where they could look more directly into each other's eyes. "I've been wishing I could get up to Carter's Creek and see you again, and something always seems to get in the way."

"And I told myself that I was never going to see you again, and that it was best that way."

"And what do you think now?"

She smiled. "Do you need to ask? I'm glad we're here."

"You know, there's too much table between us. It's a little too early to go back to the hotel, yet, and there's a dance hall down the street. Why don't we spend some time twirling around the floor?"

"Oh, my. I've never been to a dance hall. Is it," she paused, savoring her own hypocrisy, "respectable for a lady?"

"For a lady who's accompanied by a gentleman," he said.

"But will I be accompanied by a gentleman?" she asked pointedly, and instantly regretted her inability to let the obvious witticism slip by. He actually looked a little upset, so she took one of his hands firmly in both hers and said, "You've got the silver tongue, but I've got the tongue of a litigator, I'm afraid. I'm so used to verbal fencing matches that I speak without thinking. I would love, more than anything in the world, to visit the dance hall in the company of the particular gentleman I'm talking to right now."

He raised an eyebrow. "More than anything in the world?"

She blushed. "Except for the part that comes after." She was as red as the strawberries on the table. And that was just fine, because she was about to glide around a dance floor in the arms of Jeremiah Brown, and at that moment, she didn't think she could have been any happier.

• ♥ •

There seemed to be a fair number of couples on the dance floor who gave the appearance of courting, or even being married. There were an even larger number of cowboys and ranchers with their hired dancehall girls, most of whom could be hired for other things, as well. The music wasn't bad for a town that size, and although neither of them were particularly good dancers, they didn't notice much outside their immediate range, anyway. Finally, he kissed her, right in the middle of all those dancers. Surely, no one would notice.

Instantly, they heard applause from the side of the floor and someone crying "Woo! Woo!" They broke apart, and saw Edward and Jonathan, the latter red-faced and a little unsteady, and with a dancehall girl on his good arm.

"Well, who'd'a thought it," said Jonathan, slurring his words just the tiniest bit. "The Widow herself, kissin' a man, and in public, too!"

They made their way over to the side of the floor where they were standing. There was no way out of this one except to fight blackmail with blackmail. She assumed a position of as much authority as she could, considering that Jeremiah's arm remained around her waist, and said in a pointed tone, "I think that my late fiancé would understand, since it's been close onto a decade, that I might get a little lonely sometimes. I do not think, however, that Melanie would be quite as understanding about your little friend there," she nodded to indicate the scantily-clad girl hanging onto his shoulder.

"Why, Evelyn and I are just friends," he said, with as much dignity as he could muster, nevermind the lip rouge marks on his cheek and collar. "Friends. That's all."

"I think you and the lady are even," said Ed, who was a good deal more sober. The expression in his blue eyes showed just how much he was enjoying giving the young clerk an education in areas his lady lawyer mentor was unqualified to advise him about.

Jonathan nodded. "Even. I won't tell if you don't tell. Deal?" he asked Anna. They shook on it, rather emphatically on his part, and he wobbled off with his friend Evelyn draped all over him.

Ed Marcus turned to Anna. "I guess you don't let him out

much, huh? He's got no head for liquor at all. And why'd he call you 'the Widow'? I thought you and your young man were only engaged to be married when he died."

"First of all, I'm not in charge of Jonathan's off hours. Of course, we don't have too many of those, but Miss Melanie is the one to ask about them, not me. Second, they call me the Widow back home because they say I've spent longer in mourning for my fiancé than most women ever did for a husband."

Ed nodded, and seeing his company was not in demand, soon caught the eye of a young lady and whisked her off into a dance. Anna couldn't help but note that he was a better dancer than Jeremiah, though it might be that he had a more accomplished dance partner, as well.

As soon as he'd gone, Jeremiah took her hand and drew her outside. It was dark, and the sky very clear, and she pointed at Orion, the Hunter. "I always feel like he's my friend; that he'll help me to get home safely. Silly, I know."

"Are you?" he asked. "Still in mourning? You don't dress in head-to-toe black, but—"

"I told you that that night in Carter's Creek. I loved David very much, but I only knew him for three years, and he's been gone for almost nine, now. I do still miss him, but my extended period of mourning is also a way to get people to let me alone, to accept me for what I am, and not to try to marry me off. But it's a romantic enough tale that they don't just write me off as some dried-up old spinster, either. Too easy to dismiss me, that way."

Jeremiah looked at her. "I thought all respectable women like you wanted to get married. I thought you were all just born that way or something."

"I like it on my own," she said. "I thought you knew that.

You know that I've been using my poor lamented David to dodge marriage proposals for years."

He smiled and shook his head. "Lucky for me."

"Well, I'm not expecting any forthcoming from your direction," she looked him right in the eyes.

"Good thing, since right now that isn't possible." He gave her a smile that was part an apology, part a declaration, part something else, and she leaned in to kiss him to let him know that she understood. At that moment, she wouldn't have cared if Jonathan saw them, or if he'd sold tickets to half of Carter's Creek, besides. And with that, Jeremiah ushered her back onto the dance floor.

In another half-hour, they'd judged it safe to return to the hotel. When they entered the lobby, she was met with a surprise, because the desk clerk referred to them as Mr. and Mrs. Brown. Brown led her up to her room…*their* room…and when he unlocked the door, she saw his saddlebags were there along with her valise. "Surprise," he said. "I figured it would be safer this way."

"Safer except that the clerk might have noticed that Mrs. Brown isn't wearing a wedding ring," she pointed out. "I'm assuming you and Ed stayed at the other hotel in town on your way to Greenville."

"The bigger gamble was whether you and Jonathan did."

"With clients dragging me halfway across the territory, who I didn't expect would be able to pay?"

"That's what I figured," he grinned. "You must have been pretty surprised when we actually did pay you, huh?"

"You have no idea," she said.

There was a vase of flowers by the bed, and a bottle of…could it be champagne in a place like this? It popped as he uncorked it—it was! He poured two glasses, and handed her one. It wasn't very good champagne, of course, but still...

"We only have this one night, so I wanted it to be special." His deep voice was husky. He took a sip from his glass and put it down, moving toward her.

"What is it with us?" she asked. "We always only have just this one night."

That smile again. The one so bright it seemed to illuminate the room, even as he turned the gaslight down low. "I think it's that you're you, and I'm me, and that's just the way things are for us." And then he took her in his arms and kissed her and they didn't talk again for a long while.

Chapter 8

It was the following spring, when Anna took her ward, Sarah, on holiday to Colorado Springs. Right after dinner, the first evening after they'd arrived in town, Anna decided that she needed to take a turn and get some air. She refused Sarah's company, since the girl was obviously very tired, and insisted she stay at the hotel with its manageress and resident chaperone, Mrs. Grey, an almost terrifyingly respectable older woman. Anna, though, was feeling stiff and confined from the lengthy journey, and was enjoying the walk so much that even when darkness fell, she was still wandering up and down the streets. She was daydreaming as she walked, so that by the time she saw two drunken cowboys wobbling down the street, singing off key, they were nearer than she found entirely comfortable. They were in the company of a pair of women who were satin-clad and showing rather too much arm and bosom to be considered "ladies," and she thought about how lucky it was that she had left Sarah behind.

It wasn't that she believed in sheltering people, and here in the West that was hard to do, anyway. But Sarah was such a sweet and innocent girl that Anna could hardly help but want to protect her. Honestly, she didn't know much about it herself, but she'd always supposed that the saloons provided the girls who worked there with rooms right on the premises. Apparently, not the one this quartet was headed out from, however. There was something disconcertingly familiar about the two men, and as they got closer, she knew that they weren't cowboys after all. She almost wished she was a more delicate flower of womanhood, because not falling into a faint meant that she was going to have to find another way try to dodge two of her former clients and favorite acquaintances on this wide open and rather deserted section of street. Ed Marcus and Jeremiah Brown were most definitely not in a fit condition to speak with a respectable lady. From the looks of it, she wasn't quite sure they were in a fit condition to speak at all.

She knew it was already too late when Ed Marcus, his hat all askew on his dark blond hair, called out loudly, "Well, who would've 'spected to see her so far from home? Howdy, Miss Anna!" He stopped short in his path, and the quartet had a sort of collision, with Brown ending up in a heap on the ground.

She pulled herself together as best she could. Using all her courtroom tricks to keep her voice even and her demeanor unruffled, she said, "Hello, Edward. So nice to see you boys are keeping out of trouble." She looked down at the dark-eyed heap on the ground, which looked back up at her pitifully. "Hello, Jeremiah."

"Hello, Anna," he said, his deep voice hoarse from all that off-key singing.

His companion, a buxom young redhead whose ample charms were quite thoroughly displayed, tried to assist him in getting up again. She shot Anna a glance, taking in her high-necked gray dress and her disapproving expression. Apparently, there was only one possible conclusion: "Is everything okay, honey? Is that your wife or something?"

He looked miserable. "Only in my dreams," he said, trying to enunciate the words through a drink-thickened tongue.

"Didn't know you were so prone to nightmares," Anna snapped, before she'd thought better of it. It started to hit her, what he'd just said, but she shook it off. It was the whiskey talking anyway, she was certain of that. As she looked at the drunken outlaw being helped to his feet, she wondered how she could have thought that there could ever be anything real between them. Well, no matter. Right now, all she wanted to do was to get away from there as fast as she could. Remembering her manners, however, she addressed the young lady of the evening. "No, miss, it's worse. I'm his lawyer."

"You're kiddin' me," said the redhead. "You?"

"Yes, miss," she insisted. "There are professions open to women other than your own. Now, if you'll excuse me..."

"Anna, come back, honey," Brown was calling. "Don't go 'way mad."

She turned, and for a moment almost found herself wanting to relent. Those deep brown eyes of his were appealing to her with genuine longing. But just then, Ed Marcus's companion giggled loudly. "Better watch out, Lizzie. She's gonna steal your trade." The woman squealed as Marcus pinched her, and then leaned down and kissed her square on the lips.

The redhead clutched Jeremiah's arm possessively, pressing her breasts against him in a shameless fashion. Anna felt dizzy for a moment, then recollected herself. She was a lady, after all, and a lady shouldn't be subjected to such things. Looking severely at the quartet, she said, "Mr. Brown and Mr. Marcus, when you have recovered from tonight's little escapade, you will be welcome to call on me at my hotel. However, I am here on holiday with an impressionable young girl, and this is most certainly not the time for you to make her acquaintance." She turned to walk away.

"Which hotel?" asked Brown.

Anna smiled triumphantly. "The Springs Temperance Hotel. Alcoholic beverages most definitely prohibited. Good evening, Mr. Brown, Mr. Marcus, young ladies." She nodded coldly and walked away without looking back again, even when the drunken singing resumed. The whores' laughter seemed to pursue her for far longer than she must actually have been able to hear it.

When she got back to the hotel, Sarah and Mrs. Grey were waiting for her in the parlor. She made her excuses as quickly as she could and went up to the room that she and Sarah were sharing, alone. She didn't quite know what to do with herself. In rapid succession she examined the contents of her trunk, took out a poor attempt at embroidery on which Sarah had been coaching her during their train ride, put it away again, read and reread the telegram from her former law clerk and brand-new partner, Jonathan Cranbrook, which had been awaiting her on her arrival at the hotel, began to write a reply, crumpled it up, and threw it away.

She took up a book, saw it was *The Corsair* by Lord Byron, and tossed it across the room. It hit the opposite wall with a loud thud, and fell open on the floor. *What nonsense,* she thought, *the noble pirate, the tragic outlaw.* Tonight, she'd seen Jeremiah Brown in his true colors. He hadn't behaved any differently than any man of his kind would, drinking and whoring. What's more, he'd never lied about it. It was all her own fault, weaving some kind of romantic fantasy around a man she'd met twice in her life, and it was particularly her own fault that she'd taken him as her lover on both those occasions. A respectable woman like Anna didn't do things like that, and she'd only been asking for trouble. What had she been expecting, anyway? It wasn't as if he had ever made any promises.

Well, that wasn't entirely true. When they'd parted that last time, he'd looked her in the eye and promised her that he'd see her again, somehow, someday. But that had been last autumn, and she hadn't heard from him since. She certainly hadn't expected their next meeting to be like this. *What had I been expecting? That we'd fall in love and live happily ever after? Hah! A wanted outlaw and a woman who felt like she was suffocating any time a man came courting. Not likely.*

All she knew was that she thought about him too much, that she fell asleep too many nights remembering his kisses and his touch and his laughter and all the stories he'd told her. It was a stupid, foolish position she'd put herself in, and it had to stop. Besides, she couldn't have told him she was coming to Colorado, even if she'd known he was there, because she didn't have an address to write to him.

Still, she couldn't get his words out of her head.

"Is that your wife?"

"Only in my dreams."

Did he really think about her like that? And if he did, what a peculiar way to find out. She didn't know whether she wanted to laugh or to cry, so she did both, at the same time, until both the absurdity and the sadness of it all had worked its way out.

There was a timid knocking on the door, and Sarah's soft voice. "Anna, can I come in?"

"Come on in," Anna called, and Sarah found her sitting on her bed and brushing her loosened hair. She sat down next to her friend on the bed and held out her hand for the brush.

"Why are you looking so sad, Anna? With your pretty golden hair, just like a fairy princess," she murmured. Sarah was a very romantic young woman. Sarah was very young, period.

"I don't feel much like a fairy princess, Sarah. More like the old witch." The mirror on the wall told Anna she was still quite attractive at twenty-nine, but Sarah was the fairest of them all, at least as far as Carter's Creek, Montana was concerned. She had luxuriant jet-black hair, and big brown eyes, and there was something about her looks that suggested the stories were true. It was rumored that her father was a Native, and that her mama had been a captive who died of grief after her family rescued her and took her away from him.

Sarah was raised by her grandparents until she was 10 or 11, and then they died of influenza and she went to the orphanage. She believed that her father never knew about her; certainly, he never came for her. Her grandparents had done what they thought was their duty by her, but they'd never been loving, blaming her for their daughter's death. Things only got worse at the orphanage in Butte, where she was treated unkindly because of her mixed blood.

Three years earlier, shortly after her parents' death in a train derailment, Anna had gone to the orphanage on legal business, and had taken the girl away with her. Sarah was eighteen now, and with her looks, her gentle nature, and her domestic talents, Anna was determined that the girl would make a good marriage. The only problem was that some folks looked down on her as a half-breed, ugly word that it was.

“Why can’t we just stay the two of us forever?” Sarah would say, but Anna didn’t think her ward would be happy keeping house for an old maid indefinitely. She’d want children and a home of her own.

Maybe, in a resort town like Colorado Springs, Sarah might find her handsome prince. *I just hadn't expected to find mine transformed into a swine while we were at it,* Anna thought. Well, that wasn't quite fair, but lying in the gutter wasn't where she thought she’d see Jeremiah Brown next. The image of his face, flushed from the alcohol, and those longing dark eyes, came unbidden to her mind, but she quickly dismissed it. She willed herself to think of something else—anything else.

"What's that poor book doing on the floor over there?" Sarah asked, gesturing to the red volume which lay face down, some of its pages crumpled underneath it.

"It's a long story, Sarah. But let's try to get some sleep. That nice couple we met at dinner tonight said that they have a party going out into the mountains the day after next, and we're to meet the rest of the group and the guide tomorrow to see if we'd like to accompany them."

"You mean, sleep in a tent and all?" Sarah looked thrilled, which was more than Anna could say for herself, but it was the only way to see the best views. They were there, and they were going to see the best views if they had to sleep in a tent the whole time.

"Yes. Apparently, Mrs. Stevens is overjoyed to have two more ladies joining the expedition. It's herself, and her husband, and two other men. And the guide, of course."

"A real adventure!" Sarah exulted. She loved adventures, and spent as much of her free time as possible on horseback or clambering around mountains. Anna liked the wilds that surrounded their town, too, but not with Sarah's energy or unbounded enthusiasm. Sometimes, she sat below and watched her ward climbing, but she trusted to the girl's instincts and her sense of her own limits so much that after awhile, she frequently let Sarah go out on her own while she was working. She wondered if it came from her father's people, if it was in her blood.

"Good night," she said, with rather less enthusiasm, and went to sleep to dream of something other than Jeremiah Brown.

• ♥ •

"The Temperance Hotel didn't quite appeal to them?" she had asked Victor Stevens, half-facetiously. She remembered that now, thinking of her own intemperate gentleman friends of last night.

Victor had smiled. "Not terribly." He had quickly sized her up as more a woman of the world than his wife. How a spinster from Carter's Creek, Montana, could be more a woman of the world than a married lady from San Francisco was as much a puzzle to Anna as it must have been to Stevens. Anna supposed it was because she worked in a world of men as an equal, and didn't stay sheltered at home like Greta Stevens. Or maybe it had something to do with those French novels she read, that a proper lady oughtn't to—Balzac and Flaubert and George Sand and all the rest—that talked about a world of desires, of moral corruption and marital infidelity and all those things that occurred regularly in life and hardly at all in the literature written in her own language. And just maybe, it might have had something to do with Jeremiah Brown. Well, that was a train of thought she didn't care to pursue right now.

That morning they were full of meaningless small talk, as they gathered over breakfast, awaiting the rest of their party. The weather was touched upon more than once, and she began to fear that even the spectacular scenery they were going to see might not prevent this expedition from being a deathly bore. "Ah, here they are!" Victor Stevens said, as two men entered the room. One of them was young, nondescript, but with a pleasant face, and Anna wondered idly if he might not do for Sarah. He was introduced as Paul Bryant. He worked with Victor in the accounting department of a large San Francisco import/export firm that did a great deal of business with the Far East. But it was the other man who commanded everyone's attention when he entered the room. He was older than the others, with iron-gray hair, piercing blue eyes, and handsome, weathered, hawk-like features. His name was Meriwether Abel, and he told them they could call him anything but "Mary."

After the introductions had been made, Abel said politely, "It's so nice for Greta to find some ladies to join us on the expedition. I understand you're a lawyer, Miss Harrison." He said it matter-of-factly, not in that way that so many people had of making her feel like she was on exhibit in the Hall of Curiosities.

"Yes, I am."

"Well, I'm a member of the California bar, myself, although I'm mostly involved in other aspects of the business these days. I do most of the traveling to our suppliers in China, Japan, and other parts of the Far East."

"I'll look forward to hearing more about that, Mr. Abel," she said, with genuine interest, while Sarah's eyes shone with fascination. She might not have taken to her books,

Anna reflected, but would always read travelers' tales. She always had first crack at any new ones the bookseller back East sent out, to keep Anna's personal library stocked.

Abel smiled and looked around at Victor. "Paul and I found ourselves a pair of crackerjack guides, but, if the ladies will pardon me, unfortunately they're a little worse for wear this morning. They got to celebrating their good fortune in landing this job last night. But they should be here any minute now."

Anna's insides contracted. It couldn't be. It was. There they were, large as life and twice as hung over, Jeremiah Brown and Edward Marcus, making their way into the dining room at the Springs Temperance Hotel. Ed was extraordinarily pale, and his blue eyes were bloodshot, but Jeremiah looked worse. His dark hair was all messed up, and there was something in his eyes and in his gait that suggested he might not be entirely sober, even yet.

Marcus said to his partner, "Smells funny in here, Jer. Think that's temperance smell?"

Brown groaned. "Everything smells funny this morning. Come to think of it, why does this place sound so familiar? Can't be too many folks we know would stay in a temperance hotel…least, not on purpose." His expression changed as he made the connection, his brain was pushing its way past the alcoholic mists of last night, just seconds before he caught sight of Anna sitting there with his employers.

Between his poker face and her courtroom face, no one ever would have known that they had ever set eyes on each other before that moment. He swallowed his surprise as quickly as could be.

"Mr. Brown and Mr. Marcus, I'd like you to meet Mr. and Mrs. Stevens, Miss Harrison, and Miss Nicholls." They shook hands with Victor, with Greta, with Sarah, and then they paused in front of Anna, waiting for her to acknowledge their acquaintance in some way.

The two of them looked at each other for what felt like a full minute before she took his hand and with a frosty smile said, "Pleased to meet you, Mr. Brown." She turned to Marcus without the vaguest sign of recognition and did the same. "Mr. Marcus."

"Are you two in any shape to conduct this meeting?" asked Paul Bryant. He had a soft, pleasant voice, one which the group was to hear little of over the next several days. But although he rarely spoke, he always seemed to be watching, and listening. Anna's instincts were completely uncertain about him, which was unusual. She almost always got a sense of people quickly—it was useful in the courtroom. Of course, she wasn't always right, she thought, turning her attention to the guides. But she trusted herself.

Jeremiah gave Bryant one of his patented smiles, even though it looked like it hurt his face to make it. Anna couldn't help but be a bit glad, after her embarrassment of the previous night. "Absolutely. We've done harder things in worse shape," he said, and proceeded to take out a map and trace out the course of the next week for the group. They'd also planned out exactly what the party needed in the way of horses, pack animals and provisions, although Abel and Stevens kept adding suggestions to the list—suggestions that Anna suspected were entirely superfluous.

Finally, all the details had been settled, and the departure time set for eight the following morning. Abel smiled at the guides, and said, "I expect these two would like to go back to their hotel and get some more sleep."

Jeremiah and his partner nodded gratefully, and turned

away, but not before Abel offered Anna his arm, which she took, rather ostentatiously.

She managed to avoid them for the rest of the day, although they returned to the hotel several times to consult with various members of the party. Bryant and Abel lunched with the others in the Temperance Hotel, but excused themselves to meet their guides for dinner. Abel invited Victor Stevens to accompany them, but with a quick look at his wife, Stevens refused. Apparently, it was a gentlemen's dinner. Anna imagined what the conversation would be like, and was almost certain that the buxom redhead and her companion would be a central feature of it.

Tomorrow would be time enough for her to deal with Jeremiah Brown.

Chapter 9

At eight in the morning they headed out, more than fully provisioned. In fact, the San Franciscans had insisted on so many supplies that the group was trailed by an absurd number of pack animals. They looked like one of those expeditions through Africa that people like Henry Stanley kept making. Anna got the distinct feeling that their guides were more than a little embarrassed by it.

She wasn't a real wilderness type herself. Despite having grown up in Montana, she'd spent most of her life quite happily in a town, and her wanderings in the mountains had been mostly of the sort that she could do within a day of her home, with merely a horse and a pair of stout boots. When she was able to get away from her work, to go for a ramble with Sarah, she was likely to plant herself with a book somewhere partway up the slope, in a spot with a nice view, while her ward insisted on exploring every inch of the hillside.

Brown and Marcus looked quite their old selves, Jeremiah Brown so much so that Anna's heart caught in her throat despite herself when she saw him. His dark hair was partly hidden under his black hat, and he had a blue bandana knotted about his throat. His partner was wearing a leather vest, and looked so much the handsome Western man that he could easily be on the cover of a dime novel. But Anna never looked at him twice when Jeremiah was around. There was something almost magnetic about the man, an intelligence that illuminated features that were, by anyone's account, quite attractive in and of themselves. He could conceal that, however, and appear simply charming and glib, when he wanted. Anna wondered if perhaps that was the real man, and if she'd just been reading more into him than was really there. She wondered, but she kept thinking, despite herself, of moments when his insights, his thoughtfulness, came to the fore.

"Isn't he handsome?" whispered Sarah, who was riding at her side. Anna wondered which one of them the younger woman meant, but then the two men rode apart, and she saw that her ward's eyes were following Ed Marcus. Even though she wasn't actually speaking to either of them at the moment, as she reminded herself, she was obscurely pleased by this.

They reached the foothills about noon, and picnicked there. When Abel handed around a silver flask to the gentlemen, Anna thought she caught Brown stealing a glance in her direction. She didn't think for a minute he would have passed the flask on without taking a swallow, and she didn't know what to make of the gesture.

Sarah and Abel were the best riders, other than Brown and Marcus, with both of the Stevenses occupying the place below Anna in the order. At least, they were from San Francisco. She didn't have much of an excuse, except that she walked nearly everywhere in Carter's Creek, and only rode to pay outlying calls, or on the rare opportunities she had for a day off. But still, her seat was pretty good, and as the day wore on and she got back in practice with the unaccustomed saddle, she occupied a solid middle position, along with Bryant.

Mrs. Stevens, who explained that she usually rode side-saddle, but hadn't thought to ask for special provisions, was having a more difficult time with riding astride, and Anna was concerned whether she was going to make it through the week.

"Can we rig one of the saddles so she can use it as a side-saddle?" she asked Marcus. She was still more comfortable approaching him than his partner.

He shrugged, but Anna could see a certain wariness in his response. She knew he must be confused about her pretending not to know him. "No, they're constructed too differently. Truth to tell, I don't quite understand why anyone would want to ride that way. Looks a bit risky to me."

"It's what proper ladies do, you see. I learned both ways, and I often ride side-saddle at home when I need to be dressed to meet with clients. Mrs. Stevens is just used to balancing a whole different way, controlling the horse differently."

But as the day went on, Greta Stevens adapted, and proved, indeed, to be a competent rider. Considerably better than her overly protective husband, who hovered at her side the whole time, Anna noted with satisfaction. In fact, several times that afternoon she reined her horse in, in order to hold back with him.

And so they rode on, through the foothills. The guides had decided they ought to press on as long as they could the first day, so that they could make a longer-term camp for the second night. Nobody had any objections, or at least, none they were willing to voice.

Abel took particular charge of Anna, which was just fine by her, since he was full of fascinating stories. He flanked her on one side, and when the path was wide, Paul Bryant rode on the other. Bryant rarely spoke, and when he did, he generally addressed himself to Abel. But he always seemed to be watching: the horizon, Sarah, the guides, the Stevenses, everything.

Brown and Anna managed to avoid each other, all day, although she couldn't help glancing his way occasionally…or, if the truth be known, more than occasionally. Once or twice she caught him glancing her way at the same time, his dark eyes expressionless, but they both quickly looked away. She idly suspected that, if she'd been quicker, she might have caught him more often. But she told herself it didn't matter. Things were better this way, and the trip would be over soon enough. They'd go their separate ways, this time for good.

By the time they made camp it was nearly dark, which in those long summer days made it fairly late. The guides and Abel did most of the work setting up. Anna and Sarah tried to help once or twice, but were shooed back to the fire and told to sit still and enjoy the evening breezes and the fire's glow. The Stevenses and Bryant began to put questions to Brown and Marcus about what Greta Stevens insisted on calling "the Wild West," which made it sound like she was from Philadelphia or Boston, rather than from San Francisco. Anna was curious to listen, curious to hear what sorts of stories they were going to be able to tell without letting on that they'd once been Tommy Slade and Johnny Nevada, famous outlaws, and not Jeremiah Brown and Edward Marcus, drifters and occasional wilderness guides.

But there were other demands on Anna's attention. Abel was a fascinating character. His stories of Far Eastern travel were endlessly interesting, like something out of a book. He claimed both Sarah's and Anna's attention, and they both got caught up in his stories, but it was to Anna that he constantly deferred. His attentions were so marked, while always remaining within the bounds of perfect propriety, that she found herself flustered on more than one occasion.

Later, as the fire was burning low and the other group beginning to disperse, Jeremiah made his way over to the three of them. He addressed himself almost exclusively to Abel, after acknowledging Sarah's and Anna's presence with a brief smile and nod. He asked a number of questions about the Far East and about Japan, in particular, and appeared to be quite disappointed to find out that Abel had never been to India, although Anna was sure he knew even less about that country than she did. He had no great information, but an endless supply of curiosity, and she found herself fascinated by the interchange between these two intelligent, adventurous, yet very different men.

The advantage wasn't all on Abel's side, either. Brown's quick wits were evident in his contributions to the conversation, and Anna couldn't help but be reminded of why it was that she'd always liked him so much. She briefly wondered whether they were showing off for her, but neither of them seemed to be particularly aware of her presence, anymore. It didn't occur to her until later, as she was falling asleep and pondering the day's events to herself, that the two strongest personalities in any group of men were going to feel obliged to try to feel each other out, to test each other's boundaries. She wondered if that was what Nick Powell, her constant opponent in legal matters back home, tried to do, and how much it must have frustrated him that she didn't play the same game. But they had plenty of games of their own.

It was a clear night. The men were going to sleep out under the stars, while a tent had been pitched for the women. Anna thought that as she was going to have to sleep on the ground anyway, she would rather have done it out in the open, so that she might wake to see the night sky. But she wasn't being given a choice. As she made her way into the tent, she saw that

Greta Stevens quickly shoved a piece of paper—it looked like a note—into her jacket pocket. Peculiar that anyone would need to communicate with her like that on a camping trip, Anna thought, but it had been a long day, and she was too tired to think for long.

Anna asked Mrs. Stevens a number of questions about herself and her life back home, but although she was perfectly friendly, her answers were noncommittal. She seemed a little ill at ease with the lawyer, and a bit more comfortable with her ward. Anna supposed she made a certain type of woman nervous, by the simple fact of who she was and what she did. And by what that suggested might be missing from their own lives. Truly contented domestic women tended to draw Anna right into their kitchens and give her a bowl of something to mix for them while they bustled about with their business. They asked her about the courtroom and told her about their children. Greta asked about Sarah, and about one of Anna's dresses that she'd particularly admired, back at the hotel. She said almost nothing about herself.

Sarah blew out the lantern when Greta complained of tiredness in her gentle, fretful sort of way. Anna woke up once in the night with the sensation that she couldn't breathe, and she crept out of the tent. She looked up at the stars, thinking that she could almost reach up and touch them, the night was so clear and the starlight so bright. She thought she heard the sound of someone moving nearby, and called out, "Hello?" There was no answer, but it made her uneasy enough that she crept back into the tent, and pulled the covers up and close to her. She reached out and touched Sarah just to reassure herself. The younger woman stirred under the rough woolen blanket, and the sound of her soft breathing eventually lulled Anna back to sleep.

The next day Anna awoke every bit as stiff and sore as she'd feared. Greta Stevens seemed to be in a similar state, and fretted about it a little, but pulled herself together and took a brave tone. "This trip means so much to Victor and his friends," she explained. Sarah, of course, was cheerful and without a single twinge of discomfort. Anna reflected that she herself was not precisely on in years, but had to keep reminding herself how very young her ward was.

Victor Stevens came to the tent and requested that they wait inside for a little while the gentlemen were washing and dressing. In return, he promised that breakfast would be waiting. When they did emerge, to the smell of some delicious cooking, Marcus handed them tin plates heaped with biscuits and sausage and all sorts of lovely things.

"Did you make this?" Anna asked.

"Him and me. Mostly him," he indicated Brown with his glance.

"Well, my compliments to the chef," she said, and smiled at Jeremiah for the first time. He was a far better cook than she was, even the first bite told her that.

He returned the smile, his expression friendly, if a little guarded, and said, laughing, "There's something about a campfire that brings it out in me."

She could tell he wanted to say something more, but she wasn't ready for that, yet. She looked around, at the soft green at their feet, the tawny foothills which surrounded them, and the craggy blue peaks in the distance. "I can see why—the camp, anyway, if not the campfire. Everything seems so perfect—so pure, somehow. Almost like the Garden of Eden, before the Fall."

"Watch out, then. At your feet," he said quickly.

She looked down, and jumped back with a little shriek, as

a snake slithered past. "Was that—"

He grinned that wide, irresistible smile of his. "It was harmless. It was just too good a coincidence to let slip."

They rode on further that day, Abel riding at her side the whole way. She noticed Sarah was riding at the front of the group, between their guides. Well, she was sure she could trust them to look out for the girl. She couldn't help but observe that "Mr. Marcus" was particularly attentive to Sarah, but she kept stopping herself from interfering.

Victor and Greta Stevens brought up the rear, as usual, and their inequity as riders became even more apparent. Having re-accustomed herself to riding astride, which she said she'd done in her younger years on a family farm, Greta Stevens was an excellent horsewoman.

Bryant drifted between the Stevenses and Abel and Anna, quiet as ever, although he did address himself to her several times today, on very general topics like the weather and if she was happy with her horse. He and Sarah hadn't yet said a word, but then, she was so fascinated by their guides that Anna didn't think he'd have a chance. She shrugged, internally. That hadn't been the primary purpose of the expedition anyway, but she hoped her ward wouldn't take too strong a fancy to Edward Marcus.

Meanwhile, Abel's endless supply of stories had begun to wear on her by late morning. The man could certainly talk, but it wasn't at all clear whether he was any good at listening. She was just the tiniest bit piqued that he didn't seem to imagine that the adventures of a lady lawyer in Montana were worth relating. Brown and Marcus had always had their share of stories to tell, but they knew how to listen, too. She couldn't help but wonder if the awkwardness between herself and

Jeremiah Brown was a permanent state, and she had to admit to herself that she missed their former ease together even more than she'd imagined she would.

At one point, Paul Bryant fell back, and he called Abel over to him. As he tugged the reins slightly, Abel made his apologies. He needn't have. Anna was relieved that the endless stream of stories had finally come to a pause. Making the appropriate appreciative noises had become a bit tiresome.

She rode alone for awhile, enjoying the silence. The voices of the others seemed like only a murmur in the surrounding distance, even though they weren't really all that far away. The sky was a brilliant blue, with almost no clouds, and made a spectacular contrast to the tawny outcroppings of rock and the green of the straggling plants that surrounded them. And then she was surprised to realize that Ed Marcus had slowed his pace, and was obviously waiting for her. "So," he said, "I take it you're back on speaking terms with us? Since breakfast?"

"Guess so," she said.

"You know, Anna, Jeremiah would really like it if you would talk to him. But both of you are going to be stubborn and wait for the other one to say something first."

She looked quickly around. "Um, Mr. Marcus, should we be…I mean, don't you think someone might overhear—"

He laughed. "Can you hear anything they're saying?"

"Well, no, but—"

"Look, Jeremiah likes you a lot." He'd said it.

"Did he tell you that?" she asked suspiciously. "Did he ask you to say something to me?"

"You really don't know much about men, do you? He'd be pretty mad at me if he knew we were even talking about him. No, he doesn't talk a lot about you, but the idea of taking a trip up to Montana crops up a lot more often than it used to. And that town of yours seems to have taken on this vast significance. You'd practically think it was Denver or San Francisco, the way it keeps coming up in conversation. If it wasn't for the winters being so bad up there, and our luck not always being the best these days, I'm sure we'd have been back more'n once by now."

She couldn't help smiling at that. "If he doesn't talk about me, how come you knew about David? Remember, you asked me about him that night in Townsend."

"Anna, everyone in Carter's Creek loves to talk about you and David. I think you two are just about as legendary there as…who were those two? In that play that Jer made me go see in Denver that time? …*Romeo and Juliet,* that was it. You're a regular Juliet, tragedy and all. Except I guess they both died, not just Romeo." He was clearly struggling to regain his train of thought. "I must've got told about you and David by at least five people, from the deputy sheriff to the blackjack dealer to the fellow that watched our horses while we were in the lockup."

"Well, you know all about that, now. Because of my famous lost love, I get away with doing things and going places that most women can't. If they find out I'm human, I'm sunk."

Ed's smile was warm and his blue eyes almost matched the brilliant blue overhead. "Your secret's safe with me. You did a real good nun impersonation the other night, by the way."

She was beginning to accept that she might have overreacted to a situation which was probably more absurd than anything. "I'll have you know I was really shocked. I had no idea what to make of running into you two falling down drunk. Nobody in my usual circles—"

"Yeah, I can believe that, seeing how little it took to get your friend Jonathan drunk as a skunk."

She took a deep breath. "It wasn't really that part. It was the girl."

He laughed. "I knew that. I just wasn't sure you were gonna say it. Look, Anna, men and women are just different about things like that. Don't mean he thinks about some saloon girl the way he thinks about you."

She wasn't so sure about that. What had been her motivations that first night that she'd spent with Jeremiah Brown, after all? He was handsome, he was charming, and most of all, he was leaving. Nobody needed to know about it but the two of them. She just hadn't planned on developing feelings for him, and she knew that she couldn't let her judgment be swayed because of it. "That's what we hear all the time, anyway. About how different men and women are. Of course, there's a lot I hear about men and women I don't believe."

"Well, you can believe me on this one," he said. "And don't tell him I talked to you about this, all right?" And he spurred his horse on again to rejoin his partner and Sarah at the front of the group.

Soon Abel and Bryant had rejoined her. "So, did Mr. Marcus have anything important to share?" asked her constant companion.

"Just some things about the history and geography of the area. Utterly fascinating. You can ask him yourself when we stop for lunch." *Abel asking someone else a question? Hardly likely,* she thought.

They stopped to eat their picnic lunch not too long after that, and Anna noticed with a certain amount of complacency that Abel did not approach Ed Marcus, after all. Ed was particularly attentive to Sarah, helping her down from her horse when she was perfectly capable of dismounting on her own. She sat with him as they ate the overly luxurious meats, breads and fruits that the party from San Francisco had insisted on. Greta and Victor Stevens sat slightly apart from the rest of the group, talking softly between themselves.

Anna found herself sitting with Abel on one side and Jeremiah on the other, and every time she thought she might actually break the silence with Jeremiah, Abel would place another demand on her attention.

Their eyes did meet once—Brown's and Anna's. Their glances held for a moment, and both of them opened their mouths to speak at the same time, but just then, there was a loud appeal from Anna's other side, and she was forced to turn her attention to the man she was beginning to think of as her persecutor.

Although they rode for the rest of the afternoon, she was flanked by Abel and Bryant, as before, and the stories continued. When they halted to make camp, much earlier than yesterday, Anna found herself actually relieved, and not just to be getting off her horse. "We don't want to stop too far up into the mountains," Marcus explained.

His partner concurred. "This will be a nice comfortable place to settle in and make our explorations from." They were well into the foothills then, in a green, secluded space with running water, and trees on one side. Abel, of course, decided that the men should go fishing, and his co-workers and Brown gathered up fishing rods.

Marcus offered to accompany Greta Stevens and Sarah on a walk, which they gratefully accepted. Victor looked uncomfortable, but when he was certain that Sarah was going along with his wife, he seemed to relax, and accepted the fishing rod which Brown was proffering him.

Anna was included in the invitation to walk, but she'd seen a pretty spot which looked like twenty minutes' gentle climb away and she headed there on her own, with a book she'd brought along. She achieved her objective, had plenty of time to drink in the view, and was a couple of chapters further along with the story, when a shadow was cast across her page.

She looked up to see Jeremiah Brown, his black hat thrust back on his head. "If you're trying to avoid me you might try a more secluded spot. I could see you all the way down at the foot of the hill." He smiled that blinding smile, and sat down beside her. "What are you reading, anyway?"

She marked her page, and handed him the book, spine first.

"*Crime and Punishment*?" He shuddered. "That one of your law books, or are you real mad at me and trying to figure out what they'll do to me once you turn me in?"

"Neither. It's a novel by a man called Dostoevsky. Translated from the Russian. Look, Jeremiah, I'm sorry I pretended I didn't know you the other day. I was just too angry to trust myself to speak to you."

"Anna, it was embarrassing for me, too, running into you like that. But you're acting like it was the end of the world. I was just out having a good time. How was I supposed to know you were in town?"

"You hardly left me with a forwarding address."

"We don't have one. But old Leon Anderson can usually track us down."

"To what purpose?"

"Well...because you should have known I'd have wanted to see you again," said Jeremiah, exasperatingly, and tried to touch the side of her face, though she turned away. "I told you that, didn't I? Do you think I would have been running around drinking with a saloon girl if I'd known you were in town?"

She turned back to glare at him. "Probably not. Why pay when you can get it for free?"

"Is that what this is all about? Is that how you think I feel about you?"

"I don't know," she said miserably, her eyes filling with tears. "I can't say that I see much difference."

He moved closer, then, and put an arm around her shoulders and leaned down to kiss her. "There's all the difference in the world."

She pushed him away. "Is that what you did with her the other night? The redhead?"

"For heaven's sake, Anna. I'm not sure that it's really any of your business, but I couldn't go through with it, after running into you like that." He looked at her, frowning, his brown eyes fixed on her blue ones. "I ended up spending the time in the bar while Ed went upstairs to...go about his business. You might have noticed I was in worse shape than him the next morning."

She smiled in spite of herself. "I did notice, but I can't say I put together what it meant. I guess I just thought it meant you were more dissolute than he was."

He sighed, but he didn't attempt to replace his arm around her shoulders. "I had to do something with the time, didn't I? And in a bawdyhouse, the options are kinda limited. I would've played cards, but a man that'll get into a poker game when he's already drunk is asking to lose big." He stopped, sighed again, looked at her. "Look, Anna, just because we're not going to ride off into the sunset together doesn't mean I don't have feelings for you. In fact, I had Ed just about convinced it was a good idea to head back up your way sometime real soon. But I didn't expect to see you here. I just didn't think you ever shook yourself loose from that little town of yours. I thought if you did that, the evil Rick... Nick...whatever his name is—would destroy the civilization of Carter's Creek as we know it. But, here we are, and instead of enjoying our luck, you're sitting there and sniffling. So dry those tears, all right?" He pulled off his bandana and handed it to her.

She stared at his outstretched hand for a moment before reaching out to accept his offering, which she used to dab at her eyes. She found herself thinking what a fright she must look with that sort of crumpled facial expression that comes with crying—which led to her think she must be beginning to forgive him. Or forgive herself, or something. "Actually, Nick's taken his family to Europe. They're hunting for a Polish count or something to marry his daughter Lisette. I thought maybe I ought to take advantage of the time to let Sarah see some more of the world. Maybe even find *her* a husband—after all, you know how everything's a competition between Nick and me."

"Sarah's an awfully pretty girl. I don't think she'll need much help in that regard. In fact, if I weren't partial to someone else ..." There was mischief in his eyes.

"I said a *husband,* not some no-account outlaw."

Jeremiah laughed. "Who you calling a no-account outlaw? I'll have you remember I was an outlaw of quite some standing, before my retirement. At the top of my game, I might add." And with that, he replaced his arm around her shoulders. She let it stay.

"How do you two know enough about this area to serve as guides, anyway? I thought you were mostly in the Black Hills when you ran with that gang?"

"This was since we've been keepin' honest. We spent a month or two helping out an old miner just up ahead in these hills. He'd hurt his back, needed a couple of young, strong men to help him out." He stretched slightly, as though remembering past soreness, then briefly tightened his grip on her shoulder. She reached up and stroked his hand. "About a year ago. Wasn't so bad, though. We got the chance to explore around the area. Maybe we'll pay a call on our miner friend while we're out here. Your friends from San Francisco would probably enjoy that. He's a real character."

"Do you think Meriwether Abel would even notice?"

"Oh, I'm sure he would. Old Joe would become seven feet tall and a hundred years old, and one of Abel's closest friends. He'd be the stuff of legend."

"Cynic," she said, but she laughed.

And with that, he leaned over and kissed her. He pulled back for a moment and looked at her to make sure she wanted him to go on, and in answer, she slipped her arms around his neck and raised her mouth to his. For a few minutes, there was nothing in the world but his lips and tongue pressing hers, his arms around her and his body held tightly to hers, when suddenly, she pulled away.

"Didn't you say that you could see me sitting up here from way down below?"

"Yes?"

"I think we've been spotted," she said, pointing below. A flash of long black hair was disappearing behind a tree. Sarah had seen them. "Wonderful."

"What's wrong?

"Sarah sees me kissing a man who, as far as she knows, I'd never met before two days ago, and that not under the best of circumstances. Not a very good example to be setting for an eighteen-year-old girl."

"How'd you end up with her, anyway?" he asked her,

helping her to her feet. "I remember you mentioning her, back in Carter's Creek."

They started making their way down the incline, she holding her skirts up with one hand. "I pulled her out of the orphanage, over in Butte. She helps me around the house, and I give her a home, and lessons, and now, for her own sake, I'm trying to marry her off. Which, despite her many obvious advantages, is a little more difficult than you might think, because her father was an Indian, and she was born out of wedlock, besides. Some folks are a little prejudiced."

"Some folks are more than a little stupid." He held out his arms to help her down a difficult part. "You know, Ed and I were in an orphanage after our parents were killed. That's where we met—became each other's family."

"No, I didn't know that. I'm sorry. How old were you?"

"Young. Both our families were wiped out in Kansas during the War. I thought I'd told you."

"No," she said. "Everything you and Ed have told me has been about the more recent past. I guess I just thought you didn't like to talk about your childhood." She thought about her family, and how she'd been devastated losing both her parents when she was in her middle twenties. This explained so much about how two such essentially decent men could have become outlaws.

And for girls, there were even fewer options: if she hadn't come along, the best outcome Sarah might have hoped for was to end up as a servant; but there were other, more likely outcomes for a girl that pretty and that despised. For just a moment, she thought about the pair of whores who'd been with her two friends that first night in town, and her disgust for them turned instead to pity. Right there and then, she decided that if she managed to get Sarah married off, she was going to head right back to that orphanage on the next train, and take away another girl. "Jeremiah?"

"Huh?"

"Can anyone see us here?"

"I don't think so." He looked around. "No, I reckon not."

"Good." She kissed him quickly on the cheek, and then drew away again, and continued down the hillside.

She looked back and saw that he was shaking his head and smiling. A moment later, he caught her up and they walked back together, in companionable silence.

When they got back to camp, the others had already finished setting up. Nobody seemed to remark on how Mr. Brown and Miss Harrison were returning together or how long they'd both been gone, although she kept studying Sarah, looking for some indication of whether she'd really spotted them or not.

It was a fairly warm and clear night, so, once more, they'd only pitched the one tent, for the women. The men were going to sleep out, again. Anna still wished she could sleep under the stars, too, but she'd already done enough to compromise herself for one day. They sat around the campfire, eating the fish the men had caught, and Abel dominated the conversation with more tales of the Far East. Tonight, Brown and Marcus didn't even try to compete.

Anna began a whispered conversation with Greta Stevens about her walk and all the lovely things she had seen, as her husband eavesdropped, not as unobtrusively as he obviously thought. Pretty soon, Anna was sure that if anyone had seen herself and Jeremiah Brown, it was only Sarah. Greta wasn't that good a liar. It was one of those things you could just tell about her. Anna was fairly sure that if she asked her about the note from the other night, she'd be able to tell the truth from what she didn't say, too.

Bryant was silent and watchful, as always, although he addressed a few soft-spoken remarks in her direction. She noticed that Sarah seemed to be preoccupied with tending the fire and helping Marcus with the coffee and frying the fish the men had caught. Tonight, he didn't shoo her away when she tried to help, and they spoke together quietly, laughing from time to time.

Anna steered clear of Jeremiah, not quite trusting herself not to betray their acquaintance with some familiarity, especially after their recent...*familiarity.* A couple of times, as she was concentrating on other things, she was surprised by a sudden, vivid recollection of the feeling of his kisses, or the sensation of his body against hers when they'd embraced. No, on the whole it was better to avoid him. The one time their eyes met, his glance was so intimate that she couldn't imagine the whole expedition hadn't noticed. But as she looked around, it appeared they hadn't. Anyway, he and Meriwether Abel were thick as...well, maybe thieves wasn't the best word to use, under the circumstances. They were playing the same game they had been playing last night, anyway.

Abel's attentions to Anna were much less marked than previously. She wondered idly if he'd seen her and Brown together, but that didn't seem to be it. He had too many fishing stories for anyone to doubt that he hadn't left the riverside for a second. No, he seemed to be taking a hint, though. Her diminished enthusiasm was reflected by his. That, and the fact that he was preoccupied with competing with Jeremiah Brown, and he didn't know she was an object to be competed for.

• ❤ •

All that travel and the time in the open air had really tired Anna out, and she was the first to retire. Somewhere in the middle of the night, she was awoken by a scratching sound on the canvas of the tent. Her first thought was coyotes or some other wild animal, but then she heard a soft, low whisper calling her name. *Jeremiah!*

She was sleeping fully dressed, against the cold night air of the mountains, so she just had to put on her shoes and adjust her clothes a little, and she made her way quietly out of the tent. Her hair was down, and she put her hands up automatically to twist it into a knot, when she realized it didn't matter, and let it fall down again. "Have you gone completely mad?" she whispered. "You could have woken up Sarah or Mrs. Stevens."

He didn't respond, but reached out and took her hand silently, and led her away from the campsite. The moon had risen, and it was a bright night, so bright that she could see him quite clearly in the moonlight. They walked past some scrub pines and a few leafier trees, down the course of the stream. Then he suddenly stopped and turned around, facing her, and caught her to him. He kissed her, a passionate, hungry kiss—and soon, she'd lost herself in responding.

All the cautions and concerns that she'd so carefully set out for herself over the past several days didn't seem to matter, now. Not when they were alone together in the darkness like this.

When they stopped to catch their breath, he said quietly, "Not likely either of your tentmates would be waking up so easily as that. Mrs. Stevens takes a sleeping draught—her husband mentioned it—and Ed gave Sarah a big slug of whiskey in her coffee when she complained she thought she'd be too excited and restless to sleep tonight."

She didn't bother to voice her disapproval. She was sure Ed had meant well, and besides, hard as it sometimes was to believe it, Sarah was old enough to make her own decisions. About some things. "Hmm," she said. "Now...where were we?" and then his arms were around her again, and his lips were touching hers, and she lost all sense of where she was or how much time was passing. Until a twig snapped, and they leapt apart. "What was that?"

"I don't know," said Jeremiah, "but it sounds as though we have company." His trigger hand dropped to his holster, and suddenly, it struck her as peculiar that she'd been kissing a man wearing a loaded gun strapped to his leg, leaning right up against him, and she hadn't even noticed it. He put an arm out protectively, to signal her to stay behind him, and then called out, "Hello? Who's there?"

There was no response, and they stood silent, unmoving for a matter of minutes. Then, wordlessly, he took her hand again, and they began to make their way back to the campsite. They parted a few yards from the tent, as he made his way back to the circle of bedrolls around the fire, and she paused a moment before lifting the tent flap, intending to slip back inside quietly. She was worried that the moonlight might awaken her tentmates, but when a cloud passed by and the moon's brightness fell on Greta Stevens's face, Anna knew nothing was going to wake her ever again.

Chapter 10

Even in the moonlight, the ashen tone of Greta Stevens's skin was unmistakable. She was lying on her back, her eyes wide open, frozen in an expression of surprise and horror. She hadn't screamed because someone's bandana was stuffed into her mouth to keep her from doing so.

There was a pool of blood soaked into the top of her dress—since she, too, had been sleeping fully dressed against the cold mountain night—and all over the top of her bedding. A knife protruded from just over her heart.

But perhaps the most terrifying aspect of it all, to Anna's eyes, at least, was that Sarah had never even woken up. She lay curled up on her side, less than a foot away from the dead woman, sound asleep. Some of Greta Stevens's blood had seeped over, and was staining Sarah's blankets. For a minute, Anna was paralyzed by the thought that Sarah, too, had been murdered, but then she made a soft sound and shifted in her sleep.

Anna stood silently for a moment, unable to move, unable to think, unable to do anything but stare, and then she screamed for dear life.

Jeremiah Brown was the first to arrive at the scene, wearing one of his boots and clutching the other in one hand. His uneven gait would have been comical if the situation hadn't been so tragic.

"Anna! What's the matter?"

Wordlessly, she pointed inside the tent, through the open flap. He peered in. She heard a sharp intake of breath, just as the other men were arriving on the scene, and he turned around. "Stevens?" he called. "Stevens? You'd better come here."

"What's the matter?" asked Victor Stevens, groggily. He must have been sound asleep when the disturbance occurred. He had brought up the rear of the group, but now he made his way to the front.

"Don't move anything," Brown cautioned him. "We're going to have to try to figure out what happened."

Stevens entered the tent, while Jeremiah held the flap held open so that the light would follow him in. In a moment, they heard his sobs. "Greta—no! No..." He backed out of the tent, and when he turned around and they saw his face, the transformation was astonishing. The quiet accountant was as ashen pale as his wife, and looked something like King Lear in the mad scene. Meriwether Abel came up to him and led him back to the fire, where his cries and bursts of fury alternated with a deep deathly silence for the rest of the night.

Nor did Sarah continue to sleep throughout this whole nightmarish experience. As Stevens gave out his first loud cry, she stirred, and in a moment, there was a strange, low sound, like the cry of an animal. Anna slowly regained her focus, and became aware of Sarah sitting upright, her arms clasped around her legs, and rocking back and forth, whimpering. Marcus crawled into the tent, and aided her in making her way outside. He gently handed her into Anna's waiting arms.

Anna held her tightly as she screamed and sobbed, and all she could do was stroke Sarah's raven-black hair and whisper soothing things. She was steps away from screaming and sobbing, herself. The woman with whom they'd been sharing a tent for two days now was dead, in those same peaceful surroundings she'd fallen off to sleep in earlier that night. If it hadn't been for Jeremiah waking her up to take that walk with him, Anna would have been in the tent when she was killed. And unlike Sarah, or Greta Stevens herself, sleeping their different kinds of drugged sleep, she would have woken right up. Even if she hadn't been the target, she'd probably be dead now, as well.

Mostly, she was sorry for Greta Stevens, but her own close call was weighing heavily on her. She envied Sarah the free rein she was giving her emotions. Hysteria, the doctors liked to call it, whenever a woman had strong feelings. It seemed pretty healthy and natural to Anna. But then she heard Brown's voice saying, "Don't move anything," and she determined that she was going to be strong.

Marcus sounded angry. "What do you mean, *don't move anything?* The woman needs to be decently seen to."

"Someone should go get the sheriff," added Bryant. His tone of voice was sharper than she'd ever heard it before, and she wondered if what he'd been watching for had happened—in spite of, or because of, his best efforts.

"The sheriff is two days' ride away," said Jeremiah, "and how do we know that the person we send to fetch him isn't the killer?"

"Well, I'm not—" Bryant began angrily.

Jeremiah cut him off. "Each one of us is gonna say that, aren't we? Look, Mrs. Stevens was stabbed, and the murderer left the weapon right there. We need to wait until it's light, and then we need to take a closer look. But right now, we have to assume that none of us can be trusted." He sighed, running his hand through his dark brown hair. "Until then, we need to guard the tent, in teams, and not with our friends, so that nobody can claim that anyone is protecting anyone else. Bryant, why don't you take this shift with me? Edward, you help the ladies over to the fire."

"No," moaned Sarah.

"I think Mr. Stevens is frightening her," Anna said. In all honesty, some of the cries that were coming from over there were frightening to her as well. The mad scene in *King Lear* came irresistibly to mind, once again. She half expected to hear him call for the lightning to strike him down on the blasted heath. She scolded herself for thinking something so irreverent when poor Victor Stevens was suffering such a tragic loss. He had tried to protect his wife—from what?—and look what had happened.

"You'll freeze over there," Ed pointed out. "Come on."

"All right," she said, gently handing the still-sobbing Sarah into his arms. "I'll be with you in a moment," she said, and turned to face Brown and Bryant, as Marcus continued toward the fire with Sarah. "Sarah needs a shawl or something. If you two both keep watch on me, would it be all right if I grabbed something from her bags?"

Bryant looked a little uneasy.

"Look," she said, "if I had killed Greta Stevens, would I have screamed and called everyone's attention to it? Wouldn't I have run away…or something?"

"In the middle of the wilderness in the middle of the night? You wouldn't get very far on your own." Bryant said, just an edge of suspicion to his soft voice. "Come to think of it, you have your shoes and your jacket on. You're the only one of us who's fully dressed." There was a look in his eyes that made her uncomfortable, something almost wild. No, something desperate, she thought. And maybe hurt.

"Well, of course I do," she said, impatient in her own defense. "Clearly, I was awake. I had gone for a little walk in the moonlight and when I got back to the tent, I saw Mrs. Stevens through the open flap, and I knew that all was not right. I screamed for you all just about as loudly as I could."

"Or, you did that to throw suspicion off yourself," said Bryant warily. "Just why were you going for a moonlit stroll, anyway?"

She sighed and put her hands together primly. "Mr. Bryant, although I know that most unmarried gentlemen are under the illusion that ladies are not privy to certain of the more vulgar biological failings of your own strong sex, the honest truth is that I felt the call of nature." She was certain that her blush showed crimson even in the waning moonlight. "Now, may I get Sarah a nice warm shawl, please?"

Bryant looked at Jeremiah, who nodded. Anna took a deep breath and slipped inside. She wanted to be in there as little as she'd ever wanted anything, and it took all her self-control not to scream out or lapse into hysterics herself. But she'd seen Sarah shivering, and all she could do was act on her overwhelming illogical desire to provide her ward with comfort in the only way she could think of at the moment.

Brown was speaking softly through the open tent flap. "It's all right, Miss Harrison. You'll be just fine," over and over again, as she crawled past the place where the corpse lay with its eyes wide open. Sarah's bag was at the far end of the tent. She fumbled with the flap, with shaking hands, and the odor of blood seemed to fill her nostrils. Finally, she got the bag open, and fumbled in it until she felt the soft wool of Sarah's shawl. Bunching it tightly together, she made her way carefully back outside.

The night air felt cool, and the breeze was blowing the scent of the pine forests. She inhaled deeply, hoping that it would erase the memory of the horror inside. Poor Greta Stevens. Poor sweet, nervous, well-meaning lady. Who would want to kill a woman like that, anyway?

She felt Jeremiah's hand on her arm. "Excuse me, Miss Harrison, but do you mind showing us the shawl?"

"Certainly not." She unrolled the blue-and-red patterned cloth to its full size. "Nothing concealed inside. Now, if you'll excuse me, Sarah must be freezing."

"Wait," said Bryant. "How do we know there's not something else that she's taken and concealed somewhere else in her clothing?" It was peculiar to hear his soft voice take on such an aggressive tone, but she realized it was all of a piece with his earlier wariness.

"Bryant," Jeremiah protested.

"I'd say the same about any of us," he insisted. "Do you want to search her, or shall I?"

In response, Jeremiah began gently patting her down. She found it peculiar to be feeling his touch in such a manner, rather than his caresses of what must have been less than an hour ago, but felt like a century past. She was grateful it was him and not Paul Bryant. "Nothing," he said. "And sorry for the disrespect, Miss Harrison."

"It's all right, Mr. Brown. I wouldn't want to be treated differently just because I'm a lady."

He smiled despite the grim situation, and she could just hear what he wanted to say—and couldn't—in Bryant's hearing. *No, you never did want that, did you, Anna?*

It was a long, miserable night, and the dawn seemed to take forever to come. She'd made her way to the campfire, but Marcus didn't seem to be in any great hurry to leave over comforting Sarah. Anna had to ask him twice, the second time rather sharply, if he minded if she wrapped her up in her shawl. She felt like a hypocrite, intervening between Marcus and Sarah, considering her own connection with his partner. But it was plain to see that Edward Marcus was no more the marrying kind than Jeremiah Brown. Ed would be an easy man for Sarah to fall in love with, and even with the best intentions in the world on his part, Anna couldn't see that leading to anything but a broken heart for her ward. Maybe for both of them. Not that Jeremiah was any safer, except that she wasn't protecting her own heart like she was Sarah's.

Brown and Bryant returned to the campfire a couple of hours before dawn, sending Marcus and Abel in their place. No one spoke. They barely spoke at all that night, any of them. No one slept, except for Sarah, who never left Anna's side, and gradually sobbed herself to sleep in her friend's arms.

At dawn, they reassembled in front of the tent. Now, they could all guard each other. People began to make their way down to the stream, one by one, to throw water on themselves and do whatever else was necessary. Anna desperately wanted to find a way to talk with Jeremiah privately, to find out if he had a plan of some sort or if he was as lost with all this as she was. She stopped to wonder why she felt so instinctively that he was the one who could get to the bottom of things. After all, most of their dealings, so far, had centered around her getting him and his partner out of trouble. And yet now, she found herself looking to him for ideas, quite naturally.

Finally, she determined that the only way she was going to get anywhere was to throw caution to the winds. As he took his turn to make his way down to the riverbank, she called after him. "Mr. Brown, can I speak with you a moment?"

"Can't a man get any privacy?" he growled. "All right, Miss

Harrison, come along." He smiled at the rest of the group. "I'll be sending her back alone in a few minutes." A couple of the men almost laughed at that.

He didn't stop until he'd gotten well into the grove, and then he turned, and looked at her, expectantly. She frowned, realizing that he thought she needed to be held, just like Sarah had. And he was going to do his best to accommodate her feelings, but it wasn't what his mind was on. *Just the sort of thing a man would think.*

She stopped several feet away, happy to be confounding his expectations. "Sounds like you have a plan. Do you—I mean, have you got any ideas about how we can go about investigating a murder? Or wouldn't it make more sense that we all go back to town together?"

He gave her a funny look. "I'd really rather keep the sheriff out of this, Anna. There are wanted posters for Ed and me in places like that, remember?"

She nodded. "Sometimes I forget who I'm dealing with. Sorry."

"Besides, we'd lose any chance we had of finding out who did it, if we all went back into town together. No way to examine the evidence, and plenty of opportunity for the killer to cut and run." He stopped, looked around for a moment, and then paused and gave her what was clearly intended to be a reassuring smile. The worry showed right through, though. "Ed and I have been in these situations before, a couple of times. A few times one of us was suspected of something, and we had to figure out who really did it—a murder, a theft. Usually, I've managed to come up with some kind of plan to figure out who did it."

He stared off into the distance, his dark eyes inscrutable. "You and I didn't do it. We can clear each other."

"If we have to tell them. I mean, it sounds pretty peculiar, a single lady and her trail guide going off for a moonlit stroll together."

"If it looks funny, it's because thanks to you, nobody even knows that we had ever met before two days ago. I probably should have told Bryant the truth, when you started in."

"I know it was a mistake, pretending I didn't know you," Anna said. "But thank you for not saying anything. I just hope that it doesn't come up that we've both been lying."

"Wouldn't look too good, would it?" he asked. "So, why'd you come running after me?"

"Because I had the feeling you had a plan, and I knew you weren't going to tell me in front of everybody. Besides, maybe you can use a good lawyer on your team."

"Does this Jeremiah Brown even know you're a lawyer? The trail guide one, as opposed to the one that's your client, or the one that's your, you know, special friend," he paused, winked.

She blushed. "Consider yourself informed. Next time I want to pretend I don't know you, let's hope it's under less complicated circumstances."

"Next time you pretend you don't know me, watch out—I may just pretend I don't know you, either. Permanently. Now, much as I'd enjoy having you join me, I think you'd better get on back to the others and let me wash up some."

Some while later, they had all reassembled outside the tent. Anna sat with an arm around Sarah, who was still glassy-eyed and silent, and who whimpered if she felt her friend stir away from her. Ed Marcus sat near her on the other side, attentive to Sarah's every sound and every movement. Meriwether Abel, Victor Stevens, and Paul Bryant sat in a row on the other side of the fire, Stevens staring straight ahead in dumb shock. At least his ravings seemed to be stilled for now.

Brown sat apart from the rest of them, planted between the two groupings. "First, we need to take a look at what's happened, now that it's light out. We all need to be there together," he said firmly, "but not all of us need to go into the tent and look real close. Now, I know that none of us are willing to trust all of us, but since we have some ladies here, it seems more proper and decent to have a lady take that closer look. And what Miss Harrison told me, when she wanted to speak to me privately, is that as a lawyer, she's an officer of the court, whatever that means. So I figure that makes her the closest thing we've got to someone official."

"I'm a member of the bar, myself, in California," Abel added.

"Fine, then the two of you. If Mr. Stevens doesn't object."

Stevens silently, gravely, nodded his head. So Abel and Anna entered the tent together. She approached the body gingerly, not liking to get too near, and yet knowing she was going to be examining it very carefully. She left Abel to remove the murder weapon, which he lifted gingerly with his pocket handkerchief, and was nearly overcome seeing the little tug he had to give to pull it out. They both looked carefully around the body for bloodstains and for any signs of what might have taken place. Even in full daylight, it appeared that Greta Stevens had struggled very little. The bandana had been forced into her mouth, probably at the first gasp of surprise.

"I'm guessing that the killer was somebody that she knew very well," Anna said to Abel.

"Maybe," he said, "or maybe she was just abnormally calm because of that sleeping draught. You knew about that, didn't you? Her nerves were so bad she couldn't get to sleep without something." There was emotion in his voice, but Anna couldn't, for the life of her, tell what it meant.

She gingerly reached forward to remove the bandana.

"Or it could be the owner of this," Meriwether Abel remarked.

The dark blue bandanna was the one she'd seen Brown wearing when they set out on the trip. And the one he'd handed her to dry her eyes on, just the evening before Greta Stevens's murder.

• ♥ •

They made their way out of the tent, carrying the women's bags, and Anna's bedroll, which hadn't been spattered with blood, as Sarah's had. Abel slipped back in and removed Greta Stevens's bag.

Anna wondered idly about the note she'd seen Greta reading that first night, and she even worked up her nerve to look in her jacket pockets. It was the same jacket she'd been wearing the day before, but the note was gone. Anna hoped she'd never have to do something like that again. "We'll have to burn the rest, won't we? The smell of the blood is going to attract predators."

Ed Marcus nodded. "Wolves. They've been sniffing around already, in the distance. We're gonna have to bury Mrs. Stevens, as well, if you two have examined things sufficiently."

"You will not!" Victor Stevens nearly roared. "My wife is going to be buried in our family plot back in California, and nowhere else!"

"Calm down, Mr. Stevens," said Ed. "We'll bury her for now, and mark the spot. You can come back later and move her. But if we don't do it, the wolves are going to come looking for us, or the crows may get her."

Stevens practically leapt upon Marcus in his rage, and it took the combined strength of the other three men to pull him off.

"Shhh, Victor, the man's right," said Bryant, softly.

"We'll come back and get her, Victor. We'll make sure she's laid to rest at your side," Abel said, laying an arm around his friend's shoulders. "You'll take care of her," Abel murmured. "Just like you always did. We'll help you, Victor."

And the three men went off, accompanied by Marcus, to begin digging the grave.

When they'd gone, Anna turned to Jeremiah. "Well, I know you didn't do it, but would you like to explain how your bandana came to be stuffed in her mouth?"

He frowned. "Probably because everybody saw me wearing it. It was a little damp after you gave it back to me, and I left it lying on top of my pack to dry. It would have been easy enough for anyone to see it and take it, and throw suspicion on me."

"Anyone observant enough to notice you'd been wearing it for two days, and you weren't wearing it anymore." She thought of Bryant's watchful eyes, Stevens's wary glances. And Abel...well, who knew what he was noticing while he was talking? So far, he'd surprised her by having heard several things she hadn't thought he was paying attention to. Of course, as far as the San Franciscans were concerned, any of the four others—Jeremiah and Ed, Sarah and Anna—could have been guilty, too.

Then, Sarah chimed in. She'd been so silent that Anna had practically forgotten she was there. "Nothing personal against Mr. Brown, but why are you so certain that he didn't do it?"

It was clear that Jeremiah was enjoying himself, despite everything, from his quizzical look in response. "See what happens to people who tell stories, Anna?"

She sighed, and thought that she wasn't the only one in present company to whom that applied. She was making the biggest messes right now, though—that was certain. From Sarah's expression she could tell that she'd noted the use of her guardian's given name. "Mister Brown and Mister Marcus are old friends, Sarah. In fact, they're former clients. I met them back in Carter's Creek a year or so ago, when a bounty hunter mistook them for a pair of notorious outlaws. Then last fall, remember when Jonathan and I went over to Greenville to help out some old clients?"

"You're *that* Mr. Brown?" asked Sarah. "Jonathan Cranbrook can't say enough about you and your friend. I guess it was the biggest adventure he'd ever had, hunting down those outlaws with you two."

Brown frowned. It was a subject he was a little sensitive about, Anna knew. "We weren't really hunting down outlaws...just trying to recover something that was stolen from us. But Cranbrook was a big help."

Sarah smiled for the first time since the tragic events. "Not the way he tells it. But he sure was impressed with you two. He said you could do 'most anything."

"And I never did even ask what's happened with him, did I?"

"Everything, just about," Anna said. "Got married, got called to the Bar, and just two weeks ago before Sarah and I left on our trip, I made him a full partner. He and Melanie are hoping to have a large family, and I thought they'd best start saving now."

"This is young Jonathan? Sounds like he's lived about ten years this past five months."

She shrugged. "We all do things at our own paces.

Jonathan's just the kind that's made for settling down." If her fiancé had lived, she'd have been married three years already by the time she reached Jonathan's age.

"Why didn't you just say you knew Mr. Brown and Mr. Marcus back in the Springs?" asked Sarah.

"Well, Sarah, I was—"

Jeremiah interrupted her. "She was real mad at us. She caught us doing something she didn't approve of and...well, you know how she gets."

Sarah looked at him curiously. She really didn't know how Anna got, because she'd never done anything her guardian could possibly disapprove of. "If Anna doesn't approve of it, it must be something horrid, and I don't think I want to know what. I like you and Mr. Marcus too well. But it can't have been anything too bad or she wouldn't be so sure you didn't do the murder." She turned to Anna. "That's it, right? You know him well enough that you know he wouldn't do anything like this?"

A pair of slightly guilty looks was exchanged. "Well, that's true, Sarah, but that's not exactly the reason," Anna said. "Mr. Brown and I went for a walk together that night. Mrs. Stevens was alive when I left the tent, and she wasn't when I got back. It was all a matter of an hour, at most."

Sarah looked at her, a little more wisely than she was comfortable with. "I thought you two must be friends. I saw you talking yesterday on the hill."

"Well, now you know," she said. "At least, I *hope* you know I'm not the kind of woman who throws herself at strange trail guides."

"You were sitting there talking when I saw you." Sarah sounded confused. "I don't know how anybody would call that throwing yourself at someone. Didn't you teach me that if a woman has pure intentions, she can talk to any man, same as to any woman?"

"You're a smart girl, Sarah," Anna said.

"I don't get called that very often," said Sarah, truthfully. "I'm going to go down by the water for a bit. I want to wash up some. I'll be back in a moment."

When she'd gone, they began laughing quietly. "Is that what you teach her?" Jeremiah asked. "That girl's gonna wind up in a heap of trouble."

"At least she didn't see us when I thought she saw us." She stopped, thinking. "Speaking of seeing us, remember those twigs snapping last night, though? There may be someone else who's aware of our alibi."

Brown was thoughtful. "And that person could very well be the killer." And with that, he rose and went to join the other men, and Anna went to join her ward down at the water's edge.

• ♥ •

It was afternoon by the time that they assembled at Greta Stevens's makeshift grave. The women had fashioned a rough wooden cross as a marker, and Meriwether Abel led them in a brief prayer. The men took their hats off, and Sarah squeezed Anna's hand. Abel mentioned that he'd had to bury comrades in the course of several of his expeditions in the Far East, but that nothing was so melancholy as the loss of Greta Stevens, in the flower of her womanhood. He sounded sincere.

Anna couldn't help but wonder what the flower of her womanhood had really been like. The Greta Stevens she knew was a pretty faded flower, but from the brief eulogies each of the men gave, she got a very different picture. Victor Stevens was too broken up to speak much, but Abel painted the picture of a high-spirited, intelligent young woman. Anna wondered what had happened. Illness? Maybe she'd lost a child, or more than one? Or could it be something as simple as her husband's constant overprotectiveness? It sounded as though Bryant had known her the longest, since he made some reference to her childhood. He must have been quite a bit younger than her, but maybe...maybe only seven or eight years younger. Not such a difference that there wouldn't be shared memories. At any rate, his remarks were brief and inscrutable, but there was no doubt that he'd cared very much for her.

Afterward, they retired to the campfire, which had been relit in order to provide them with coffee. Even though it was a warm day, the flames somehow drew them all.

Brown began the discussion and took charge of it so readily that Anna could see how he'd once been a leader among outlaws. "Look, I think you all know that the bandana which was used to gag Greta Stevens was mine, so let's just put our cards on the table about that one. You probably all saw me wearing it. Anyone could have gone into my things and gotten it, especially since I'd left it out in plain sight."

"You'll admit that it weighs against you, though?" asked Bryant, in his soft-spoken but determined manner.

"I don't see it that way, and I've just given you my reasons why. But I can't stop any of you from thinking what you're going to think. Next piece of evidence, the knife. Nothing remarkable about it, either, except that it looks fairly new. Something that anyone might have bought outfitting for a trip like this one."

"Why are you assuming that the killer was necessarily a 'he'? Are you implying that it was one of the three of us?" asked Bryant, emotionless. He indicated himself and his two San Franciscan friends. "And what if the knife was new? You and Marcus could have bought something for the trip, as well. Even a lady might carry a knife in the wilderness." He was measuring facts rather than making accusations, but Anna felt oddly under scrutiny.

"I'm not implying anything," said Brown, "except that as far as I can figure it, it must have been one of the seven of us. If any of you think differently, I'd be glad to hear about it."

Stevens spoke up for the first time. "Can't it have been an outsider? An Indian, or an outlaw, haunting these hills?"

"To what end?" asked Marcus.

"What do you mean, to what end? Do we understand why Indians or outlaws act the way they do? Just because."

"If someone's feeling ornery or vicious, they don't walk past five sleeping men, creep into a tent with three sleeping ladies, and choose to stab only one," Marcus responded. "If the ladies will forgive me, stabbing probably isn't what they'd do." Sarah grabbed onto Anna's arm and squeezed it; both ladies knew exactly what was meant.

Abel had been unnaturally silent throughout the discussion, almost as though he had ceded his dominant position in the party to Brown, and therefore, had no further function. But now, he cleared his throat. "I'm afraid there may have been an outsider among us last night. I was unable to sleep myself, and I took a walk down by the stream bank. I saw Miss Harrison walking, too—that yellow hair is hard to mistake, in the moonlight—and she was with someone. It looked like it was a man. And, begging your pardon, Miss Harrison, but she seemed rather…familiar with him."

"It wasn't one of our party?" asked Ed Marcus.

"I couldn't see him well enough to tell. It may have been, although, frankly, I didn't think any of us knew her quite as intimately as this fellow seemed to." Anna didn't much appreciate the way he looked at her as he said that.

"I went for a walk, Mister Abel, but what you're implying is—" She stopped, not wanting to dig herself any deeper into the lies she had already surrounded herself with.

He continued, unheeding. "I woke up in the middle of the night—I have no idea when it was, but I needed to, if the ladies will forgive me, relieve myself. The moon was bright, and I was restless. I decided to take a walk. I saw Miss Harrison ahead of me. As I said, I recognized her by the shine of the moonlight on her hair. I was about to call out when I realized that she wasn't alone."

She remained silent, and felt all eyes upon her. Sarah looked at her curiously, clearly wondering why she didn't speak up and defend her innocence. Anna was ready to sink into the ground and die of shame.

"You sure it was a man?" asked Marcus. "Could've been Miss Sarah."

"It was a man, all right. Miss Nicholls is a lot smaller than Miss Harrison, and this person was taller than she is."

At that moment, Anna decided she was never going to lie ever again, no matter what the provocation. But that vow would have to wait until she managed to get out of this mess, somehow.

She had just opened her mouth when Brown spoke up. "It was me. I was on watch and I saw her, so I caught up with her."

"Well, now, going gallivanting off with our trail guide, Miss Harrison? Hardly something I would have expected of a lady like you," said Abel. Anna had the feeling he wasn't used to anyone else's company being preferred when he was around.

"Let the lady explain herself," came Ed's voice, cool and

hard. She was sure he could figure it out, but he was bound to be the only one who'd know for sure.

"Miss Harrison is an old friend of ours," Brown intervened again, seeing she was at a loss for words. "She's handled some legal matters for Edward and me when we've traveled up Montana way. We were just having a talk that night about the awkward position she'd put us in, pretending not to know us that day."

"Why on earth did you do that, anyway?" asked Abel, now genuinely curious.

She blushed. "Do you remember the condition these two were in that first morning when we all met with them at the hotel? Well, I had encountered them the night before, extremely drunk and with a couple of the girls from one of the saloons, when I'd gone for what was clearly an ill-advised evening stroll. I was so mad at them I didn't trust myself to speak. A lady shouldn't have to see such things, and especially not when she's acquainted with the gentlemen in question."

The men laughed.

"Trust a lady to overreact," Ed said.

Abel continued. "Except that I saw them in the moonlight, and it didn't look like they were talking business to me. It looked a lot more like they were kissing."

Anna blushed deeper and stammered, "Well, n-n-not exactly." She fell silent, praying to the patron saint of litigators for an inspiration. Only, there wasn't one, as far as she knew, litigators and saints not holding much truck with each other.

"Well, Miss Harrison, we're waiting to hear all about what you *were* doing that night."

She opened her mouth and began to stammer something, but once again, Brown jumped in first. "I'm afraid I was a little overcome by the moonlight and how pretty Miss Harrison looked in it. She made it clear very quickly that my attentions were unwelcome. I apologized and we're friends again, aren't we, Miss Harrison?"

Marcus looked at Anna, just to see how she was taking it. One glance and he could tell she was on top of things. She couldn't even face Sarah, though.

She cleared her throat, and managed to blush, although probably not for the reason they thought she was blushing. "Well, it was just the tiniest little bit flattering, Mr. Brown. An old maid like me, and all. But what I'd like to do is to ask Mr. Abel why he was following us, anyway."

Abel looked abashed. "Just concerned, that's all. Didn't mean to intrude on your privacy, Miss Harrison. I'm awfully sorry if I interpreted things the wrong way."

• ❤ •

Later that afternoon, Anna came across Marcus and Brown sitting on a couple of rocks alongside the stream. As she approached them, Ed, always the more polite of the two, rose and offered her his rock.

Jeremiah was staring down into the stream, as the sunlight played off its quickly-moving waters, almost as though it was going to give him the answer, if he stared long enough. He didn't turn as she sat down, but just said, "Anna. Glad you came and found us. We were just talking about what we've figured out."

"Which is?"

"Well, we've been through everybody's bags, and we haven't found any unaccounted-for gloves. And we've examined everyone's clothes, and there aren't any bloodstains that we can find."

"So, the killer was neat?" She wasn't sure what this proved.

"Maybe. Or maybe he disposed of whatever got

bloodstained."

Ed spoke. He'd walked downstream a few paces, and was squatting at the water's edge, almost as if he, too, thought he would find inspiration somewhere in the rushing stream. "We haven't found any place where it looks like it's been dug up to bury anything. And we've checked the underbrush, as best we could."

She thought for a moment. "Could he have sent something floating downstream?"

"Could be. We haven't found anything, though."

"How are our friends reacting?" she asked.

Jeremiah turned now, and gave her a funny look. "Haven't you been with them this afternoon?"

She shook her head. "No. I needed to think. I took a walk. Remember that place I climbed to yesterday afternoon?"

"Uh-huh."

"Climb up another fifteen minutes' worth and there's this plateau. Very pretty." She tossed him something sparkly, which he caught, quickly, with one hand.

"What's this?" he asked, examining the stone that now lay in the palm of his hand.

"Fragment of a geode, it looks like. Nothing valuable, just pretty. They're lying all over, for the picking."

Ed rose and walked over to stand just behind and between the two rocks on which the other two were seated, and his partner handed him the geode, which he looked at and returned to Anna.

"Meanwhile, did all your climbing and thinking suggest anything to you?" asked Jeremiah.

"Not much," she admitted. She paused. "Did you find anything in Greta Stevens's luggage? A note, or anything similar?"

"No," said Brown. "Was there something?"

"I saw her reading something the first night. She put it in her jacket pocket. I checked the body, but I didn't find anything." She shuddered at the memory.

"Ed, you want to go and take another look?"

"Why don't you?"

"'Cause I'm thinkin'," said Brown, without moving. He'd resumed staring into the stream again, focusing his thoughts.

Ed sighed. "Okay." He turned to Anna and smiled. "But if he makes any more unwanted advances, yell real loud and I'll come running."

She laughed. "Don't worry. I'll just push him in the river."

"You always hurt the one you love," Jeremiah shot back, with a wicked grin.

"That's it!" she said. Something that the men had totally overlooked, but that she should have seen. "I've been really slow on the uptake about this, but...who's in love with Greta Stevens?"

"Well, Victor Stevens," said Ed.

"Obviously—or maybe not. Husbands and wives don't always stay in love, unfortunately. But who else? I mean, I couldn't figure out why someone would send her a note in the middle of a camping trip, but making an assignation would be difficult on a trip like this when there's always someone around." She looked at Jeremiah. "We got caught, and that was in the middle of the night."

He looked thoughtful. "So who would want to get Greta Stevens alone? Well, obviously not any of us. And probably not Bryant. Somehow she doesn't seem like the type who'd appeal to a younger man."

"Bryant is one of those still waters that runs deep, though," she said. "I certainly don't have him figured out, and he was riding along with Abel and me as often as not. But I don't think he was in love with Greta. Also, it sounds like he knew her when he was a child. I could be wrong, but I don't think that would tend to encourage that kind of thing, especially with her being so much older."

"It's funny, though," said Ed. "When we were digging the grave for Mrs. Stevens, he was almost calm about it. You could tell he was upset, but he was keeping things under control. Not like Abel, who—"

"Abel?" asked Jeremiah curiously. "You think a man who travels around the world like that was in love with a little mouse like Greta Stevens? There are some stories he told me about the women in Japan, Anna, that I couldn't repeat in front of you."

"Haven't you ever heard of finding solace for a broken heart? Maybe he's had adventures with half the women in Japan, Polynesia, and even China, but I'll bet almost anything that it was after Greta became Greta Stevens." Not like some men she could mention, she thought; but somehow, the thought seemed almost amusing this time. In any case, she felt a rush of emotion, and it wasn't anger, but it wasn't tenderness, either. Affectionate bemusement? She turned to look at Jeremiah's profile, as he stared into the water, but found she had to look quickly away. Confusion. She certainly was feeling a fair amount of that.

"You think so?" asked Ed.

"I'm sure of it. Whenever she was around, he couldn't pay enough attention to me. But it was clear that it wasn't me he was interested in. He never was quiet long enough to learn the first thing about me. What he was interested in was in showing Greta that he was over her, which was a transparent falsehood."

"And this means?" Jeremiah frowned at her, a crease appearing between his dark brows.

"Maybe nothing at all, as far as her death goes. Maybe that he killed her. Maybe that he was the motive for someone else to kill her. But in any case, it means something. Jeremiah, remember how quickly he dropped his accusations against us when you claimed you'd been…um…surprising me with your attentions? Why, exactly? We could have been standing several yards apart talking about politics or horse racing, or he might have caught us being a little—ah—more friendly than we were. It doesn't change the suspicious circumstances. It doesn't mean that it wasn't your bandana she was gagged with, or that I wasn't the first person on the scene of the crime, not to mention the only person who was fully dressed. Or that you were the second there, minus exactly one boot, as I recall. Face it, there are plenty of reasons to suspect that it was either or both of us. And one little word and he can't tell us he's sorry enough. As though it were a situation he could imagine being caught in himself."

The frown was replaced by a fleeting smile. "Let's just not rush to tell him you were kissing me back, then, all right? But what we're coming down to is exactly where we started out. It wasn't any of us, or Sarah. It could have been any of the three men Greta Stevens arrived with."

She had a peculiar thought. "You know that book I'm reading, *Crime and Punishment?*"

Jeremiah nodded, while Ed looked like he was about to ask the same kind of question his partner had asked when he first saw its title.

"Well, it's about this student, Raskolnikov—"

"Who?" asked Ed.

"Some Russian in this story she's reading," explained

Jeremiah.

"Anyway, he commits this senseless murder, just to show that he can, to prove a theory he has about...the inherent nature of man, or something. The woman is an unpleasant person, a pawnbroker who preys on others. He doesn't even keep her money, though he's desperately poor. There's no reason for anyone to suspect him, and in fact, nobody does. Except that after he commits the crime, he becomes very ill—delirious, in fact. And he admits to just about everything. Only his friends don't believe it for a second—you know the things that people say when they're delirious. But one of his friends has a relative who happens to be investigating the case, and he's not so sure it's just rambling."

Ed smiled. "Jeremiah tells everyone who we are when he's delirious."

"Just once. I had a really high fever, and the doc in that town dosed me with laudanum, which only made it worse. You try it sometime, Ed, and see if you don't do the same thing."

"Yeah. It's a good thing that doc had a taste for his own laudanum. Afterwards, he didn't remember much about the evening."

"Anyway, I haven't gotten that far along with the book, what with everything that's been happening, but I peeked at the ending, and I think his conscience gets to him in the end. But it's too bad we don't have a way of inducing delirium."

The two outlaws looked at each other and began to laugh.

Jeremiah finally caught himself, and looked at Anna, his eyes dancing with mischief. "Oh, but we do. You're just not going to like it very much."

"Try me?"

"Break out the liquor. In all those extra supplies our city

friends insisted on bringing along is probably enough whiskey to float a small ship. They said it was for snakebite, but there aren't that many snakes in North and South America together. We can have a sort of an Irish wake. People get talking when they're drinking. They let things slip they'd never say otherwise."

She thought about that old phrase *In vino veritas,* and she thought again about what Jeremiah had said about her a couple of nights ago in the Springs. She wondered if he'd meant it after all, if he fantasized about her being his wife. But all she said was, "It might work, although I'm not happy about exposing Sarah to all those drunken men. But what about you two?"

"We'll drink just enough to make it look good, and pretend the rest. It's a pretty standard trick, to get information."

Anna nodded. "So, what's your plan? This evening around the campfire?"

"Probably so. Why?"

"I'd rather get Sarah out of here. I just don't like the idea of—"

Ed interrupted. "Sarah's not a child, Anna. You can't treat her like one."

"She's had a lot of sad things in her life, and I guess I keep thinking I can work that fairytale ending for her. Besides, she's such a pretty girl, and I just don't want..." She trailed off. It wasn't really that she thought that any of the members of the party would threaten Sarah's honor. It was a kind of nameless dread she had on her ward's behalf.

Jeremiah frowned. "Sarah's a good rider, isn't she? And you trust her on her own?"

"You saw for yourself. She puts me to shame, that's for certain. Every chance she gets, she goes off riding on her own.

I go with her when I can, but often I have too much work, and she's never given me any reason to worry."

"Okay, then, here's the plan. We won't wait for this evening. Say in half-an-hour, you and Sarah go off for the rest of the afternoon, to take a walk. Everyone knows you won't get anywhere on foot, so nobody will try to stop you. And they won't find it too peculiar that the two of you want to do a little exploring while you're here, to take your minds off things. You can show them your geodes or something. When you two are gone, we make some remark about how now that it's just us men we can relax a little, and we break out the whiskey, see if we can get these men talking. Only, Ed'll go now and bring one of the horses around so that when you've gotten to the other side of the hill, one'll be waiting for Sarah. Remember that old miner we know up this way? I told Anna about him, Ed. Sarah can reach him before dark and be back in the morning. He might be a useful reinforcement if things don't go the way we hope."

"You really think she'll be okay?" asked Ed, frowning.

"Do you trust this old man?" Anna asked.

"Sure," he said.

Anna nodded thoughtfully. "Sarah will be fine. Give her some landmarks and she'll find her way there. I'd feel a lot better about it, actually. Especially in case things get messy." She turned back to Jeremiah. "But what about me? I don't think these gentlemen are going to sink too deep into their cups or start sharing their innermost secrets if I'm there. Do I go with Sarah, or do you have another idea?"

"How are you at climbing trees?" he asked, and gave her a mischievous smile.

Chapter 11

Anna looked at Jeremiah in surprise. "Climbing trees?" she asked. "Fair to middling when I was younger. Not something I've attempted in quite a while."

"Any good with a gun?"

She pulled a small pearl-handled derringer out of the leather pouch she had slung across her shoulder. She handled it gingerly, with all the distrust with which she regarded firearms, even her own. "Terrible. I can hit the broad side of a barn on a good day. If I'm standing close, that is. What's all this about, anyway?"

Ed made a face. "Anna, with one of those ladies' little pop guns, even I can barely hit the broad side of a barn. Those are just for scaring off people who are coming too close. You could have used it last night to show Jeremiah just how unwelcome his attentions were." He winked, then turned serious. "You need a real gun."

"Are you offering me yours?"

He laughed. "Nope. I'm making Jer offer you his, though."

His partner sputtered. "What?"

"Well, that's your plan, isn't it? Have her listening to what's going on, and cover us, just in case?"

"Yeah, but why does that mean she needs my gun? Don't we have a shotgun someplace she can use?"

"Wonderful," she said. "You're having me climbing trees

without being detected, eavesdropping, and brandishing a firearm about ten times the size of anything I've ever handled. And we've already established that I'm about as far as you can be from a crack shot without being publicly disowned by the Territory of Montana. Anything else I'm not good at you might want me to try? I'm pretty dreadful at cooking, and I was my mother's despair since I couldn't sew a straight line. Any way we can work those into the plan?"

Brown laughed. "I don't think that will be necessary. And you'll get to the tree before we bring the conversation over there." He looked critically at her long skirt. "You going to be able to climb a tree in that, or you want to borrow a pair of trousers?"

She shuddered, but then thought about the last time she'd climbed a tree, and why it was the last. She was all of twelve years old, and she distinctly remembered tangling her favorite summer frock in some branches. At the time, she was sad—because she'd ruined the dress beyond repair—but now, all she could think about was how her father had to come and untangle her. "I can see why Jonathan thinks you two are so much fun. You get people doing things they never imagined they were going to be doing. All right. I'll wear your pants, and I'll climb your tree, and I'll carry your shotgun. But don't expect me to do anything more than fire it in the air and make noise with it."

"That's all we're asking," said Jeremiah. "If it's even necessary. The distraction would give Ed and me the chance to draw, if somebody's already got a gun on us. But the main thing is, that you're listening to whatever results from the conversation."

"Good girl, Anna." Edward helped her to her feet. "Come along and let me give you some pointers for the shotgun."

• ♥ •

Anna really didn't know how Brown and Marcus thought they'd be able to do all of this undetected. But both Stevens and Abel were sunk into a sort of morbid distraction. Bryant had risen to the occasion, and was concerning himself primarily with the state of his two friends. Anna tried to interpret his expression whenever he looked her way, but he was as unreadable as ever. She thought she saw pain reflected in his light eyes; but then, in a moment, the expression had flickered and disappeared.

Both Sarah and the horse left without anyone seemingly any the wiser. A little concerned to be going off without her guardian, Marcus was able to reassure her that it was the best thing to do. She seemed to trust him implicitly, maybe more than she should have, Anna thought.

Thanks to a boost on Ed's shoulders, Anna was concealed among the boughs of a leafy tree. It was so uncomfortable that she was thinking about sleeping in the tent nostalgically. She was wearing a pair of Jeremiah's trousers along with her own shirtwaist and boots, and had to admit they were more comfortable than she'd expected. She was tall for a woman, and since he was slim, the fit wasn't too bad, although she still had to belt them in. The not-being-able-to-move part was the worst of it, though. Her gold locket dangled forward in her bent-over position, and she quickly tucked it inside the high neck of her shirtwaist, afraid all the while that she was going to lose her grip either on the tree or the shotgun.

She felt like she'd been crouched there forever, and she was beginning to wonder if one could suddenly develop a fear of heights in one's adult years, when the voices got louder.

"Don't see why we shouldn't start a new fire over here," said Jeremiah. His black hat came into her line of sight, as well as a very peculiar view that consisted primarily of the tops of his shoulders, and then, as he squatted to clear away space for the fire, part of his thighs in those faded black trousers he usually wore.

"What's wrong with the old one?" his partner asked him, testily, and promptly provided a similar view, of hat, shoulders, and thighs. She thought she could detect just the slightest thickening of their voices, and despite herself she began fretting about whether they'd stuck to their plan about faking most of the drinking they were going to be doing. She didn't doubt their self-control so much as wondered whether, like most men, they might not be a little optimistic about how much whiskey they could handle.

But when the trio of San Franciscans came within clearer earshot, she stopped worrying so much about Jeremiah and Ed. She could hear the drink in the others' voices much more obviously.

"Less start a new fire. In her mem'ry," came Abel's voice. She hadn't noticed the bald spot at the back of his head before, but it was prominent from her new angle. He was followed by some drunken mumbling and sobbing that must have been Stevens.

"Ligh't'n up now, boys," came Bryant's soft tenor, sounding a little less intoxicated than Abel—but just a little. "She wouldn't wan' us to be all sad in this beau'ful wilderness she wanted to visit so much..."

Anna had always wondered what men talked about when there were no ladies present, and the next hour or so was an education. Stevens didn't say much, but the remaining quartet boasted and bragged about adventures they'd had, in terms they hadn't used in mixed company. Even Bryant had a few stories to tell—admittedly they were mostly about the cleverness of accountants, but apparently, he was quite athletic, as well. Brown and Marcus did a remarkable job of telling stories that had, no doubt, happened to them, without crossing over the line into outlaw territory. What with all the stories that were current about them, it must have been difficult to pick ones out that nobody knew about. But the silver-tongued Brown, always the spokesman for the partnership, was particularly expert about this. She recognized a few that they'd told her, back before she'd known they'd once been Tommy Slade and Johnny Nevada.

As time went on, and more liquor was consumed, the stories began to take a turn that was, for their secret listener, frankly more than a little bit uncomfortable. Bluntly, the bragging and boasting turned to exploits with women. She found out a lot more than she had ever known about, ranging to acts she hadn't even dreamed were possible, largely in connection with Abel and his Polynesian travels.

Brown and Marcus were surprisingly modest, although she suspected that had a great deal to do with the fact that they knew she was listening. They made reference to a couple of legendary cathouses, in Denver and San Antonio, but they weren't too specific about the goings on. They were specific enough to surprise her a few times, though.

Bryant was quiet about this—he probably had a respectable sweetheart or something—and Stevens, naturally, wasn't going to participate. But then, he'd been awfully silent, except for some sobbing and moaning, anyway.

Finally, Abel did what Anna had dreaded he would do. "So, Brown, tell us the truth? Was Miss Harrison really pushing you away when I saw you last night? 'Cause it kinda looked like she was kissin' you back." When Jeremiah didn't respond, he went on. "Wouldn't blame you...I kinda had a fancy for 'er myself. A little too proper, I thought. But I put that down to bein' a spinster, and all. Nothin' a man couldn't fix."

She wondered idly if he would still think she was too proper if he knew she was sitting in a tree, wearing a pair of trousers, and holding a shotgun. She also hoped he'd stop that line of thought before it went any further. After all, she *was* holding a gun on him.

In an attempt to draw the conversation away from a direction that was awkward for their secret sharer, Ed and Jeremiah suddenly broke into a drunken song, and Anna cringed a little. Fond as she was of both men, neither could really carry a tune. At least, it served its intended purpose. But with one hand hanging onto the tree trunk for dear life, and the other holding the shotgun, she wasn't in any position to stop up her ears. Besides, who knew when snatches of drunken song might not turn into a confession? They were singing something to the tune of "Sweet Betsy from Pike" but the words were a bit bawdier—actually, a great deal bawdier. In fact, despite her not being quite so proper as Abel imagined, she wasn't sure what all of it meant.

After awhile, it was noted that Victor Stevens had passed out. "Poor thing," said Bryant, in a maudlin tone. "S'hard on him. S'hard on all of us..." Anna wished she could see his expression, because his words gave her a funny feeling. She remembered *in vino veritas* and wondered if it was universal.

"Drink to that," said Ed, passing around the bottle again.

"*He's* not the poor thing," slurred Abel. "*He's* not the poor thing at all. Greta...*she* was the poor thing. You should have seen her before she married him. She was the prettiest little thing in those days. Just sweet, and trusting, and pretty, but spirited and brave, too. You saw her ride, once she got accustomed to riding astride, again. And nerves? Not one bit of it. He did that to her, with his constant criticizing and his treating her like she needed protecting all the time."

"You loved her?" asked Jeremiah, in a seemingly careless tone.

"Anyone would have, in those days. But I never got over her, poor sweet Greta."

So, she'd been right! It was all Anna could do to keep quiet, up in that tree. If only Jeremiah asked the right next couple of questions...now she wished she hadn't been so eager to avoid their little party, although she knew it never would have happened if she were there, anyway. Her litigator's instincts were keyed up and ready, and it was frustrating not to be able to leap into action. Now she knew how Ed Marcus must feel whenever he couldn't go for his gun.

"Was Stevens your rival?"

"You know why she married him and not me? And this'll really get you," he said confidentially to everyone for miles around. "Because she thought he was steadier. He wouldn't always be gallivanting off on her to the Far East—he never went any farther than the accounting department."

"Hey, what's wrong with that?" asked Bryant, defensively, but he seemed to catch himself. Anna really wished she could see him, since his voice gave away so little.

"I would have shared the great wide world with her, taken her with me. He kept her in such a small little world, it was pitiful to see."

"So that's why you killed her?" asked Ed impulsively. "Because you felt sorry for her?"

"Me? I didn't kill her. I'd have done anything in the world for her, but not help her out of it!"

"Then, who did?"

Jeremiah drew his gun quietly, and pointed it at the man

slumped on the ground. "I think we can all guess that. Who gave her the sleeping draught every night and could have given her a stronger dose on the night he didn't want her to wake up until it was too late? Who was so jealous of his wife that he couldn't let her out of his sight for a minute, unless she was safely chaperoned by other ladies? Remember how he never left her alone unless she was with Miss Harrison or Miss Nicholls, and hardly even then?"

"Who turned the sweetest, most beautiful girl I ever had the privilege to know into the worn-out mass of nerves you all met several days ago?" slurred Abel. He must have been really drunk, because Anna would have thought what was going on would have sobered anyone. But then, what did she know about it, anyway?

Ed Marcus had drawn now, too. But suddenly, Stevens sat bolt upright, and said in a dead cold sober tone, "I think we all know the answer to that, Abel. I couldn't bear it anymore, knowing that my wife was carrying on with you like that."

"What?" asked Abel, his drunkenness momentarily swallowed up by his disbelief. "I never touched her. She was a married woman and I'd never— But Victor, you were out cold a moment ago."

The cold voice continued. "Well, it's possible I was doing her an injustice, of course. But it was just a matter of time, wasn't it, with you always watching and waiting, and... I wasn't *planning* to do it. I loved her. But I kept seeing how you looked at her, the whole time you were pretending to make such a fuss over Miss Harrison." He paused, and laughed flatly. "Did you really think I'd let myself get stinking drunk with the four of you watching my every move? Don't think I didn't know you suspected me, Abel. Bryant, too. You aren't the only ones pretending tonight, Mister Brown and Mister

Marcus—or, should I say, Mister Slade and Mister Nevada? Somebody pointed you out to me once, when you were in San Francisco many years ago. I didn't recognize you right away, but it came back to me the other day. I'm good at remembering faces."

There was a sharp intake of breath from Ed, as Abel drunkenly muttered, "What the—"

"I'm right, aren't I, gentlemen? Those *are* your real names? Tommy Slade and Johnny Nevada? I'm not sure what a pair of outlaws are doing, serving as wilderness guides, but it sure makes things convenient. So, you can see why I'm not particularly worried about your testimony in a court of law. How convenient for me that you sent the ladies away. A pair of outlaws and two men so drunk they can hardly stand—not much in the way of witnesses to a confession."

"These are our real names," said Jeremiah. "Brown and Marcus. Anything else, well, you'll have to talk to our lawyer. She's heard your whole confession, by the way." He looked right up at Anna. "You can come down, now, Miss Harrison."

"You're faking it. She's not really up there," said Stevens.

Anna surmised he couldn't imagine a delicate flower of womanhood like herself climbing trees. On another day, she would have agreed with him about that.

"I'm afraid I am, Mister Stevens," she called down. "And in all my years as an attorney, that was one of the cruelest admissions of guilt it's ever been my unhappy duty to listen to." She clutched the shotgun under her arm the best she could, and she began to make her way back down. There was a seven-foot drop at the bottom, and she paused, frightened. She couldn't drop the gun, for fear of setting it off, but she didn't want to jump with it.

Jeremiah noticed, and holstered his own gun to come to her

aid. Stevens wasn't likely to bolt for it if he suspected it was Johnny Nevada covering him. She handed him down the shotgun, and began shimmying down the tree trunk, in a most unladylike fashion that she could remember being very fond of in her youth. Wearing trousers helped her get a grip better than she could have in her usual clothes, but unfortunately, there was some moss on the trunk, and she slipped partway down. She fell to the ground with an inadvertent yelp of pain where she landed on her left ankle. Ed turned just for a moment to see what was wrong, but that moment was enough.

Victor Stevens, with more speed than she would have given him credit for, had grabbed the shotgun—and for Anna, herself. "I'm leaving here right now, and you're not going to try to stop me, or she dies."

She heard Jeremiah's anguished voice. "Ed, do something."

"I can't get a clear shot at him. Not the way he's holding her in front of him."

If Ed Marcus couldn't do it, nobody could. She caught a glimpse of Jeremiah's expression and she was deeply touched—or would have been, if she hadn't been so preoccupied with being terrified. Nonetheless, she focused on controlling her voice. "You're just making it worse for yourself," she said, trying to reason with her abductor.

"Be quiet, you whore," he hissed in her ear.

So much for her vaunted ability to persuade people, she thought. Judges, juries, maybe. Madmen holding shotguns uncomfortably near her head…no. Stevens continued to back away, dragging her with him as he went.

What happened next, happened so quickly that she had to put it together later on from talking to the other people present. Meriwether Abel admitted to remembering very little of the incident, so it wasn't surprising that nobody quite recalled what he was doing. Paul Bryant, apparently sobered by the shock of hearing his friend confess to murder, and watching him prepare to commit another, had sprung forward, flinging himself at Stevens in complete disregard of his own personal safety. The shotgun discharged straight into his chest, but in the meantime, Anna was able to break free, and roll away. Bryant fell backwards, dead, and a moment later, so did Stevens, hit square in the heart by Ed Marcus's bullet.

Jeremiah Brown ran to her side, and knelt down to where she was trying to get up. "Anna, you okay?" In the middle of her pain and shock, she heard the way his voice cracked, and she was touched by it.

She clung to him as tightly as she could, burying her face in his shoulder, and her heart pounded so hard and fast she thought it was trying to go somewhere without the rest of her, but she willed herself not to cry. He held her, and stroked her hair.

Despite her best efforts to control them, a few tears leaked out onto his shirt. "You have terrible judgment about employers, you know that?" she asked, when she finally could trust herself to speak.

He laughed and kissed her on the top of the head. "Yours about traveling companions isn't so great, either." She felt him pull away, just a little. "Ed, you okay?"

"Been better." Anna turned and looked at him, his gaze steely when he looked at the still form of Stevens, and regretful when he looked at Bryant, torn up and bloody from the shotgun blast. "I can't help thinking if we hadn't fed him so much whiskey, he might not have run right at a man with a loaded shotgun like that."

"Don't know, Ed. Guess we'll never know."

"I think he would have," she said. "He didn't do that for me—not mainly, at least. Remember how we thought Greta Stevens had a lover? I thought it was Meriwether Abel. I guess I was wrong. I guess I read Bryant all wrong."

"So, what do we do now?" asked Ed.

"Well, it's getting close to dark, and we can't leave these bodies, or they'll attract wolves," Jeremiah replied. "Don't look like Abel's going to be of any use to us in that department." He reluctantly pulled away from Anna altogether, and they gathered what they could and covered the bodies. Afterwards, they built another fire as close to them as possible, not that far from the first one. Abel was snoring away—Ed said he guessed he was out until morning. Anna just sat there and watched them, growing ever more conscious of the throbbing in her ankle.

After a bit, Jeremiah threw his partner a look. "Mind looking after old Abel by yourself, Ed? I don't think Anna should have to sit watch on the bodies."

Ed just smiled in reply. Anna felt as though something that should have been very secret had somehow been exposed. But only Ed Marcus was going to know, and it was foolish to think he didn't know, anyway. She believed what he had said; that Jeremiah hadn't talked about her, not directly. But the two men were obviously so close. If there was one person in the world who Ed Marcus could read like a book, it was his partner.

As Jeremiah helped her to her feet and led her back in the direction of the original campfire, it didn't seem to matter so much. The ankle she had landed on was barely supporting her weight, so she was leaning on him heavily, which made her all the more aware—between twinges of pain, anyway—of how his body felt against hers. Of how much she wanted him. How she could think of something like that after all this, she didn't know. She supposed she was just naturally turning to him for comfort. That was her excuse, anyway.

He sat her gently down on a heap of bedding, and went to gather some more, as well as to stir up the ashes of the fire and get it going. She sat watching him go about his business, admiring the well-knit lines of his back as he bent down, and his lean, strong legs as he rose again. Finally, he came and sat beside her.

"Sorry I couldn't be of any more help," she apologized.

"Shhh," he said, and kissed her. After a while, he pulled his mouth away from hers, and she felt his kisses on her cheek, her neck, her earlobe. "Do you want me to stop?" he whispered. "I could move my bedroll to the other side of the fire if you—"

"No," she said simply. "I want you right here." She wanted him to hold her all through the night, and not let go. She reached back to let down her hair, and he smiled in appreciation.

"Anna," he said softly, and his mouth met hers, again.

She finally got her wish about sleeping out under the stars that night, and somehow, the ground didn't seem so cold and hard for once.

• ♥ •

When Anna woke the next morning, in the gray light of dawn, he wasn't there. She looked around in a bit of a panic. She could tell from the way her ankle felt that she wasn't going to be getting anywhere on her own, so she'd just have to wait for Jeremiah to get back. She noticed that the bedding had been rearranged to make it look as though someone had slept on the other side of the fire, but she was certain he'd been with her all through the night.

Presently, he did return, accompanied by Marcus and by a very hungover-looking Meriwether Abel. Ed was carrying some fish.

"Good morning, Miss Harrison," said Jeremiah. So, they were back to formality, for Meriwether Abel's sake. "Sleep well?" She couldn't help but notice the twinkle in his eye as he asked that.

"Very well, Mr. Brown. But Mr. Abel looks like he had a rough night."

Abel looked a little green. "I'm ashamed to say I don't remember much about it. I know you and Miss Sarah went for a walk, and we broke out the whiskey, and after that, it's a little hazy. Something about you falling out of a tree, and Stevens confessing," he stopped, tightening the muscles of his mouth. "Stevens confessing to Greta's murder. And Bryant attacking him and then getting killed. And then you, Mr. Marcus—"

"I had to shoot him," said Marcus, quietly. He busied himself over the fire, with the fish, so that his face was turned away as he said this.

"I know you did," Abel replied. "I'm just sorry I wasn't in any condition to do it myself. I don't quite remember what all I said last night, but I loved that woman more than life itself. Victor was such a quiet, respectable-seeming man, but he had the soul of a monster. If only Bryant and I could have persuaded her to leave him, but she wouldn't have any of it. She said married was married for life."

Anna spoke, softly. "I'm sorry. I knew her as a sweet, kind of worn-down lady, but it sounds like she must have been a lot more."

He nodded. "She was. Of course, Bryant and I used to fight about it all the time, which one of us had the better right to protect her: the rejected suitor or her half-brother."

"Half-brother?" she asked. If the note was from Bryant, it wasn't a love note, after all. She looked at Brown and Marcus, and she could tell they were wondering the same thing she was. "Bryant was her half-brother?"

"I didn't realize you didn't know that," Abel replied. "It wasn't any secret. Of course, he's so quiet...was so quiet, around folks he didn't know. He was a good man, and he loved his sister." His sorrow was obvious, and he had to stop talking for a moment.

There was silence for a few minutes, as Abel visibly composed himself.

"Seeing as you got us all mixed up in this, Mr. Abel, would you mind tellin' us something?" asked Jeremiah.

Abel shook his iron-gray head, and said, "Go ahead."

"Just what was the purpose of this trip, anyway?"

"Well, I guess Bryant and I were afraid of...not of what happened, but of what he might do if he got angry at her, or jealous. As soon as we heard about the trip, we invited ourselves along. He could hardly say no to such valuable coworkers. I guess all I can do is hope that we did the right thing. I'm afraid we didn't, but then, who knows if he wouldn't have gotten jealous if it had been just him, her and a guide." He smiled ruefully. "Now you know what I was doing watching you and Miss Harrison that night. I couldn't sleep for worrying about her. You can imagine how pleased we were about Miss Harrison and Miss Nicholls being added to the party. Safety in numbers, and all that. And we knew that Stevens didn't get jealous of her talking to women, or not as much, anyway." He paused, looked around. "Where is Miss Nicholls, anyway? Is she all right?"

"She'll be back later," Anna said. "Mr. Brown and Mr.

Marcus sent her off to a friend's—a miner in the hills—in case things got out of hand last night."

Abel smiled benevolently. It looked like it hurt him, and she wasn't entirely sorry, remembering some of the things he'd said the day before. "There was something else about you two, Mr. Brown and Mr. Marcus, wasn't there? But I'm afraid I can't remember what it was."

• ♥ •

When Anna had the chance, she caught Ed Marcus alone. There was something she needed to say before Sarah returned. She had to bite her lip, because she knew what a hypocrite she was going to sound like, but it couldn't be helped. "Take it easy with Sarah, all right? She's a vulnerable young girl, and her whole future depends on her making the right choices. As you probably know, I stand *in loco parentis* to the girl."

Ed frowned at that. "You stand as a crazy parent?"

She sighed. "Lawyer-Latin. Everyone in my family used to talk that way, even mother. Someday, I'm going to learn to speak like other people. Maybe. I stand in the place of a parent to her. I'm the only one looking out for her interests."

"Well, I would never do anything to harm those interests. She's a fine girl, and you're right to say that I'm not the one to give her the future she deserves. But I think there's something she needs to tell you herself."

"What?" she asked.

"I told you—she has to tell you herself. I gave her my word. But I think it'll make you happy."

"There's not much will make me happy," she smiled at him. "Besides, you must think I'm a complete hypocrite, considering me and your partner and all."

"Look, Anna, you and Sarah are completely different women. She's a young girl, and you're—"

"Not."

He laughed. "I was going to put it in much more flattering terms. You're a grown woman, not someone who needs protecting, like Sarah does. And I think you're good for Jeremiah. You keep him on his toes." He looked at her, seriously. "And you don't seem to be expecting something that can't ever happen. Or at least, can't happen while things are the way they are right now. You know there's no future, for any woman, with either of us, until that statute of limitations runs, in more than one jurisdiction, and it's still well over a year away before we're free and clear. A lot could happen between now and then, especially while we've each got a reward on us." He trailed off, having made his point.

"I haven't been thinking about the future, funny as that might sound," she said. "Considering I'm a woman and we all know about what women are like." She didn't bother to tell him about the suffocating sensation she got when anyone came courting. She'd long suspected that she wasn't the only woman who felt that way, but that she was unusual in being lucky enough to have the choice. She thought about David and she wondered whether they would have been happy. She was so young then, and she hadn't gotten used to being on her own yet, and she rather thought they would have been.

And then, she thought about Greta Stevens, and the weight that Victor must have been on her. Funny, but for all he annoyed her at times, she couldn't understand why Greta hadn't had Meriwether Abel instead. That would have been a fine life for her, with all that travel. She was a little sorry he was too old for Sarah. But he'd probably never love another woman, anyway, and certainly not a naïve young girl.

"Anna?" She heard Ed calling her name. "Where'd you go off to?"

"Sorry." She gave him a sheepish smile. "Just thinking... about being a woman, and life, and Greta Stevens."

"Not about Jeremiah?"

"I do think about other things once in a while, you know." She laughed. "Make sure he knows that. I wouldn't want him to get conceited, or anything."

"Guess you've got lots to think about." He smiled at her. Was it an expression of relief she detected? "Got any interesting trials coming up?"

She rolled her eyes. "When Nick gets back from Europe, it's going to be dreadfully busy. Everything's backed up right now, waiting for him." But just then, her ankle took the moment to remind her of its existence and she groaned aloud. "I think I need to see a doctor."

Before the sun had risen too high, Sarah and Old Joe, the miner, had made their way into camp. The gray-bearded old man grumbled a little, but he agreed to keep watch while the party made their way into town to go see the sheriff. Meriwether Abel made him a gift of many of the pack animals and the extra supplies, which cheered him up a great deal. He wrapped up Anna's ankle for her, before they left for town.

Chapter 12

When they got to town, Anna and Abel were able to handle most of the business with the sheriff. A pair of lawyers, even if one of them was an explorer from California and the other a woman from Montana, was enough to gladden the sheriff's legalistic heart.

Brown and Marcus were able to have a minimum of contact, and Anna didn't once see the sheriff's eyes go toward the "Reward $5,000" posters for both of them that were pinned right to his wall. Abel never seemed to remember what he'd heard that night, so it appeared that the memory was gone for good.

That evening, Sarah and Anna made their way back to the Springs Temperance Hotel. If it had seemed excessively genteel before, it felt stifling now. "So," Anna said, taking a deep breath, "you seemed to be taking a real shine to Mr. Marcus, but when I asked him about it, he just said that you might have something to tell me."

"Oh, that," Sarah smiled mysteriously. "Edward Marcus is a wonderful man. He certainly is handsome, and brave, and he understands the wilderness. But I was just trying to throw you off the track. You see, I have a sweetheart, and I couldn't tell you 'til he'd got his daddy to say it was all right for us to get married."

"Why on earth not, Sarah?"

She looked down. "Cause it's Ray Powell." She handed

Anna a piece of paper. "While the bellboy was helping you up the stairs, I checked to see if I'd gotten a transatlantic cable, and I have. It's definite now."

It was tersely worded, but it was a proposal and a consent from his father, all right. "You're marrying Raymond Powell? Son of my dearest adversary?" A quote sprang to Anna's mind, not one that she had consciously known that she knew. "'My only love sprung from my only hate! Too early seen unknown, and known too late! Prodigious birth of love it is to me, that I must love a loathed enemy.' Well, all I can say is, I'm glad I made you read *Romeo and Juliet* and not *Julius Caesar* or *Richard III*!"

"Ray's nothing like his father."

That was something Anna couldn't disagree with, although she wasn't so sure the difference was in the boy's favor. There was something to Nick beyond greed and showiness, even if she was one of the few people who knew it. But Sarah seemed so happy. Well, Ray served as an intermediary between the local cattle rancher's association and the stockyards in Chicago. He certainly had a bright future, and at least he didn't practice law with his daddy. That would have been a little too Montague and Capulet, Anna reflected.

"That's wonderful. But if Nick was so opposed to the match at first, what happened?"

"Well, he wasn't opposed to it because of you, if that's what you thought. He just felt like his son should marry someone who could help him with his business interests. But after Lisette found herself a Polish count, and then he turned out to be not only just after her money, but a complete fraud and from New Jersey, Nick decided that maybe Ray's impulse to fall in love with a local girl was a sound one after all."

"Did the cable tell you all this?"

"There was another one...not for you to see." She blushed.

"Well, even old Nick can live and learn. That's wonderful!" Anna hugged her ward, but then drew back and frowned. "Only, this makes me and Nick relatives, almost, sort of. I'll tell you a secret if you promise never to tell anyone, especially not Ray."

Sarah gave her guardian an inquiring look.

"I like old Nick. He may be unscrupulous, and he may lie awake nights trying to figure out how to embarrass me in court, but I like him. And he likes me, too. We're friends, kind of, even though you'll never get either of us to admit it." The funny thing was, next to Jonathan and Sarah, Nick Powell was probably the best friend Anna had in the world. She vaguely wondered where Jeremiah Brown fit into the scheme of things, but he was from outside her world, and she wasn't sure that he fit into it at all.

Sarah laughed. "So, you'll stand up with me?"

"Of course. Just let me heal up some first, okay? So that I can manage the actual standing part." And they embraced again, but Anna's ankle gave out, so Sarah helped her sit down on the bed, and went to get the doctor.

The doctor said it wasn't so bad as it looked at first, but that she ought to stay off it for a week, as much as she could. As soon as he left, she groaned loudly. "So much for the rest of our holiday, Sarah. I'm not going to be able to get out and about much."

The younger woman looked at her hesitantly. "There's a big camp meeting up at Red Rocks, near Boulder. Mrs. Grey asked me if I'd like to go. It'll be most of the week, starting the day after tomorrow."

Anna snorted in disbelief. "Sarah, I can't even get you to pay attention to the sermon in church. How many times have

I asked you what you thought about it, or about the gospel reading, and all you can tell me is what a pretty day it was outside, and doesn't Mrs. Wilkins look lovely in her new bonnet? It's kind of Mrs. Grey to ask you, but you don't really want to go and listen to all that fire and brimstone preaching, do you?"

"It's supposed to be real pretty around there, and I did love it when we were off in the mountains, until all those horrid things happened."

"This won't be you and me and half a dozen other people, Sarah. This will be you and Mrs. Grey and a couple of hundred, most likely."

"The stars will be the same, and the mountains. And this may be my only chance to get up that way, since Ray and I will be getting married pretty soon." How could someone claim that she was approaching the happiest day of her life, and all Anna could think of was it sounded like a prison sentence?

"All right, Sarah. Leave your poor crippled friend here all by herself." She feigned martyrdom.

Sarah blushed. "Well, I'm sure Jeremiah Brown would be happy to help you get around town." After a pause, during which Anna said nothing, she continued. "And Edward Marcus, too, of course. And tomorrow, we'll go out and get you the prettiest walking stick."

Anna wondered all over again what Sarah had figured out about Jeremiah Brown and herself, and decided she was better off not knowing.

The gentlemen joined them for dinner. Meriwether Abel accepted the invitation to dine at the Temperance Hotel with the alacrity of a man who could still recall a recent, painful hangover, and Brown and Marcus were forced to concur.

Besides, it was just down the stairs from Anna's room, and everyone was kind enough to agree that her limited mobility was a factor in making plans. The cooking was not too bad, anyway, although she was a little concerned about what it might be when the cook was not under the watchful eye of Mrs. Grey. Well, she'd have to let the worries of the next week be sufficient unto themselves.

Meriwether Abel was going to leave for San Francisco the following day, and he'd decided to accept a permanent posting in the company's new Shanghai office. It went unsaid, but was understood by everybody, that only Greta Stevens had been anchoring him in San Francisco, anyway. He was unusually subdued, and for the first time, he really asked other people questions about their own lives. He turned out to be an intelligent and attentive listener, and he was particularly interested in hearing about the contrast in Anna's life, between the way the community in Carter's Creek accepted her for what she was, and the way that people outside still treated her like some kind of oddity for being a lady lawyer. He hadn't missed the sheriff's reaction when she'd told him. But Brown did most of the talking, and even the quieter Marcus had quite a bit to say, about the wide-open spaces of the West.

"I will miss this country," Abel said thoughtfully. "And I regret that I haven't spent more time getting to know this part of it. But I won't be in China forever, after all. You know, there's a place just outside of town where the sunset is one of the prettiest things I've ever seen. It's nearly that time, now. Would any of you like to accompany me?"

Sarah accepted with alacrity, and the others rose to follow her. "Have a nice time," Anna said gently, and Jeremiah Brown dropped back.

"We're going to find you still sitting here when we get back, aren't we? Let me help you out to the porch or something," He called out to the others. "You three go on. I'll keep Miss Harrison company."

One thing Anna couldn't complain about with the ankle was that it gave her a reason to lean on him in public. It wasn't going to be as much fun once she got her walking stick. But who knew how much longer he and his partner were even going to be around, anyway? When he'd settled her on a wicker settee on the hotel's front porch, he took out a cigar from his breast pocket. "Do you mind?"

She made a face. "They make me cough."

He rolled his eyes, but he replaced it. "You're a hard woman, Anna Harrison. Never mind, I'll smoke it later, at the saloon." He saw her expression, and knew she was thinking back to that first night in town. "You're not going to tell me you have objections to my playing a little poker, are you? You wouldn't want me to get out of practice."

She laughed. "Certainly not. Since that's how you get the money to pay your attorney's fees, as I recall. I'm bound to encourage anything with that beneficial side effect."

He sat down next to her. "How much longer are you in town for?"

"I'm not going anywhere until the end of the week. Probably literally, with this ankle. Sarah got herself invited up to some camp meeting up at Red Rocks by the lady that runs this hotel. She's leaving the day after tomorrow, and I guess she'll be gone for about a week. Nick won't be back in Carter's Creek for another couple of weeks, and Jonathan's handling things just fine on his own." She fingered the telegram in her pocket, with its greeting to "my old friends Brown and Marcus."

Jeremiah shuddered. "A week-long camp meeting? Better her than me. So, you'll be here all on your own?"

"Looks that way."

"Well, you know, Ed and I are in no hurry to move on. Abel paid us in full, with a generous bonus for all we had to go through. I'm sure we could think of something to amuse you. At least, I'm sure *I* could." And the way he looked at her then, she had no doubt he had some ideas on the subject.

But she couldn't let things go that easily. She never could. "Maybe you can show me how to play poker?"

He looked horrified. "Anna, you're a fine lawyer, and the next time I need to send someone up a tree with a shotgun, you're at the top of my list. But poker's a man's game. Leave us something."

She contented herself with muttering something about bankrupting him at whist, because she knew he'd never call her on it.

• ♥ •

They saw Sarah off early in the morning, two days after that, Anna from the porch in front of the hotel where she waved and smiled, and Brown and Marcus from the coach's side. Jeremiah soon joined her on the porch and flashed her one of those smiles of his. "You up to a ride? In a stagecoach, I mean?"

"Certainly, if I don't have to walk anywhere." She looked ruefully at the delicately carved, but strong, walking stick by her side. "Where to?"

"There's a pretty little town just on the other side of the pass where nobody knows us. Ed and I just rode through it a couple of weeks ago, but we didn't stop. I was thinking we could go there until you have to get back to meet Sarah. The hotel there looked nice and...well, you wouldn't have to walk much." He looked at her expectantly, and she blushed.

Someplace where nobody knew they didn't belong together. A little hotel where they would register as Mr. and Mrs. Brown, and no one would be the wiser. "Sounds good to me, if your partner doesn't mind." She raised her voice a little, to include Edward, who was standing just below the porch railing, waiting to be drawn into the conversation.

Ed Marcus winked at her. "There's plenty for a man to do in this town. I'll be just fine until you get back." She knew he was thinking of that first night she'd run into them.

So, a few hours later, she and Jeremiah Brown were in a stagecoach all to themselves, with a four-hour ride to what was probably going to be the longest time they were ever going to be alone together in their lives. She looked at him and couldn't help fretting, "What if we don't get along? We've never actually spent so much time together."

His brown eyes sparkled. "Well, if you'd be quiet and kiss me, and stop worrying about everything, I think you'll find we get along just fine." And he matched his words to his actions, and proved himself right.

Chapter 13

At the end of the week, Mr. and Mrs. Brown caught the stagecoach back to Colorado Springs together. This time, they were not entirely on their own, but shared the ride with an older couple and two younger men. As the miles rolled past, they slowly drifted out away from the role they'd been playing, and into another—not strangers, but for the sake of propriety, acquaintances with a noticeable layer of formality as they addressed one another.

If any of the other passengers had been observing closely, they would have seen the two stiffen slightly, keeping as much of a distance between them as the crowded coach allowed for. He became Mr. Brown, and she Miss Harrison.

When they arrived in Colorado Springs, she arranged with the driver to have her baggage delivered to the Springs Temperance Hotel, while he grabbed his smaller case. Noticing the cane she was walking with, as though for the first time, he offered to accompany her to her destination, which she quickly accepted.

"There was something strange about those two," Mrs. Benson said to her husband. "I could have sworn I saw them together in the hotel dining room every night last week. But they were acting like they'd barely met until the trip back."

Mr. Benson shrugged. "Perhaps they're carrying on an illicit affair, Maude."

Mrs. Benson gave her husband an annoyed look. "I was imagining something much more exciting, Henry." But she refused to give her husband any specifics, or admit to him she'd imagined that perhaps they were government agents, on an important mission, playing roles and keeping secrets.

• ♥ •

He saw her to the hotel door, assisting her up the steps.

"I'm really walking much better now," she pointed out, but took his arm anyway. "Sarah should be back tomorrow; will you and Ed wait to say goodbye?"

"I'll see you tomorrow," he said, and walked away quickly.

That evening, though, he came calling. "I'm sorry—there's been a change of plans. Ed got a telegram at the hotel the other day, and it looks like we've got a big job waiting for us in Denver. We've got to be out on the last train tonight."

"Sarah will be so disappointed."

He smiled, ruefully. "I hope she's not the only one."

"We've had more time together than I ever expected. Let's just be happy for that."

"All right." He paused, and took a deep breath. "Anna, I'll find some way to see you again."

She found herself unable to respond, other than to say, "I certainly…that is, I hope so. You know where I'll be."

But right there, on the porch of her hotel, there was nothing more they could do but clasp hands quickly. She watched him walk down the street until he'd disappeared into the crowd.

• ♥ •

Four months passed before Anna heard from Jeremiah Brown again.

Sarah was soon to be married, and she had been holding her guardian a captive audience for days now, as she went about her preparations. Anna wasn't quite certain why her presence was necessary, since Sarah was managing everything quite satisfactorily on her own, from sewing her dress to making the arrangements with Reverend Thompson.

Sarah, however, saw things differently. At least, every time Anna tried to make her excuses and head downstairs to the office, her ward stopped her in her tracks with a sad, sweet, helpless look in those big brown eyes.

On this particular morning, when Anna had finally managed to escape the prison of white satin and heavy cream paper in which she'd been entangled, and head downstairs to the safe haven of her office, it was closer to noon than she wanted it to be. Jonathan was sitting at his desk and giving her a peculiar look.

"Morning, Anna," he said. "There's a telegram on your desk."

"Client?" she asked.

"In a sense," he said. There was mischief in his light green eyes, and it was clear he was keeping his aquiline features expressionless only with the greatest effort.

"Someone's either a client or they aren't," she responded. "I assume it isn't an emergency, or you'd have come up and rescued—I mean, interrupted—me."

"Now, Anna," he grinned, "I don't want you to miss out on *any* of Sarah's joy." Jonathan really was the little brother she'd never had.

She restrained herself from doing anything childish in response, and crossed the room to her desk, where the telegram sat prominently on top of one of the "to-do" piles. As soon as she read it, she saw the reason for his amusement.

TO: A. HARRISON ESQ CARTERS CREEK MONTANA

MUST SPEAK TO YOU ABOUT MUTUAL CLIENT J

BLACK. URGENT. MEET ARTHURS CORNERS, WYOMING IN THREE DAYS. CHARLES STANTON ESQ EN ROUTE FROM DENVER COLORADO

"I assume that J. Black is a clever disguise for J. Brown?" remarked Jonathan. She really didn't appreciate the knowing smile he was flashing her.

"I suppose so," she said, as nonchalantly as she could manage. "Jonathan, where is Arthur's Corners, Wyoming, and how on earth does one get there?"

He rather triumphantly produced some railway maps and a sheaf of notes, and proceeded to demonstrate that if she left town on the noon train tomorrow and made three connections, she could be in Arthur's Corners on time. "That is, of course, if you're going."

"Well, this Charles Stanton doesn't seem to be giving me any option, since he's indicated that he's en route there himself."

"It's kind of peculiar, isn't it, that a Colorado attorney should want to meet a Montana attorney in Wyoming in order to discuss a mutual client of no fixed address, isn't it?"

"Well, um, you know, I guess Jeremiah Brown has been spending time in Wyoming lately and—"

"As opposed to Tommy Slade and Johnny Nevada—who, as I recall, were clever enough to know that Wyoming has no statute of limitations, and steered clear of the place altogether during their criminal heyday."

She stared at him. "What does Tommy Slade have to do with anything?"

"Come on, Anna," he said. "It's okay. I've known who your friends Brown and Marcus really are since that time we defended them in that civil suit over in Greenville. Some of the fellows we retrieved that stolen property from kindly identified them for me. I was afraid maybe you didn't know, since you seemed to be getting a little..." he cleared his throat, "*partial*, shall we say, to Jeremiah Brown. But I figured that was why they called you in on that case in the first place, because you knew who they really were, from that first time you met up with them here in town." He smiled and shook his head. "Well, that, and because Jeremiah Brown seemed to be a little partial to you, too."

She sighed, deeply. "There's no point in trying to lie about it, is there? Except that you've got it the wrong way around. Jeremiah Brown isn't really Tommy Slade, because Tommy Slade never really existed. Our friends Brown and Marcus went into their life of crime with an exit strategy already in place. Not too bad for a pair of teenagers who got kicked out of an orphanage, yes?"

"Not too bad," Jonathan said. But then his expression turned serious. "You're not telling me— There really *is* something going on between the two of you, then?" He paused as she nodded wordlessly. "I kind of figured he might be interested in meeting up with you again, but I didn't think that you'd...well, I tried to convince myself that whatever happened between you and him that night in Townsend was just the same kind of mistake that I made with that dancehall girl."

"So you thought the notorious Tommy Slade was pursuing an old maid lawyer without the slightest bit of encouragement?" she asked, looking him straight in the eyes.

"I hoped so. That's just sort of charming in its way."

"Worth teasing me over, instead of lecturing me about?"

"This is another story, Anna. A more dangerous one. Look, Sarah thought he was sweet on you when the two of you ran into them in Colorado, but she didn't think that you...and I didn't want to think… You must realize it's not exactly the best judgment you've ever shown." He reached over and put a hand on her shoulder. "I'm not going to say it doesn't worry me, because it worries me a lot. But I did get to know Jeremiah Brown a little bit, and I can understand that there's more to him than his—or rather, Tommy Slade's—criminal reputation would suggest. Anyway, I guess matters of the heart don't have much to do with reason or logic, do they?"

"How would you know, Jonathan? You married the prettiest, sweetest girl in town, and the two of you have been ridiculously happy. Your heart showed pretty good judgment."

He shrugged. "Just lucky, I guess." They both reflexively looked at the staircase leading to the second-floor residence, hoping that Sarah's choice would turn out to be as fortunate. He turned back to her, stepped forward, and put a hand on her shoulder. "Be careful, Anna. I don't want to see you getting hurt. There are so many ways this can go wrong on you. I really do think he's basically a good man, despite his past, but he's not like us."

She gave him a little smile and said, "I know, and I don't want to see me getting hurt, either. Jonathan, they're trying to stay out of trouble while the statute of limitations runs out on their last crimes. They spent the first two years on a friend's ranch in Texas, but he had heart troubles, and died very suddenly, and since then, they've been keeping on the move, trying not to stay anyplace too long. They're a little over a year away from being free and clear everywhere. But they showed pretty bad judgment coming back to Montana that second time—their gang rode in the Black Hills, mostly, but they made it across the border more than a few times. They've been sticking south of here, for the most part. Even so, the law's got a long arm; or, at least, some of the railroad companies do."

He raised a single eyebrow, a talent she'd always envied. "I see. Well, then, maybe your judgment isn't quite as bad as I thought it was."

"I wouldn't say that, exactly. I'm afraid that Jeremiah Brown's partiality for me might be leading him to take some unnecessary risks. I'd feel a lot better if any telegrams I got from him were coming from New Mexico, or California, even. I guess I'd best make that clear to him when I see him, in a day or two."

Jonathan smiled in a way that made her a little uncomfortable. She hated to disappoint her partner, but she was not planning on coming home from this expedition with a new fiancé.

• ❤ •

Two days later, her train pulled into Arthur's Corners, Wyoming. She hadn't the slightest idea what Charles Stanton, Esq., looked like, and since the telegram was to A. Harrison, Esq., she wasn't even sure he'd be expecting a woman. It would be just like Jeremiah not to tell him, in order to see his expression when he realized that this blonde woman was the other attorney he'd wired to come to town.

If there even *was* a Charles Stanton, Esq., of course. If Jeremiah Brown, or Black, or Slade, or whatever he chose to call himself these days, was even in trouble. She stepped off the train, onto the platform, and looked for an unfamiliar figure, possibly accompanied by one or two familiar ones. What she found was one very familiar one, all alone, and looking extremely pleased with himself. She tried to recall the expression—the cat that swallowed the canary? As always, she got that funny feeling inside when she caught sight of his lean form, his handsome, distinctive features, and those dark eyes. And as always, she did her best not to let on in public that theirs was anything other than a strictly professional relationship.

"Hello, Mr. Brown," she said, putting down her suitcase, and extending her hand for a formal handshake. "Where's Mr. Stanton? I got his wire, and here I am. I can tell you it took some doing to get me here in time for this meeting."

He took her hand, but instead of shaking it, he held it in his own, for a moment, before releasing it. "Well, hello, Anna. How was your journey? You're looking lovely, as always." He grinned at her, then shook his head. "Didn't your ma ever teach you about polite conversation?"

"Yes, but my father taught me it was a waste of time for a busy attorney. Is Stanton meeting us somewhere?"

"Only if you'd like to accompany me back to Denver."

"Is this a joke? And where's Ed?" she asked, suspiciously.

"No joke, Anna. I missed you. I couldn't exactly wire you and say 'Meet me in Wyoming because I want to see you again before we head south for a long spell,' now could I?"

She looked around to make sure no one else was within earshot. "Well, I appreciate the sentiment, but maybe for future reference we could work out some kind of code we both understand? Because I came here prepared for a meeting, and it's a little unsettling to be surprised like this. Not to mention that this is an extremely busy time for me, and I had a hard time getting away."

He laughed. "There's ever a time that isn't? If I waited until you had some free time, next time I saw you might be a few years from now, and I didn't really want to wait that long." He picked up her luggage in one hand, and then offered her his other arm. "I didn't figure you did, either. Come along back to the hotel, now. I told the desk clerk that Mrs. Brown would be joining me this afternoon."

"Yes, dear," she said, with as much sarcasm as she could muster, though it was hard to be sarcastic when even the touch of her hand on his arm was sending shivers through her.

The hotel was quite near the depot, and Jeremiah Brown ushered her inside, explaining to the desk clerk that his wife was tired after her long journey, and needed to rest. It had been a long journey, and she was tired, but she didn't expect that resting was on the agenda.

When they got to the room, he closed the door and turned the key in the lock. Then he put his arms around her and gave her a long, lingering, breathtaking kiss. She forgot all about being annoyed with him, and thought to herself that it had been well worth the long and complicated train journey to get there.

Apparently, Mrs. Brown was quite tired, because the couple never emerged from their seclusion for the next several days, except for one foray into the hotel's dining room. Two days later, Anna caught the train home, arriving in time to help Sarah with her final wedding preparations.

Chapter 14

It was a crisp autumn evening when Jeremiah Brown and Edward Marcus returned to Carter's Creek, Montana. Anna was not expecting them, but it later occurred to her that perhaps she should have been. After her first meeting with Jeremiah in Wyoming, he'd done the same thing several more times: telegraphing from various locations requesting her presence on urgent legal business which always turned out to be entirely pretextual.

Jonathan, having caught on quickly on the first occasion, continued to watch with both amusement and a modicum of alarm. "I like him very much," he'd say. "I like both of them, for that matter. But this is still very dangerous for you, Anna."

And every time, she told herself it would be the last. But every time she got a telegram, she hurried off again.

Whenever they'd met, he reminded her that the date when the last statute of limitations ran out on the crimes of his younger years was drawing nearer. But there'd been no indication that it had finally run, and none that he was coming to visit. She'd never thought of him as the knight in shining armor on his gleaming white horse, come to rescue her, either. Rescue her from what? Her life was already exactly the way she wanted it to be, and his presence would only complicate that.

So when the figurative white charger came riding into

Carter's Creek, she was caught completely unawares. She didn't actually know what color horse he was riding, because she was in a meeting in the back office.

The first thing she knew about it, she heard a commotion in the front office, and Caroline's voice saying, "You can't just go back there, Miss Harrison is—"

The next thing she knew, the door had burst open, and there was Jeremiah Brown, a bit travel-worn but otherwise looking every inch the handsome outlaw, from the dusty black hat that was pushed back over his brown hair, right down to his boots.

She'd stepped to the door to see what was going on, and when he caught sight of her, he slid his arms around her and gave her a long, deep kiss, the kind that would have taken her breath away if she hadn't already been breathless and speechless. When she'd collected herself enough to tap on his shoulder, he pulled away, but immediately started in. "It's finally run – the last statute of limitations has run! We're not wanted men, anymore."

His eyes were locked on hers, but he finally looked up as a tall figure approached him from over Anna's shoulder.

"Mr. Brown?" It was her partner, speaking in a soft but agitated voice.

"Cranbrook," he said, and put out his hand. "Good to see you...I'm sorry, I didn't even notice you were there. Did you hear what I was telling Anna? The statute's finally run, in the very last of the jurisdictions—we're free and clear with the law."

"Statute? As in statute of limitations? I knew it! You *were* wanted!" came an exclamation from across the room. "I knew you were Tommy Slade, all along." Nick Powell had jumped from his seat, his broad face even redder than usual.

Anna was surprised at Nick's vehemence. Certainly, the bounty hunter who'd tried to turn Brown and Marcus in on that fateful day had lost out on a whole lot of money, and that meant that Nick Powell had lost out on some substantial fees. Money was something that Nick didn't let go of very easily, and the only grudges he ever held were financially oriented. But he'd never held one against her before, certainly not over cases won or lost. Whether money was involved or not, it was all part of the game between them. He'd always just moved on to the next opportunity, figuring that if he lost this one, he'd demolish her the next time. There was something about his vehemence, now, that seemed unlike blustery old Nick, even when his avarice had been thwarted.

She looked at Jonathan and then at Jeremiah Brown, and said helplessly, "Welcome to the Carter's Creek Bar Association. I think you know all the members—Mister Nicholas Powell, Judge Harold Clayton, and of course you know Jonathan Cranbrook."

"Did you know this all the time, Anna?" Nick was as agitated as she'd ever seen him, his normally red face a frightening shade of scarlet. "We had Tommy Slade and Johnny Nevada in jail right here and *you got them out*? Do you have any idea what those two have been responsible for? It's a miscarriage of justice! Not to mention that my client was cheated of his reward money." He loved to scream in court, but then there was always a twinkle of humor in his eyes when he did it. She scanned him anxiously, but she couldn't detect that twinkle.

"I didn't know it until afterwards, Nick," she protested, "and then it was protected by attorney-client privilege."

"He and his partner were worth $10,000, and notorious outlaws, besides. We could have turned them in ourselves!"

Nick had lost his temper entirely, now, something she'd never seen before, and it was catching.

"Nick, that was privileged information. I could have been disbarred for even thinking that! Besides, they'd gone straight years before they crossed our paths—think how long it took for that statute to run out on them." She found that was beginning to shout back, and Jeremiah, who was standing behind her, put his hand on her shoulder to quiet her down.

It was a well-intentioned gesture, but somehow seeing Jeremiah Brown touching her set Nick off even worse. "Look at him, laying his dirty outlaw hands on you! And the way he just walked in and kissed you, without so much as a by-your-leave. Like he knew he'd be welcome."

"Calm down, Nick," said Jonathan. His eyes met Anna's for a moment, and she could see he was as shocked by Nick's outburst as she was.

"I will not! You really had us fooled, Anna Harrison, pretending to be all pure and proper. And here this—this *criminal* just walks in and kisses you like he's done it before. No man in these parts is good enough for you, but here she is—the Widow and her outlaw fancy-man."

Jonathan took him by the arm and tried to propel him toward the door. "Nick, I think you should take a minute to think about what you just said. You know Anna as well as I do, and you know she's a lady and would never do anything so improper. Why don't you leave now, and come back when you've calmed down? Just think about it for awhile, and you'll realize that you're misinterpreting what you saw." But of course, he knew that Nick wasn't misinterpreting anything, and that was the worst of it. She'd been doing exactly what Nick was suggesting, and possibly worse. She was breaking the rules, and she'd just been found out—or suspected, which was almost as bad, since the suspicious mind would be able to piece the evidence together and discover the scandalous truth. There was enough of it, if you knew where to look. And Nick was a master of evidence.

"I am not," he spat out in response. "I know exactly what I just saw. And I remember when she came to my office to tell me you two were going to go out of town to help Mister Brown and Mister Marcus out of a jam they'd gotten into over in Greenville. How long have you known about this, Jonathan? Huh? He's not just a grateful client, is he? He's an outlaw, and he's her *lover*."

Jeremiah spoke up, now. "I'm sorry if you took this the wrong way, Mr. Powell. I've been kissing a lot of ladies to celebrate getting clear of the law. I didn't mean nothing by it. Miss Anna's just been a good friend to me and Ed, that's all."

"And if you expect me to believe that—" He shook his head in disgust. "We're out here in the middle of nowhere, and you show up just by chance. If you're about to tell me you're visiting every lawyer who's ever helped you out, well...there's one born every minute, but I'm not one of 'em."

He turned to Anna with cold, hard fury in his eyes. "My wife will certainly have a story to tell her sewing circle this afternoon, I can promise you that." He stormed out of the room, leaving her torn between laughing at the absurd picture of Nick as an enraged bull, and trembling about what might happen.

Not only did Nick seem like he was in the mood to do her some damage, but Cora Powell was more than likely to be willing to aid and abet. She had never liked Anna. It was almost as if she was jealous, for some absurd reason, of the professional interests that the two lawyers shared, and she was a well-connected woman, with a very sharp tongue.

Usually, Nick put out the fires she started, but when he chose not to, life could be pretty uncomfortable for her targets. Anna Harrison associating with a notorious outlaw and letting him kiss her, maybe worse? That was going to be the best piece of news she'd had to share in a very long time.

But that wasn't the worst of it. While Brown kept watching in the direction in which Nick had stormed away, Jonathan and Anna turned back toward the conference table, where a single, elderly figure sat.

It was Judge Clayton's expression, as he sat there silently, that was the most painful thing to see. It looked like his own heart was breaking. He was David's uncle—David, her long-lost fiancé. In fact, when David came to Carter's Creek to clerk for Anna's father, it was because Judge Clayton had arranged for it. And when they fell in love, there was nobody happier about it. When David died, the judge was with her. Anna's subsequent period of extended mourning, her decision to clerk for her father in David's place, and her whole existence thereafter as a single lady and lady lawyer were Judge Clayton's one and only romantic tale.

And now, it was shattered for him. Even if it had only been that single kiss he'd witnessed, the idea of another man looking at her, touching her at all…the pedestal that the judge had put her on was a high one, and a hard one to balance on. The idea that just maybe her entire life didn't revolve around David's memory anymore was bad enough. She didn't suppose he believed the rest of what Nick had suggested, but that didn't matter. She'd been proved human.

The judge had always seemed much younger than his years. Right now, he looked every minute of them. Jonathan had to assist him out of the room.

A moment later, Jonathan returned, accompanied by Ed

Marcus, who must have been waiting outside to give his partner a little privacy. She appreciated his consideration. He couldn't have known that half of the town was going to be in the room already.

He looked puzzled. "What's going on in here, anyway? That Nick what's-his-name looked pretty mad, and the old man looked ill."

Jeremiah turned to him. "What's going on is that I was so happy to see Anna here, that I didn't bother to look around the room before I gave her the good news. Apparently, I just surprised a lot of people."

Ed frowned. "You never walk into a room without checking it out first. What were you think—oh. You *weren't* thinking, were you?" He smiled an odd little smile.

Anna took up the thread. "There was a meeting of the Carter's Creek Bar Association in progress. You've met them all in a professional capacity before. I'm not sure if they were more angry to find out you two really were who you'd been suspected of being, or offended by the rather familiar manner which Jeremiah, here, took in informing me about the fact that you're now free and clear in the eyes of justice."

Ed started to laugh, but he stilled himself when he realized that nobody was laughing along with him.

Anna continued. "I, for one, would like a change of scenery. If you gentlemen wouldn't mind retiring upstairs to the parlor? Caroline, honey," she called in a louder tone, "come and help me with the tea things."

Caroline was Sarah's successor as the resident ward, a fourteen-year-old orphan girl. She was about as different from Sarah as could be, though. A plain, small, thin girl with lank light-brown hair and washed-out blue eyes, she was never going to be much better at cooking or housekeeping than

Anna was, but she was clever with her books, and the boldest, brashest little piece of baggage it had ever been anyone's qualified pleasure to meet.

Anna had already asked her if she wanted to be a lawyer when she grew up, and she'd thought about it and said that she might, but right now she had her heart set on moving East and teaching French or German or something. Since she didn't know any French or German when she'd firmly declared her decision, and had never been any further east than perhaps an hour from Carter's Creek, Anna thought this was an interesting choice. Interesting, and brave.

The house was full of French and German grammars now, but the uncomfortably frank French novels by Flaubert and Gauthier were hidden away under lock and key. Anna tried to get her to take an interest in learning Spanish, thinking that it might come in some practical use, but she studied it only dutifully, without the passion that she brought to her other work. Spanish was a beautiful language, but presumably it wasn't impractical or obscure enough for her. Caroline not infrequently expressed annoyance that Anna hadn't kept her Latin grammars, and unbeknownst to her, a set had already been ordered for her for Christmas.

There were sometimes, though, when her boldness was not so welcome. Now, for example. "So, has that man kissed you before, like old Nick said? He sure is handsome."

"Caroline, that is none of your business. But if I catch you kissing any man before you're married to him at least five years, you're going to be sorry you were ever born."

"Don't be silly, Anna. Married people don't kiss each other."

"You don't think Jonathan and Melanie kiss?"

"Well," she reflected, "maybe Jonathan and Melanie do.

But not most of 'em. People kiss people they're not married to."

Where had the child gotten those notions? "Did you find those old books, Caroline?"

"The French ones? That you had locked up in that trunk? I figured you just forgot about 'em. You would have given 'em to me otherwise, wouldn't you?"

"Not *Les Liaisons Dangereuses*?" Anna shuddered, both horrified at the notion of de Laclos's decadent aristocrats forming any part of Caroline's store of knowledge, and at the same time, thinking about how she herself had been involved in a very dangerous liaison, indeed.

"Wasn't that so sad at the end, when Valmont realized he really did love Madame de Tourvel and it was too late, so he went and got himself killed in that duel?"

"Caroline, I'm going to 'prentice you off to the Pinkertons to be a detective if you keep it up like this."

"They don't take girls anymore. I already asked."

Sometimes, Anna reflected, she really wished she hadn't encouraged Sarah to get married and leave her.

They brought the tea things up into the parlor, and then Anna shooed Caroline back down to the kitchen to work on her German grammar. The girl pouted as she left. She hated to miss anything interesting, but her guardian was determined she was going to keep whatever shreds of innocence remained to her.

Marcus and Jonathan were sitting in the two armchairs, and Brown was on the settee, which left her no other real option than to join him, unless she wanted to ostentatiously drag over a side chair from the dining table.

As she poured from the silver pot into the delicate china cups, she began, trying to keep her tone light. "Jeremiah, we've really got to talk about your timing. You're free and clear with the law now, and will be for the rest of your life. You couldn't even send a telegram to let me know you were coming to town, but just burst into my office without so much as a by-your-leave right in the middle of my monthly Bar Association meeting."

He was unusually subdued. "I'm sorry. I figured you'd know why I was here, when we'd agreed I should stay away 'til things had worked themselves out." Their eyes met and she could tell he was remembering the last time they had sat on this couch together, back on that first night they'd spent together. Could it really have been just a couple of years ago? It felt like they'd just met, and yet like they'd known each other for a very, very long time.

He took a cup from her, a little awkwardly, and their fingers brushed. The sensation seemed to travel all through her body. There was no doubt how she felt about this man. It was just that feeling that much for anyone frightened her. She'd loved David and that had seemed safe and then he died. Loving Jeremiah Brown was in no way safe. And there was the other thing, the thing that maybe he wouldn't understand.

Jonathan turned serious. "Look, we don't know that this is going to turn into anything. Nick gets mad, and he gets over it. Probably by the time he sees his wife, he'll have thought better about spreading gossip."

Jeremiah stared at him, and then at Anna. "What does it matter what folks say? I didn't think you cared about what other people thought of you, anyway, Anna. You don't exactly live like everyone else, living all by yourself, doing a man's work. You do what's right for you, not for some proper young lady. That's one of the things I like about you."

"Don't you remember lying to a bunch of people back in

Colorado a while ago?" she asked him. "Telling Meriwether Abel that when he saw us kissing in the moonlight, it was because you got carried away, and I was some innocent, injured party?"

"Well, yeah, but you'd gotten things so tangled up, pretending you didn't know me in the first place. I just didn't want things to look any more suspicious than they did already."

"And what about those telegrams you sent me, summoning me on urgent business regarding my client J. Black?"

"I kind of thought someone in the telegraph office might pick up on it if I gave my real name. There was still a price on my head at the time, if you recall."

"I meant the urgent business part. Jonathan figured it out before I did, the first time."

Brown gave his winning grin. "You caught on quick, as I recall."

But before he could take the reminiscences any further, Jonathan interrupted, his young face grave. "You really don't get it, do you? She's a lady, a respectable lady, and one of the leaders of this community. You do understand that carrying on with any man, much less a stranger of somewhat dubious background, is against all the rules for someone like her, don't you?"

Jeremiah Brown gave him a strange look. "I'm not entirely lacking in sense, you know. This isn't how I wanted to do this." He turned to face Anna. "There's a reason I came back to town. I—can we speak privately?"

She nodded to Jonathan, who nodded to Edward, who sat, fascinated.

No one spoke for a moment, until Jeremiah cleared his throat. "Ed, would you mind?"

At that, his partner stirred and rose, and the two men headed down the stairs, Edward turning his head several times to look back at his partner. "I'll be at the saloon if you need me."

The former outlaw fixed his dark eyes on Anna's. "I was hoping it'd be a little more romantic, but—I thought now…now that I'm free and clear, well…" He stirred uncomfortably in his seat, then leaned toward her and took her hands in his. "I never thought— I wasn't looking— The thing is…" He trailed off, giving up explaining.

"Jeremiah, I—you know I…"

He took a deep breath. "Would you…that is, would you do me the honor of becoming my wife?"

Her eyes had widened, but for a moment, she said nothing.

"Anna?"

Her expression was troubled, as she said, "I thought you understood. This was never meant to—that is, I—I can't."

"What?" Now his expression was disbelieving. "One minute your partner is telling me how I'm compromising your honor, and the next, you're telling me you won't marry me?"

"Not won't. *Can't*. Have you ever heard of the term coverture? Married women's property laws?"

"Property?" he said, his dark brows drawn into a frown. "*That's* what this is about?" He rose abruptly. "You don't trust me. Well, hell, Anna—it's not like I wanted to settle down, anyway. I just thought we had something, you and me. Something worth trying to make a go of. But if you don't, then…hell with all this." He turned and was down the stairs before she could get a word out.

The stairs let out into the back office, and he was nearly to the door before he realized Jonathan was calling him.

"Brown, wait a minute."

"Why? I'm gonna go to the saloon and get Ed, and see how quick we can get outta this town."

"Jeremiah, look, she's scared. There are things you don't know about, things you need to understand."

"Can you tell me at the saloon? Kinda not feeling real welcome here, at the moment."

"I'd rather we talked privately. Come back to my house. I'll give you a drink, try to explain things, then you can meet up with Ed at the saloon afterwards."

Brown looked at the younger man, his anger and his sadness warring. "Why the hell not? But this had better be good."

Jonathan's house was on the outskirts of town, but as there wasn't much of a town, it didn't take them too long to walk there. While Jonathan was pointing out his home in the near distance, they passed a big white house, with a wraparound porch and boarded-up windows.

"That's a nice place," Jeremiah said, to fill the silence. "Pity it's all deserted like that."

"It's Anna's," Jonathan said. "It was her parents' and then it went to her when they died. But she and Caroline can't live there all alone. It's just easier and safer for her to live upstairs from the office."

"How did they die, anyway? She's never told me."

"She doesn't talk about it much, to anyone. Train derailment. Four or so years back. I was meant to clerk for Ben Harrison, but I ended up with his daughter, instead. And she's been the best lawyer I could ever have trained with." He looked around, then led Jeremiah toward the house. "Let's sit here awhile, instead of going back to my place." There were some wooden chairs on the porch, and he sat in one, so the former outlaw followed suit. They were surprisingly comfortable. "Look, don't think she doesn't love you. I know her better than anybody does, and believe me, she has feelings for you, and they run deep. But she's afraid."

"I know she lost that fiancé, but we've all lost someone. Hell, Jonathan, I lost my whole family to raiders, in the war, and I was just a child."

"It's not even that."

"She said something about...coverage? And married women's property. It—it didn't sound like her. I'm the mercenary one, not Anna. Sounded like she doesn't trust me, to be honest."

"Coverture. See, a married woman loses most of her rights under the law. In a couple, there's only one legal person, and that person is the husband. Her property would all go to him, including her earnings. Well, other than a certain loss of dignity, that needn't matter much, as long as she had a husband who respected her, and treated their property as mutual."

The dark brows creased. "But she'd lose her independence. She'd have to come to me for everything?" He had to admit, he wouldn't like it much if the shoe were on the other foot. He'd never thought much about what it would be like to be a woman—most of the women who he'd ever met were farm wives, or they sold their favors to survive. He'd steered clear of anyone who looked like they might need something from him. The fact that Anna hadn't needed him, just wanted him, had been a big part of what had drawn him to her.

"She couldn't even be party to a contract."

"All right. I can see how that'd be a problem. Would I... would I have to sign everything for her?"

"Or I could, as partner. But it means that I'd be the one legally responsible for everything—and I was her clerk just a year ago. Think about what that means to her—just proof again that everything she's worked so hard for is almost nothing in the eyes of society."

"But she was gonna marry that David."

"They were studying law together. They would have been equal partners in everything."

Jeremiah quirked a smile. "So, if I want her to marry me, I gotta become a lawyer?"

Jonathan laughed. "I suspect your boredom threshold would be reached long before you got near a bar exam."

"I'd be pretty popular in the criminal defense line, though." Jeremiah couldn't help but chuckle, himself.

"Could be. Listen, Brown, I can see the two of you here, in this house, happy. You just have to understand it's got to be handled the right way."

"And that is?"

"Let her come around, slowly. It's not that she doesn't want those things—a home, a family, a man who loves her. It's that she wants more besides, and she's had to fight for those other things. And she's terrified of having to let go of them."

"I don't want her to give up anything. I like that she's the way she is. Could we…is there any…well, lawyer thing you can do, to work around it?"

"Maybe. There are other women in her position, scattered throughout the country, and some of them are married—I don't think all of them to their law partners. Anna belongs to this corresponding society, made up of lady lawyers. It's called the Equity Club. Let me get in touch with some of the members, do some research on it." Jonathan looked down the road, toward his own house. "You run along and have a couple of drinks, and we'll talk tomorrow. Just…don't do anything foolish. Promise?"

"I'll do my best," said Jeremiah. "Least the one place in town I know I won't run into Anna is the saloon."

• ♥ •

After he'd stormed out on her, she remained sitting in the upper parlor, considering the evening's events. Again and again, she ran over what he'd said, what she'd said, Nick's surprising reaction. She wondered what Jonathan had said to Jeremiah afterwards; Caroline, with her honest curiosity, watched from the window and saw them head to the left, the opposite direction from the saloon where Ed Marcus waited for his partner.

It had been so sudden and unexpected. She hadn't explained herself well, but she also hadn't had a chance to think things through. In the courtroom, she planned for every angle ahead of time. In her own life, she'd been caught unawares.

Caroline sat and read beside her, apparently unruffled. But Anna could tell, from the girl's frequent glances, from her quick movements, that she was restraining herself from asking endless questions. Finally, the younger woman rose to retire for the night.

"Did you hear that?" she asked, suddenly.

They stood there and listened, and there was a distinct rapping sound coming from the direction of the back door. He wouldn't have, Anna thought, with mixed emotions. Motioning to Caroline to stay where she was, Anna rushed down the stairs, and opened the door, and hurried her visitor inside.

It was Jeremiah Brown, and he'd been drinking, of course. After all, it was the saloon where he'd joined his partner, and what else, she supposed, was there to do there? He was just drunk enough to make him reckless, no more. She'd seen him really drunk only once, that time in Colorado Springs, but this time, he seemed to be in control of himself. His dark hair had been combed back, but it was starting to fall forward around his face, and his intense expression gave his handsome features a particular charm. "I'm sorry," he said. "I just couldn't stand it, anymore, me bein' there and you bein' here."

"Did anyone see you on the way over?"

"I don't think so."

"You don't think so?" Her voice rose despite her best efforts.

"Not that I could see. I tried to be careful. Anyway, I don't get the big scandal. I came to town to ask you to marry me; just can't see what's so shocking about that."

She sighed. He was here now, and it would just draw more attention if she sent him away. She turned to find Caroline standing behind her; of course, the girl hadn't listened. She only hoped her ward wouldn't be ruined for life by all this. She'd have to have one of those long "do as I say, not as I do" talks with her later. Tomorrow. The honest truth was that she didn't want to send Jeremiah away.

"Okay, Caroline," she said. "You're going to sleep down here, tonight, all right? Just in case anyone else tries to come visit us in the middle of the night." Caroline had her own bedroom upstairs, but she was small, and easily curled up on the office sofa, on the rare occasions when her room was needed for company. Or in this case, when her guardian didn't want to corrupt her any further with what she might overhear.

"All right," she said, far too affably. The child was frighteningly aware sometimes. "*Bonne nuit.*"

Anna led the way upstairs, with Jeremiah following close behind. She could feel his breathing, and the air was practically crackling with the electricity of his presence. He wasn't making things easy, that was for sure.

She closed the door at the top of the stairs behind them.

"You shouldn't have come."

"Are you really going to tell me you don't want me here?"

"No, just that you may have made things a lot worse, if anyone saw you coming here." She looked at him, at those deep brown eyes, at his sensual mouth, at his lean form, and sighed. She couldn't pretend to herself that she didn't want him, and want him badly. Her breathing came shallow and heavy as she felt his nearness in the air all around her, the whiskey scent of his breath. "Of course, I want you here. Just tell me—why am I such a hypocrite?"

His look was frankly sensual, as he ran his hand down the side of her face. "Anna, you're human. The only thing that's hypocritical about you is this idea you have that you ought to stifle your feelings." He lowered his hand to her breast and cupped it through the thin fabric of her nightdress. She moaned a little, in spite of herself. "You want me just as much as I want you. You've always been so honest about that. It's one of the reasons that I—" He stopped himself short. "I want to marry you, Anna. We can be like this always. Why can't you just say yes?"

She sighed. "Because you're asking me when you're drunk. Because you're Tommy Slade, or you were, and people around here have feelings about that. Because a lady like me needs to guard her reputation, and if I marry you now, everyone's going to know that whatever it is that Nick is saying, is probably true." She paused. "What is he saying, anyway?"

"Word at the saloon was pretty mixed, to tell the truth. A couple were muttering about how dare I show my face around here, but more of 'em were wantin' to hear stories of the old days. 'Fraid I let a few too many folks buy me drinks. Some of 'em were congratulatin' me on…what was it? ...provin' that you were human after all?"

"That's not a good thing," she said. "Human means fallible—and fallible is something I can't afford to be."

"Honey," he said, "people *are* fallible. You are so wonderfully human and alive, and there is nothing wrong with that." And with that he kissed her, hard and deep. The feel of him was intoxicating, and soon she was responding in kind, lost in the sensations of touching and kissing. In the back of her mind, she kept thinking that she was forgetting something, but she couldn't hold onto a coherent thought long enough to remember what it could be. He was passionate, urgent, different somehow than he'd ever been before, and she shut off that nagging part of her that was telling her that instead of the beginning she'd sometimes let herself imagine, this was, had to be, the last time.

The night passed quickly, and all too soon, the clock on her mantel was warning them that it was a quarter-to-five and that she'd better get him out of there before it got light.

Chapter 15

Ed Marcus, still half-asleep, rolled over and looked at his fully-dressed partner, sitting on the other side of the bed. "Well, that was a pretty stupid move, Jeremiah. I turned my back for a minute, and you disappeared on me. I don't think I need to ask where you went."

"The desk clerk was asleep when I came in. Probably had been for hours. Nobody saw me."

"Jer, we're talking about a lady's reputation, here. A lady you claim to care about."

"Ed, I do care about her. More than I ever thought I'd care about any woman." He paused. "Why is it anybody's business but hers and mine? Yesterday, you were more certain of that even than I was."

"Yesterday I hadn't heard the talk. These townsfolk are pretty vicious, if you ask me."

"What talk?"

"Some fellow came into the saloon after you'd left. Apparently, his wife is in a sewing circle with Nick Powell's wife. He had some pretty harsh things to say about Anna, and the story was spreading like wildfire. When he figured out who I was, he turned on me, and I had to show him a thing or two." Edward blew on his knuckles as though they were still sore.

Jeremiah looked away suddenly, unable to meet his

friend's eyes.

"And then it got worse. One of the saloon girls remembered you from the last time we were here. She recalled seeing you kissing Anna outside her door, and then following her inside. She said she watched for awhile and you didn't come out again."

"How'd she know it was me? That was well over a year ago, and it was dark. For all she knew, it could've been some other man, another client stepping into her office. You know, for legal papers, or something like that."

Marcus had the good grace to look embarrassed. "She knew it was you, all right. That is, she knew it was my partner. See, I spent some time with that girl that night, and apparently, she remembered me real well. And she distinctly remembered feeling pleased to know—what was it she said? 'That high and mighty Miss Anna Harrison wasn't no better than she was.'"

Brown shook his head. "Guess there are no secrets in a little town like this."

"Jer, Anna's a respectable woman. She's not like a lot of the women that we know. You knew that, from the beginning. And since Colorado, this thing of yours of sending her telegrams calling her out of town on business. How many times have you done that? Three times, four? Even I would get suspicious about that. Cranbrook clearly knew what it meant." He looked curiously at his partner. "Anyway, she's lived in this town her whole life. I don't think she knows anyone who'd call her out of town on business except you." He sighed. "I knew it'd lead to trouble if you kept on this way."

"I never meant to hurt her, Ed, and I never made her do anything she didn't want to do. I never told you this, but that first night, I was just giving her a goodnight kiss. Like you and me both do with the girls we know we can't touch. She was the one who invited me in."

"I don't want to know any more about it. I know you meant well, and that you'd never do her harm on purpose. But she's not like us, and I don't think we can really understand what's going on here. Just that this whole 'respectable' thing means a whole lot to a lot of folks, and she's stuck living with 'em."

"What do you think I ought to do, Ed? You're the one that usually attracts all the respectable girls. What do you do about them?"

"Well, that's the thing. A woman like her, only thing you can do is marry her. Or you have to let her go. And from what you've said, sounds like she's already turned you down a couple of times. I just don't think...well, I just don't think you can keep carryin' on with her the way you have been. 'Cause in the end, she's the one that's gonna get hurt."

Jeremiah looked away. "It always seemed so natural with her, you know? No guessing games, no flirtation. If she was mad at me, I knew it, and if she wanted me, I knew it. And when I didn't, it was because she was confused herself, not because she was playing some kind of woman game. I guess I should have known it couldn't be that simple."

Ed looked at his partner sympathetically. "Get some sleep, Jer. Might be that she'll be seeing things a different way, soon enough."

"Mmmm," muttered Brown. He pulled off his boots and lay down on top of the covers. He knew he wouldn't sleep at all. All he kept thinking about was how Anna had looked when he left her earlier that morning, before it was even light, her normally keen eyes all soft and sleepy, and her fair hair spread on the pillow. He thought about how nice it would be to wake up with her like that, every morning. But as soon as he thought that, he remembered that she'd turned him down, twice, in less than twenty-four hours. His heart tightened in his chest, with the loneliness of it, but then he thought about the passionate lovemaking that had followed her second refusal. Surely that showed that she wasn't ready to quit him, that it was just a matter of time before she knew her own mind.

Funny thing was, he'd never seen himself marrying. And now, all he could think about was how to get this lovely, frustrating, brilliant, maddening spinster to agree to be his wife. As the words cycled around in his head, again and again, and as he imagined her there in the hotel bed with him, he drifted off to sleep.

• ♥ •

Ed had gone out, had breakfast, picked up a paper, and been back in the room and halfway through reading it, before Jeremiah finally woke up.

When they left the hotel, early in the afternoon, they ran into Jonathan Cranbrook and his wife Melanie on the street. Melanie, a very pretty young woman of about her husband's age, had a great deal of curly, pale brown hair, a button nose, and huge eyes. She was obviously expecting a child. Brown recalled Anna telling him that Cranbrook's promotion to full partnership had been in anticipation of them starting a family, and they'd clearly followed through. Jonathan's wife clung to his arm as she shyly expressed her delight at meeting them; sweet, but tentative as she looked at the strangers, and adoring and trusting as she looked at her young husband.

Brown couldn't help pondering the fact that this man, who spent most of his waking hours with Anna, had fallen in love with a woman who couldn't be more different. He probably needed her peacefulness and tranquility after a long day at the office with his charming but often demanding and all too quick-witted law partner.

After they'd gone, he turned to Ed. "Well, I guess we should go face the worst of it."

"You really want to hear what the talk is in the saloon?" his partner returned.

"I think we'd better. Don't you?" He needed to know what Anna was up against, if it was as bad as Ed had suggested. He hated to think that it might take that to get her to change her mind about marriage, but there was a little part of him that had to admit, he didn't much care how, as long as she said yes. He knew he could make her happy, once she agreed.

"Just warnin' you. It ain't gonna be pretty."

They walked between those swinging doors, and a profound silence fell almost as soon as they did.

"You got some nerve, showin' up here," muttered a short, heavy man. "After what you did to poor Miss Anna."

"We just came in to get us a drink," said Jeremiah placatingly, but he was ignored.

"Poor Miss Anna?" spat another man. "That whore? This was just the first time she got caught. She's probably been up to stuff like this all along, with lots of men. This poor fellow is probably just another one of the black widow's victims."

"Just 'cause she turned you down," said one of her defenders.

"And you, too," said someone from the sidelines.

"Yeah, but to be fair, I'm not good enough for her," the man said, shrugging.

"Well, she ain't even any good at trappin' 'em," said a third man. "Or keepin' 'em, anyway."

From the continued conversation, it was apparent that there were two camps: one blamed Brown entirely, and felt that Anna was innocent womanhood injured. The other somewhat larger group seemed to glory in the way she had fallen off her pedestal. They ranged between commiserating with Brown for getting caught up in her vicious web, and leeringly asking him, "What she was like, if ya know what I mean."

This last was too much for Ed, who dropped his hand to his gun. "I'm getting a little bit tired of hearing the lady's name treated like that, mister," he snarled.

"Oh, yeah, drawing on us like the big gunslinger you are, Mister Marcus—or should I say Johnny Nevada? We know who you are," said the object of his anger, scornfully. "You one of her men, too? Well, go ahead, and see how long this new so-called honest life of yours lasts. Trash like you." He spat.

Edward Marcus's eyes burned cold blue. "Why you—"

Jeremiah put up his arm to stop his partner. "Listen, mister, we don't want to fight you. We just want to clear up a little misunderstanding. What you heard about me and Miss Harrison, it ain't true. She's helped us out, as a lawyer, a couple of times. It's true I kissed her, 'cause I had something to celebrate. If you folks know who we are, guess you also heard all about that, how me and my partner are free and clear with the law, now. Well, there she was, lookin' so pretty, that I couldn't help myself. I can tell you it came as a big surprise to her, and she wasn't much pleased by it, either. Do you really think a lady like that would even look at a man like me?" He took a deep breath. "Anyway, I did ask her to marry me, and you can't blame me for takin' my chance, someone like her don't come along every day. She turned me down, too, boys, just like I hear tell she does with everyone."

"You mean her bein' so rich," said someone, scornfully.

"Hey!" he exclaimed, nettled. "We got friends on Nob Hill in San Francisco. If I was just after money, there's women out there with a lot more'n she's got." He cut himself off, realizing that the line of discussion wasn't getting him anywhere. *Never thought of her as rich, anyway. She works so hard. Rich ladies usually just like to spend their money…*

"None of us are outlaws, Tommy Slade." One of the men got right up in his face. "We know who you are, too. And how she'd get mixed up with the likes of you, anyway?"

"Thought everyone in town knew she was our lawyer."

"Right, because even a shyster like Nick Powell wouldn't handle your case. We heard about that, too."

"Way we heard it is, she did a lot more than look," leered another man. "Way we heard is, you were seen leavin' her place early this morning."

Brown turned to Marcus and shrugged. "Guess there's no use in talking, huh, Ed?"

"Guess not," his partner responded, and in a moment his fist had connected with the last speaker's face, while Jeremiah threw a punch at the other man. A few minutes later, Ed's opponent was flat on his back on the floor, while Jeremiah's was draped oddly over a nearby chair. Two new fighters moved forward.

These new men were just about to engage with them when a sudden hush came over the crowd. A tall, burly man was heading toward them, brushing people aside as he went. "What's goin' on here?" he demanded. "What you boys think you're doin'? We'll have none of that in here. The Carter's Creek Saloon is a peaceable place, unless it's *me* throwin' the punches in order to keep folks in line."

"They insulted a friend of ours," said Jeremiah. "Me and my friend didn't much appreciate some of the things that were bein' said."

"Well, you can cut it out now, Mister Tommy Slade. And your friend, Johnny Nevada, too. We know all about who you are, even if you call yourselves something different now," said the man. "Miss Harrison was always actin' like she was better'n us, just 'cause her daddy was some big important man around here and she inherited his business. Couldn't stay in a woman's place, like she ought to, but always had to be messin' around with men's work. And now, we know she was no better'n anyone. And you," he turned to Ed, "breakin' poor little Nellie's heart by not recognizin' her last night. She ain't changed so much since then. She's as pretty as ever."

Jeremiah hesitated for just a moment, knowing that a man the size of this one could flatten them both, but not wanting the insult to Anna to go unavenged. His partner, normally the quicker-tempered of the two, looked troubled at hearing about the hurt he'd inadvertently caused the saloon girl. There was a movement behind him, and Jeremiah turned around, to see a vaguely remembered figure coming in through the saloon's doors. He touched Ed's arm, indicating that he should look, too.

"What's going on here, Sam?" asked the man, a blond giant wearing a tin star on his vest. His bass voice had an odd singsong accent. If the man who was speaking to them was six-foot-four, this new arrival easily had to be six-eight.

"Why, Deputy Rasmussen, nothing at all. Just a little friendly discussion," said the bouncer.

Jeremiah had some half-remembered notion that Deputy Rasmussen was a particular friend of Anna Harrison's, in addition to being one of the biggest men he'd ever met. "We were defending the honor of a mutual friend."

Karl Rasmussen frowned. "Seems to me you had something to do with getting that honor besmirched. Seems to me you need to do a bit more for her than get into some childish barroom brawl."

"Yeah, Deputy Karl, just 'cause everyone knows she turned you down when you went a-courtin' a couple of years after your wife died," sneered a man. "Don't know what you did wrong, since she seems to give it away to any man comes along, even lowdown outlaws."

Rasmussen turned to the man. "I never even thought of courting Miss Anna. She's way too good for a man like me...or for a man like Jeremiah Brown, here, either. But I think that there is one thing that Mister Brown would agree with me on, and that's that folk like you shouldn't be allowed to talk about a lady like that." He unpinned his tin star, and dropped it ostentatiously on the nearest table. "So happens I'm off duty right now, and if anybody wants to talk about my good friend Miss Anna, they might as well say it to me."

There was a hushed silence. Pretty much all of Carter's Creek was afraid of Karl Rasmussen, between his size and his quiet strength. He calmly removed his gunbelt, and then his vest, and rolled up his sleeves. "Anybody? Anyone at all?" He walked toward the man who'd spoken last, picked him up with one hand, and flung him across the room. "Next?" asked the giant, but there were no takers. He grabbed Sam by the collar and pulled him close to his own face, practically lifting the burly man off the floor. "I don't want to hear about nothing like this again, Sam. Anything you say against Miss Anna, remember, I'll take it personal." Then he replaced his vest and his belt, and finally his star, and escorted Brown and Marcus out of the saloon.

"Think about what I said," were his parting words to Brown. "You owe her something."

The two former outlaws returned to their hotel room, where Jeremiah paced like a caged animal. His partner lay on the bed, watching him, but inside he didn't feel much better.

"Ed, how'd this get so complicated? I can't believe someone saw me leavin' her place this morning. I thought I was so careful."

"Guess it was bound to happen, sooner or later, that one of us would do something stupid over a woman. I just always figured it would be me." Ed smiled wryly.

"Me, too. I wouldn't have given you any odds on this happening."

"Jer…if she changes her mind. If you—you know, get married." He paused and took a deep breath. "It won't make any difference between us, will it? We'll always be partners, won't we?"

"Did you even need to ask that? There's no woman alive that could split us up." Jeremiah was thoughtful. "Anna knows we're a team. She always has. I thought you knew that."

Marcus nodded. "Yeah. I guess I just wanted to make sure."

"Didn't think we even had to talk about it." He looked away. "So, she's turned me down twice, but the second time, well…she said no, then took me straight to her bed. So, I figure I got one more shot before I give up. Maybe give her a few days to think about it."

"See if things get worse for her, with these folks here in town?"

Jeremiah sighed. "Don't exactly want to be the lesser of two evils. Let's just say—let her miss me a little bit."

On the way out of town, they stopped at the Cranbrooks' house. Jonathan opened the door, and there was no sign of Melanie. "Come into the library," he said. His curly, dark hair was nearly standing on end, and the reason why was apparent as he ran his fingers through it, even as he led them to the rather pretentiously named room, which was actually quite small and contained a desk, a few straight chairs, and a couple of bookcases.

Jonathan turned to face them, and for the first time, Jeremiah noticed just how pale he was. His green eyes glittered with a strange light, and his tall, thin form seemed tense, like a bow, strung and ready. He was still in his early twenties, but at that moment, he looked strangely old and young all at once. "What the hell is going on?" he said softly.

Jeremiah opened his mouth to reply, but Jonathan went on. "I've had three very interesting conversations, today. One was with Karl Rasmussen and another was with young Caroline. The third was with a man who saw you leaving Anna's place early this morning and couldn't wait to share the news with anybody who'd listen. What the hell are you trying to do? Ruin her life permanently? And why the hell did you go back there last night? Are you really that stupid?"

"No," protested Jeremiah, while his partner remained silent. "I went back to propose again. Guess I was having a hard time accepting the fact that she'd turned me down. What happened after…well, that's between me and her."

"Are you a complete idiot?" the younger man snarled. "I told you she needed time to get used to the idea of marriage. I didn't mean try again later that same day, with a snootful of cheap whiskey in you. You know she gave up on the whole thing almost a decade ago, when she lost her fiancé. You can't just wave your hand and wipe all those years away. Instead of which, now everyone in town knows the two of you spent the night together, and you're fooling yourself if you think otherwise. Could you be any more irresponsible? Anna isn't some plaything for you to amuse yourself with when you feel like it. She has a life here, and you can just ruin it and ride away like it was nothing."

"I never thought of her as a plaything. I care about her, a

lot. Never thought I was gonna get married, either. Always thought I'd either die young or grow old bein' bachelor uncle to his kids." He glanced at his partner. "Now, all I can think about is how to get her to say yes. Look, I'm gonna go off for a bit, give her some time to get used to the idea. Come back and ask again. Don't know what else to do at this moment."

"You'd better do right by her."

"What's that supposed to mean? I already told you my intentions. Who are you to—" Jeremiah stopped short in surprise, as Jonathan jumped up and his fist connected with Jeremiah's jaw. Instead of responding with a blow of his own, though, he stood silently, rubbing the place where the younger man had struck him.

"I'm her best friend. She hasn't got anybody else to look out for her. And I don't care who you are, because if she gets hurt, and it's your fault, I will kill you." That strange light in his green eyes glittered more intensely for a moment, and then he pushed his way past them, out of the room.

After a moment or two of silence, the visitors found their own way out.

Jeremiah rubbed his jaw again, and looked troubled as he faced his partner, outside the door. "Well...he's loyal. I just couldn't bring myself to hit him back, considering he's defending the honor of the woman I love."

"Yeah, guess he *is* loyal, at that. But she calls him her partner, just like you and me. So I guess he would be," said Ed. "What are we gonna do? Come back, what do you think, in a week?"

"Ride down to Helena, maybe over to Billings. I dunno. Someplace where I can distract myself for a week." He sighed. "Play some poker, drink enough that I don't have to think too much."

• ♥ •

They didn't get as far as Helena, but stopped at a saloon in a small town, where the poker was good enough to keep Jeremiah occupied, but not so good that he was at much risk of losing. Ed, who'd been remarkably patient with his partner's preoccupation, took the opportunity to find himself a pretty redheaded saloon girl. He disappeared upstairs with a bottle and enough of Brown's winnings to keep her company exclusive for a few days.

Jeremiah played poker for thirty-six hours straight, went to the hotel and slept for almost a day, and then went back and did the same again. Ed emerged long enough to treat the redheaded gal to a fine meal, and then collected some more of Jeremiah's excess winnings and took her right back upstairs. Finally, Jeremiah had run out of opponents, and that meant his self-enforced sobriety—he wasn't foolish enough to gamble drunk—had run its course.

He ordered a bottle of whiskey and sat there, lost in thought, remembering to pour himself a glass and drink it every so often, but then drifting off into his thoughts again. Of all the women he'd ever been entangled with in any way, Anna was the only one he'd ever imagined a future with. But what if she was right? What if neither of them was suited for marriage, for family? This idea that he'd marry her, settle down in Carter's Creek, was it all just a fantasy bred of too much time on the dodge?

Maybe Anna was right. She came from one world, and he came from another, and he couldn't see how those two worlds could ever fit together, not day-to-day. Was he really planning to stay in that small town? And how could he ever expect her to leave it? He didn't like the idea of living off her—of all the unpleasant things people said to him in the Carter's Creek

Saloon, there was nothing that had stung him more than the notion that he was after her for her money—which was apparently considerably more than he'd imagined.

Anyway, Anna was the absolutely least domestic woman he'd ever met. Sure, he admired her independence, her intelligence, but like most men of his time, he associated marriage with an angel in the house, bustling around the kitchen, keeping the home fires burning while tending to their children and providing him with a sanctuary from the cold, hard world. But the woman he'd fallen in love with couldn't keep house if her life depended on it. She could barely cook, she was a hopeless seamstress, and she had practically no idea of what it took to run a household. Those orphans she took in did most of the cooking and sewing, but they'd better know about it beforehand because she didn't teach them anything like that. Instead, she taught them French and similar useful stuff, and would probably have tried to turn them into lady lawyers, too, if they'd showed any signs of wanting it. Might still, with Caroline, who was more like her than Sarah could ever be.

Anna had chosen to develop other aspects of her abilities to the exclusion of the more usual feminine accomplishments. All well and good for her, but she wasn't really suited for hearth and home. If she'd married that other lawyer, the one that died, they'd have had to have a housekeeper, for certain.

But he had a responsibility for what was happening to her now. When he thought about the cruel jeers in the saloon that afternoon, he was upset and angry. She'd worked so hard to be accepted for who she was, and the townspeople were so quick to revert to stereotype and mockery. The same townspeople who probably a week before had been bragging in letters to their relatives back East about what an up-to-date town they lived in, what with having a lady lawyer and all. The thought of it made him so furious that he found himself wishing he could have pounded a few more heads before the deputy intervened. It made him want to hurt all those people who were hurting her. But wasn't he the one responsible for her troubles?

And he thought about the moments he'd caught her looking scared and vulnerable. She was so appealing then, the kind of woman a man could protect and cherish. For crying out loud, he sounded like Ed. Did he ever fall for women like that? No, the few women Jeremiah Brown could claim to have been sincerely partial to had all been well able to take care of themselves. Of course, most of the time, they'd been out for themselves—and themselves alone.

Maybe that was why he kept coming back to Anna. She'd always been able to take care of herself, but she also cared about other people. She kept surprising him, because she never had a hidden agenda, and never seemed to be out for anything. When she was with him, it was because she wanted to be with him, not with someone who could get her something. But what did that mean? She'd been very clear from the beginning that the only future they had together was the occasional meeting. He'd been the one to try to break that bargain. And much as they had both cherished those meetings, maybe the time for that was over.

Should he give her one last chance to turn him down, when he already knew the outcome? Did he really want to humiliate himself like that? After all, it was Anna herself who had indicated that she had no intention of getting married, to anyone, ever. Certainly not to Jeremiah Brown. She'd made that clear all along. She liked her life just fine, and she'd never again give anyone a chance to do to her what her David had done, by going and dying on her.

As he was thinking this, the level in his bottle was getting lower and lower. He had the strangest feeling that in all his thinking, there was something he was ignoring, but he was getting so tangled up in it, that he couldn't quite figure out what it was. There was a brunette saloon girl with an insouciant smile sitting at the table next to his, and she kept looking over at him, encouragingly. Finally, he smiled back, and she approached him. "Care to buy a girl a drink?"

"Mind whiskey?"

"Not one bit," she said, and gulped down the first glass she poured him. She looked at the level of the bottle. "Judging by this, I've got some catching up to do."

He grinned at her, as he refilled her glass. "There's more where this came from."

"You smile nice," she said. "I was afraid, watching you sit over here by yourself, that you were just some Gloomy Gus. And I thought that would be a real waste. Don't get 'em in here as handsome as you too often."

Jeremiah ignored the compliment, but not the girl. "Just thinkin' about some things. But now that I'm with you, I'll cheer up real fast. Promise." They clinked glasses over it.

He looked at her. She was very pretty, with rich brown ringlets spilling down her back, her hair a few shades lighter than his own, and hazel eyes, that looked green one minute, brown the next, depending on what she was looking at. Her figure was like ripe fruit, bursting forth, round and ample above and below her tiny corseted waist, and the low cut, clingy dress she wore made the most of her assets. Anna's slender, graceful figure in her usual prim shirtwaist and skirt rose unbidden to his mind, but Anna lacked the voluptuous charms of this glorious example of womanhood.

Her name was Maggie, she told him, but she didn't seem very interested in talking about herself. Instead, she laughed delightedly at everything he said that was amusing, she was suitably impressed by everything else, and she drank freely. He'd made some reference to poker, and she'd immediately said, "Saw you playing, over these past few days. You're really good, aren't you? I bet you have some good stories, don't you?"

Not only did she launch him down the path of retelling some of his triumphs at the poker table, but it was clear she knew the game. Her eyes were shining with admiration as he told her the stories. He couldn't help but contrast that with the blank look in the blue eyes of a certain other woman, as he and Ed had tried to share some of their gambling exploits with her, and the constant, puzzled questions. Not to mention the complete lack of comprehension of his gambler's spirit. Well, he wasn't going to think about...*her*...for the moment. He poured himself and his companion another round.

Maybe he was crazy, continuing his pursuit of Anna. This was his kind of woman, he thought, as she listened raptly to his storytelling, chiming in with delighted laughter. Easy to be with, and without those complicated twists and turns and prickles that made some women such a challenge. She wouldn't judge him, wouldn't suggest that maybe he'd had enough to drink or point out what was wrong with one of his plans. She would never deflate him with some clever remark. All right, she wasn't particularly bright, but she didn't need to be. He had brains enough for both of them. *Hell,* he thought, *if I was really thinking about marrying, a girl like this would be the right kind.* She'd always be grateful for being taken away from the saloon, and she could never hold his past against him, when she had a past of her own. She'd probably be a real hard worker, too. By the time the bottle was empty, he was half-convinced that he'd found the answer—just leave Anna be, like she wanted him to, and court Maggie, instead. Or forget that, and stay footloose and fancy free. There were girls like Maggie, though not always quite so pretty, in every saloon along the way.

But when Maggie took his hand, with the clear intent of leading him upstairs, he found himself unwilling to go. He shook his head no.

"Awww," she said. "Gettin' a girl's hopes up like that. All right, what's her name?"

"What?" he asked, his voice slightly thickened with drink.

She looked at him, leaning over slightly to emphasize her abundant charms, and said, "Thought I had a live one, here. Don't get 'em in here as handsome as you, too often—like I told you before. You and your friend, but he marked out Lucy Belle practically the moment he walked in here."

"Sorry," he said.

"Well, I know you think I'm pretty, 'cause nobody looks at me like that if they don't. I'm thinkin' there's only one possibility. You must be in love with someone, 'cause otherwise, we'd already be upstairs. So you go along and you get that girl—and if for some reason she's crazy enough to say no, you come right back here and I'm gonna show you such a good time you'll forget all about her. You promise?"

"Sure, Maggie."

He went back to the hotel room that they'd taken when they arrived in town, but had spent hardly any time in, and got into bed, but he didn't sleep at all that night. As he tossed and turned, all he could see was the smile that sometimes crossed Anna's delicate features, and the times when her clever, brittle wit was replaced by a real sense of joy, and she broke forth into genuine, wholehearted laughter. He knew that he was one of the few people who could make her laugh and forget about her various preoccupations for a moment. She couldn't say no, again, could she? Not now that she'd had time to think about things. He was the only man who really understood her, and accepted her for who she was.

They belonged together.

As soon as it was light, he began making ready for the trip back to Carter's Creek.

Ed turned up at the hotel shortly after dawn, looking like a cat who'd gotten into the cream. "That Lucy Belle sure knows how to show a man a good time," he said, stretching contentedly.

"Sure you don't want to stay with her awhile longer?"

"You're the one lookin' to get married, not me. I stay with Lucy Belle another couple of nights, and she's like to start thinkin' of me as her beau, rather than a customer. That ain't fair to her, and it ain't fair to me, either." Now, Ed's eyes grew distant. "Least you've still got a chance with Anna. Wish I'd met…well, doesn't matter now."

And soon they were gone, on their way back north.

Chapter 16

Anna knew that things were bad early that day when old Jake, the man from the general store who delivered the groceries, didn't stop to chat when she paid him. And she knew they were worse pretty soon after, when she and Caroline ventured out on some errands and were roundly snubbed by just about everyone they passed on the street.

Except for Sarah Powell, of course, who rushed up to her at once, forcing them to take a longer walk than she'd originally intended. When her husband caught sight of them, he looked angry, but Sarah ignored his glares and tightened her grip on her friend's arm.

Anna and Caroline soon retreated back to the safety of their rooms and their books, and the older woman caught her ward's lip trembling on several occasions as their eyes met. Caroline had never been affectionate, like Sarah was, but today she kept hovering about until Anna wanted to ask her to go away. She didn't, though. She had a feeling she was going to appreciate her loyalty more and more. With Caroline's vivid imagination and her inappropriate reading, Anna suspected that the girl was afraid that she was going to waste away like the character Madame de Tourvel had after Valmont seduced and abandoned her. It was too late to wish that Caroline hadn't understood what had happened between Jeremiah Brown and her guardian that night.

Jonathan told her about the saloon girl who'd remembered seeing her kissing Jeremiah Brown that night a year-and-a-half ago and then leading him inside, and about the man who'd seen Brown leaving her place early the other morning.

Apparently, Ray Powell had added some weight to his father's tale, too. The story that was going around was that he and Sarah had been disagreeing about something and she'd cited Anna as an authority to prove her point. He'd dismissed the lawyer's opinion by calling her a "dried up old spinster." Sarah, instead of pointing out the irrelevance of her friend's marital status to the subject of the discussion, had angrily jumped to her defense by mentioning that when they'd been traveling in Colorado, there had been two men who were sweet on Anna. One was presumably Meriwether Abel. But the one that concerned Ray was, as he said, "some rough fellow named Brown, who Anna'd known from before. I think we all know who that was, and what she was doing in Colorado." He had then gone on to say how Anna had dragged his poor innocent Sarah into the middle of all her shameless behavior.

As her partner told her this, she smiled in spite of herself. She had distinct memories of that week and of her attempts to shelter Sarah not only from any knowledge of what was going on between herself and Jeremiah Brown, but from drunken men, saloon girls, and most particularly from an innocent flirtation with Ed Marcus. Thinking about the man her ward had married, and about the former outlaw who'd been so courteous and even chivalrous to the girl, she wished she'd encouraged her to run off with Marcus, even with the threat of the law still hanging over his head.

The younger lawyer told her about his various conversations with Karl Rasmussen and with Brown and

Marcus, and he seemed awfully proud of having punched Jeremiah. Anna knew he'd been pretty good at fistfights from his stories of boarding school, back East, but he'd never hit anyone in the entire time she'd known him. Sometimes, she forgot just how young he was.

The next morning was Sunday, and she dressed and went to church, the same as usual. She noticed a certain coldness in people's greetings, the few who would actually speak to her. Most people cut her altogether, as she made her way to her pew. Caroline took her hand and squeezed it. She heard whispering all around. "Some nerve to show up here... everybody knows...that outlaw...no better than she should be...hypocrite..." They went on.

She made her way through the service until the sermon. Reverend Bliss decided that this was the Sunday to preach on the woman taken in adultery, and he didn't quite seem to get around to Jesus's message of forgiveness. Instead, he started going on about scarlet women, and all kinds of unpleasant things from Paul's Epistles and from the Old Testament. All eyes were on Anna and the whispering was pretty loud. Just when he'd gotten to Jezebel, a loud bass thundered from the choir.

"You've forgotten the rest of the story, Reverend. Don't you remember? Let he who is without sin cast the first stone!" And Deputy Karl Rasmussen was making his way down the aisle toward them. He offered one arm to Anna, and the other to Caroline, and escorted them out the back.

Et tu, Reverend, she thought to herself. She recalled her favorite novel, *Middlemarch,* and how a whole town could turn against a person.

Karl and Caroline led her back to the rooms above the office, and to her parlor, where she made her way to the settee.

She sat there, contemplating the ruin of the edifice she'd so carefully begun constructing all those years ago when David died. What she'd thought was built of solid masonry turned out to be just a house of cards, scattered in the wind.

Sarah and Jonathan called on her that afternoon. Jonathan made his apologies for Melanie, but she was so close to her time that he wanted to keep her away from any more upset. Apparently, he'd distressed her quite a lot last night, after he'd left Anna's place, drinking whiskey alone in his study and then treating his wife to a long, drunken ramble about the hypocrisy of most of his fellow townspeople. The same reason kept him from staying long. Sarah just sat next to her friend on the settee, silently, her head resting on Anna's shoulder. Anna stroked Sarah's thick black hair mechanically, thinking to herself what it had cost her friend to get away from the sacred Powell Sunday Dinner, which took the place of church as the central observance in that family.

She overheard Caroline asking Karl in a whisper if he didn't think Sarah was a little touched in the head.

He smiled and said in his deep voice, "Just loyal. People show their love in different ways. You show Anna you love her by making her proud of you with your lessons. Sarah's way is different."

"What about Mr. Brown's way?"

"Well, now, people ought to save that way for when they're married. But sometimes people make mistakes. Miss Anna has lived a very good life. She's made one big mistake, and people are punishing her for it much more than she deserves."

Caroline hesitated for a moment. Finally, she chimed in with something that had been a subject of great curiosity for her for some time. "Is Swedish anything like German?" she asked.

He laughed. "Not really. Maybe a little bit. Let's go down to the kitchen and you can show me your German books. I'll see if I can understand them at all, and we can get something for Miss Anna to eat."

• ♥ •

It was later in the afternoon when Jeremiah Brown arrived, looking as though he hadn't slept in a day or two. Caroline showed him upstairs. He sat down and looked at Sarah, who was still sitting slumped against Anna's side. She looked doubtfully at Anna, unsure whether she should leave her friend alone with the author of all her disaster. *Sarah always did have an uncomplicated view of things,* Anna reflected.

"That girl sure is fond of you," he observed.

"More than I deserve, sometimes," she said, flatly.

"I've been hearing the talk, or hearing about it, anyway. I'm sorry." He paused for a moment, took courage and continued. "It's all my fault. I should have understood your position. I should have realized you weren't just some girl who could be dallied with."

She looked him straight in the eye. "*Dallied* with? I wanted you." Where had this come from, she wondered. He'd been getting lectured, and he'd bought it, at least that's how it seemed.

"I should have controlled myself. It wasn't right, what I did. Not with a woman like you."

"A woman like me? Would you like to explain exactly what 'a woman like me' is? Because you're sure confusing me. A woman like me is capable of making her own decisions—and her own mistakes. I seem to recall I was there at the time, and I had something to do with what happened between us."

"But you're—you know...respectable."

She threw up her hands. "This respectable thing which

everyone is so fixated on. Which I've been so fixated on. Well, apparently, I'm *not* so respectable. At least that's what I hear. Look, it doesn't seem fair that this should have consequences like this for me, and be just a romance along the way for you. It doesn't seem fair at all. But I knew the rules when I broke them. This isn't something you did to me."

"Anna, I know you're afraid. Jonathan told me all about the legal stuff...what happens to married women in the eyes of the law and why you don't want that. But he also said that you're not the only one. That some married women have figured out how to make it work. Honey, if that's what's scaring you, well, I'll do whatever it takes. Whatever you need to be happy. Just—don't turn me down again. Anna, let's get married. Please?"

She didn't say anything.

"Anna?"

She hadn't known what she was going to say until she said it. From the first night they'd spent together, she'd wondered what would happen when he was straight with the law, and he didn't have to keep on the move anymore. He'd taken her by surprise with his first proposal, the other day, and he hadn't been entirely sober when he'd asked the second time, so she'd discounted it. Now that she'd seen the townspeople's sudden change of heart toward her, here was her way out, and with the man she truly cared for. The man that, she had to admit to herself, she loved. But since David's death, she'd promised herself that she'd never rely on a man to rescue her. That she'd never let anyone become her whole world, not ever again.

"How long has it been since you've lived in one place for more than a few weeks or a month at a time? I know—your friend's ranch in Texas, a few years back. But have you even thought, now that you're clear with the law, of what you're going to do with the rest of your life?"

"I thought I'd stay here with you."

"And do what? You know that I have no interest in making a home, like a woman's supposed to do. I've known what my future would be since I was thirteen years old and Daddy told me about how Belle Mansfield had just been admitted to the bar in Iowa. I don't see anything about my life changing much, and after awhile, you wouldn't be happy with me."

"What if I think different?"

"Then I'd say you don't know yourself as well as you think you do. You've never spent more than a few days with me at a time. A few weeks, at most. I know that you're feeling responsible for what's happening to me. But you wouldn't be happy here. You wouldn't be happy with me."

"But, Anna, isn't it already a little late for that? Haven't we already promised ourselves to each other, with our hearts, with our bodies, in every way possible?"

She took a deep breath, and she readied herself to set him free. "Look, I don't have a lot of experience with this kind of thing, but…you do. How am I different from the other women you've…known? I am an adult and I am responsible for my own behavior. I invited you in that first night, and I could have sent you away loudly, that last night, proclaiming my injured innocence at this presumptuous man. I didn't do any of those things."

"Folks around here are not being very nice to you. If you don't want to stay here, I could take you anywhere you wanted to go, to start over. I need to start over, myself. I'd like it to be with you. I *need* it to be with you. Say yes, Anna. Please. Marry me."

She looked him straight in the eyes, those beautiful deep

brown eyes, and she said what she had to say. "The answer is no. It wouldn't be fair to you, and in time you'd come to see that. And I don't think it would take very much time, either. I think it would be soon." She took a deep breath, and hoped he wouldn't see her eyes filling with tears. "And it wouldn't be fair to me. I don't expect you to stop being who you are, and you can't expect me to stop being who I am. You think that you want me, but once you've settled down, you'd want a wife who put her home, her man, her children first. And you'd start to feel stifled, living here, no matter what you think now. But this is where I've built my life, and I can't just run away from that. I know that right now most of the so-called decent folks of Carter's Creek are cutting me on the street, but all my history is here. This is my home, and in time..." She trailed off, unable to speak anymore.

He looked at her for a moment, as he realized that there was no point in asking her to change her mind. "Well, if you really feel that way, there's no point in my hanging around anymore. I've asked you to marry me three times, which is three times more than I've asked anyone else. There's not going to be a fourth. Goodbye, Anna. And this time, it really is goodbye."

When she heard the door slam shut downstairs, she ran to the window, and watched as he disappeared down the street and out of sight. She knew that she would never see him again, and she could feel her heart breaking as she stood there, clutching the window frame.

But she never for a moment doubted that she'd done the right thing.

• ♥ •

Ed Marcus was sitting on the bed in his hotel room, his long legs stretched out in front of him. He was idly pretending to read a newspaper, but he was really counting the cracks in the ceiling and pretending he wasn't waiting every minute for the door to the room to open. If she accepted him, it might be some time, he thought. In fact, Jeremiah might forget that his partner was sitting there wondering about the outcome. The outcome that would make as much difference in his own life as in Jer's, he thought, and then felt selfish and miserable for even entertaining the thought.

When he heard the door handle turn, sooner even than he'd expected, he figured that it meant either good news or bad. From his partner's expression as he walked in the door, he could guess what happened, and now that he could, he had to admit he was surprised. But he wasn't going to let on. "What happened, Jer?" he asked.

"Let's go," Jeremiah replied. His dark eyes were unreadable to anyone but his longtime partner, but Ed Marcus could see that all the joy had been extinguished right out of them. From the way he tightened his fingers on the doorframe, it almost seemed like he was angry. "No point in staying around here anymore."

"She turned you down?"

"Yeah, she did. Like I should have known she would." He gave a wry smile, but he almost spat out the words. "You know, I never even wanted to get married. She just got under my skin. So why am I feeling so…" He trailed off.

Rejected, filled in Ed mentally. Surprised? Unhappy? Disappointed? "Never mind, Jer. It's better this way." He spoke with an assurance he didn't feel. "At least you offered to do right by her. You can't blame yourself about anything, now. So let's get out of here and go someplace where we can have us a real good time and you can forget all about Miss Anna Harrison."

"Maybe later. Right now, all I want to do is get on out of here and keep riding." He went to the wardrobe and flung his few things into his saddlebags with quick, decisive movements. "Come on, Ed. I mean right now."

Ed stood up and hefted his own saddlebags. Even though this wasn't the outcome he'd expected, he'd packed already, just in case. He'd long ago learned to prepare for all eventualities, especially for getting out of town quickly. "We're gone."

• ♥ •

It was days before Jeremiah Brown got over his fit of silence. Then, one evening, as he and Marcus were sitting down to play cards at some saloon in a town in Wyoming they'd never been to before, something seemed to shift in him. He was lively, that night, and very amusing, almost unnaturally so. He lost at cards, for once, because he wasn't paying much attention, and he spent the evening flirting with two saloon girls simultaneously. They willingly allowed him kisses and other small liberties, but he didn't take either of them upstairs. In the end, he got so drunk that Ed had to assist him back to their hotel, and he sang loudly and tunelessly almost the whole way.

The next morning, he woke up complaining of his throbbing head, but after that, he seemed to return to normal. Well, normal except for his determined silence about Montana and some of its inhabitants. Ed tried to shrug it off as natural, but he kept wondering how badly his partner had been hurt by everything that had happened.

Chapter 17

Things didn't get better, not for a long time. It hurt to be betrayed by a friend, but she knew that Nick had felt betrayed, as well, and she could understand his reasons a little, if not fully. But there had been another voice in all the scandal that she couldn't understand, the saloon girl who said she'd known about Jeremiah Brown and Miss Harrison since that first night, well over a year ago. Anna was surprised the girl would remember something like that after all this time, but even if she did, she couldn't understand why someone who didn't even know her wanted to hurt her that way. Not when this girl, out of anyone, must have known what scandal was like.

She asked Karl Rasmussen to bring the girl to see her, since he was about the only person she knew well who ever frequented the saloon. Well, other than Nick, who she clearly couldn't ask to help her out now. Jonathan would pop in now and again for a whiskey, just to keep up his membership in the unofficial fraternity that sprang up in such places, but he didn't talk to the girls. And they certainly didn't waste their time on someone who, though young and handsome, was hopelessly in love with his own wife.

But Karl talked to everyone, or rather, since he was a quiet sort, everyone talked to Karl. Politely. That was just the effect he had on folks. He reported back that he'd spoken to the girl and that she said she'd only come if she was paid for her time, since it was time she'd have to take away from her business. Anna inquired after her usual rates, and told him to tell her she'd pay triple.

So one day, not too long after it all happened, Karl arrived at her flat with a blonde woman in tow. There was a superficial resemblance between them, though the soiled dove was shorter than Anna and her hair was wavier and more luxuriant. Her green eyes, tip-tilted nose, and generous mouth suggested Irish ancestry. She was pretty, but worn-looking, and Anna supposed she was about her own age, around thirty, but that she'd just lived harder. It wasn't until later that she learned the woman was in her early twenties.

Caroline was hovering at the doorway, but she darted to her guardian's side and whispered, "*Une courtisane*?"

"Caroline, honey," Anna said, "Why don't you go down to the kitchen and start supper? Or do your German—or something."

"Not suitable company for the girl?" spat out the woman. "She lives with you, don't she?"

Anna took a deep breath and held back her rising anger, just as she'd learned to do when Nick baited her in the courtroom. "It's not the company, but the proposed topic of conversation, that I consider unsuitable for the girl. Karl, would you take Caroline downstairs?"

He looked doubtful, as though he ought to stay. She wondered if he was afraid that they were going to claw at each other's eyes, as jealous saloon girls were rumored to do. After a moment, he sighed. "All right, Miss Anna. Miss Anna Harrison, this is Nellie. She works at the saloon."

"Nellie...?" she asked, waiting for more. She gestured to a seat, which Nellie took.

Karl was already escorting Caroline down the stairs. She

had the distinct feeling he was anticipating fireworks.

"Does it matter?" she asked, bitterly.

"I'd like to be able to address you properly, Miss—"

"So now I'm a lady to be addressed properly, am I? But whenever I pass you on the street, you look right through me."

"I'm—I'm sorry." Anna might have passed Nellie dozens of times or even hundreds, but she'd never seen her—all she would have seen is one of *those* women. And a lady like she was didn't speak to those women. It was the way people looked through her on the street now, and she found herself feeling sympathy for the fallen sisterhood, for the first time. Many a formerly "respectable" woman in her own situation, without the annuity and the property her father had left her, or the too-generous insistence of Jonathan in adhering to the letter of their partnership and continuing to split their fees—now almost exclusively *his* fees—would have ended up as one of them.

"I'm certain it was wrong of me. Have you...have you lived in Carter's Creek long?" A fatuous question—she must have lived here for at least as long as Anna had known Jeremiah Brown.

"Quite a while, thank you," she said, sarcastically. "Long enough."

Anna examined her pretty, worn face, pale and tired-looking beneath the rouge she wore. Her jaw was clenched and her eyes were filled with anger. "Why do you hate me?"

"Because he came back for you. Jeremiah Brown, Tommy Slade, whatever his real name is. He came back. That night he spent with you must have meant something to him. I had left the saloon to go for a breath of fresh air that evening, and I saw the two of you in your doorway, kissing. I saw him follow you into your office, and I knew you lived above. Everyone knows that." The very room they were speaking in now. "And that's what I told when I first heard the rumors."

"Why did you keep quiet for so long? And why did you speak up when you did?"

"Because I liked knowing you were no better'n me, Miss Pillar-of-the-Community Harrison. I liked you for it, and I liked knowing that it was a little secret that only you and me knew, even though you didn't notice me any more than you notice the dirt under your feet. And I felt sorry for you. You see, that night I went back to the saloon and I met up with his friend, Edward Marcus, that they're now saying is Johnny Nevada. He spent that same night with me that Jeremiah Brown spent with you. And it was…he was like no man I've ever been with, and I've been with plenty. I've never been able to get him off my mind, since. I figured it was probably the same for you." She seemed to have forgotten her anger in her sadness, but it flared up again in a moment.

"And what happens, but this Jeremiah Brown comes back to town to throw himself at your feet! You, Miss Anna Harrison, the ice queen, the one they call the Widow because you're s'posed to have made your whole life around the boy that you loved who died. And instead, we find out you and this outlaw have been carrying on all this time, Miss Respectable Harrison."

Her eyes were filling, and her nose was turning red. "And I've seen Ed Marcus in the saloon and on the street since they came back, and he hasn't even noticed me." She sobbed a little. "I knew he wouldn't. I knew he'd have forgotten that night a long time ago, even if I can't, but…why is it different for you? Just 'cause I'm the kind of woman I am, and you're the kind of woman you are. Life just ain't fair."

"I'm not sure I'm the kind of woman I am anymore, either.

At least, most folks around here don't seem to think I am." Anna paused. "Well, you've got your revenge now, haven't you? You and Nick Powell. You know Nick?"

Nellie laughed through her tears. "'Course I know Nick. All the girls do. He—well, you know his wife, don't you? What I hear, she'd drive any man to seek some comfort with us. But Nick likes me special. He told me once, when he was a little drunk, that I looked a bit like some girl he was in love with."

Anna tried to hide her shock, probably unsuccessfully. She'd never heard of Nick being in love with anyone. But then, she'd always assumed he was faithful to Cora, and she'd thought he was a friend, too, so what did she really know about him? Just that he was a hypocrite, running around with saloon girls and then blaming her for having taken a lover. At least she hadn't deceived anyone with Jeremiah, even if they were saying she'd deceived everyone. She'd thought it didn't matter to Nick that she was a woman. She'd thought wrong.

"Did you try to talk to him—Ed Marcus, I mean? He's a good man. Of course, he would have been bound to be a little bit angry at you now, for his partner's sake, maybe for my sake. But—" she stopped short, thinking of what Ed had said to her, about Jeremiah, in Colorado that time. *"Look, Anna, men and women are just different about things like that. Don't mean he thinks about some saloon girl the way he thinks about you."* Maybe it wouldn't have been such a good idea. Anyway, he was long gone, and she didn't expect to see him again. Like she didn't expect to see Jeremiah Brown again.

"Are you crazy? What would I have said to him? 'Excuse me, but you were one of my customers once a few years ago and even though there've been hundreds since, I still remember you?' He'd just have thought I was loco or somethin'."

"I'm sorry." Anna didn't have anything more to say, so she

rang the bell to the kitchen for Karl to come and escort Nellie out. She walked over to her secretaire and counted out the money.

"Yeah, me too," Nellie said, taking it without looking at it. "Sorry I ever met Edward Marcus. Sorry I have to be reminded I'm a whore like this, in case there's any danger of my ever forgettin' it for a moment or two." She smiled quickly, almost sympathetically. "Sorry yours ran out on you in the end, too."

"No," Anna said. "He didn't. I sent him away. He asked me to marry him, but...I sent him away."

Nellie looked at her like she was looking at a certifiable lunatic. "You—you *what*? Most women would give anything for a chance like that, especially one that's just lost her reputation. You turned him down? Not good enough for you or something?"

"Nothing like that. But I don't think you'd understand," she said, simply, "and I don't think you're alone in that." They fell silent until there was a knocking on the door and it was Karl, come to see the visitor out.

Anna never saw Nellie again, and when she inquired after her, months later, she learned the woman had left Carter's Creek for good, shortly after their meeting. She hoped that Nellie found what she was looking for, but she was afraid of what the answer might be.

Chapter 18

Anna wasn't herself for some time after Jeremiah Brown left town. Jonathan thought that she'd always known that she and Brown were bound to part someday. She'd said to him once, "It wasn't like we were ever really together, Jonathan. It was more like this sort of bubble in time that would spring up whenever he crossed my path. Like one of those fairy-places they talk about in the Irish legends, where time passes differently, and you watch things happening to yourself that don't seem to have any basis in your everyday existence. . . ." she trailed off. "You know, I think the men in town will forgive me first. How many of them haven't sowed a few wild oats? And they half think of me as one of them already, even though they'd never admit it. But the women, they're the ones who won't let it go."

He wished she'd at least given the idea of marriage a chance. But everything had happened so quickly, and she'd let her fears control her. And now Jeremiah Brown was long gone.

Sarah Powell and Melanie Cranbrook were the only "decent" women in Carter's Creek who would associate with Anna for a long while. Sarah and her husband, Ray, barely spoke anymore, although she continued to cook his meals and care for the house. She'd come over to see to Anna as much as she could. Jonathan noticed that sometimes she seemed to move a little stiffly, or rub herself as though she had aches and pains, despite her youth, but he didn't think much of it at the time. Sarah had always seemed so healthy, with her love of the outdoors, but it turned out she was delicate after all. The demands of an entire home seemed to be too much for her. Once when she raised her arm to get something off a high shelf, and her sleeve fell back, he noticed some odd bruising on her forearm. She told him she'd been clumsy. Later, he recognized how stupid he'd been not to see what was really happening.

Melanie had always been a little uncomfortable with her husband's law partner, who seemed to her the living embodiment of that admirable yet terrifying creature of whom she'd read, the New Woman, with her independent ways and unusual interests. But uncomfortable or no, she figured that if Anna was Jonathan's dearest friend, why then, Anna was *her* dearest friend, too. And at this complicated joyous time when her daughter was born, Melanie turned her back on the gossipy, spiteful women of her sewing circle, who tried to gather around her, and stood by Anna just as firmly as her husband did.

A few times when Anna was awkwardly trying to hold the baby, Jonathan caught Melanie looking at her strangely, but he never really asked her why. Everyone knew that Anna Harrison was hopeless with the things that were supposed to come naturally to all women. She no more had the instincts of a domestic angel than she did of an Apache tracker.

That first month, Anna never left the flat above the office unless she was accompanied by Sarah or Caroline. Some officious busybody tried to get young Caroline to move in with a more respectable family, but she let the lady know just where she stood in no uncertain terms. Jonathan overheard the conversation, and began to wonder if the girl might be their next law clerk, in a few years. But other than that, Carter's Creek was united against Anna.

In keeping with everything else, the larger number of the firm's regular clients indicated that although they would not withdraw their business, they preferred that the junior partner represent them from now on. So, while he handled the majority of their ordinary work, Anna interested herself in the plight of a tribe of Indians who'd been forcibly resettled by the Federal government a few hours outside of Carter's Creek. She became obsessed with their claims against the government, to the point where she rarely slept. Caroline used to tell Jonathan that she'd wake up any time of the day or night and find a light burning, or hear Anna's footsteps pacing above or below stairs. Her clients used to see her in the back kitchen, sitting at the old wooden table, since many of them objected to sharing a consultation room with "dirty Injuns"...or with the firm's senior partner, although that went unspoken.

The older families, the ones who'd come out from Massachusetts along with the Harrisons at Carter's Creek's founding, were the ones who turned most definitely against Anna. They'd always held themselves to a higher moral standard, one which she'd now failed at. Some of the ranchers, and the ordinary townsfolk, seemed more willing to relent—but then, with the shortage of women in the region, some of them had found themselves wives in the saloons, and weren't as much inclined to condemn Anna for "being human, after all," as one of the shopkeepers had said to Jonathan the other day.

It was about three months after Jeremiah Brown and Ed Marcus left town, when it happened. It was very late one evening, and Melanie had already gone to bed, while Jonathan was going over some documents, and planning to follow her shortly. There was a knocking on the door. He went to the drawer where he kept his gun, pulled it out, and went cautiously to the door. Nobody in Carter's Creek was likely to call on them at that hour unless it was an emergency, or something worse.

It was Caroline, her lank brown hair streaming around her face, and her eyes wide with terror. "It's Anna. I don't know what's wrong with her, but she's breathing funny and she won't wake up or move."

He put down the gun. "Have you called the doctor?"

"Doc was there this afternoon. She got a funny look in her eyes when he left, but she seemed okay until I went in to check on her just now, before I went to bed."

"I'll be right there," he said, "and you go wake up the Doc."

She nodded, a little hesitantly, almost as though she blamed the doctor for bringing on Anna's trouble in the first place. But at Jonathan's prompting, she went.

When she arrived at the rooms above our offices, he found that Caroline had not exaggerated her condition. Anna was flushed and breathing with difficulty, and nothing he could say or do roused her to consciousness. His first thought was that she'd finally been driven to poison herself, but that didn't seem like her. She saw things through, you always had to give her that. And then he remembered something from one of her books, one she'd gotten him to read. It was called *The Woman in White,* by some fellow called Will Collins or something like that. There was a woman in it called Marian, and she was a strong, brave woman, the kind Anna liked to read about. Under an excessive strain, though, she'd collapsed and fallen into something called "brain fever."

The doctor arrived shortly afterward, and found Jonathan

cradling Anna's head in his lap. He realized that was probably indecorous, but she was like a sister to him. He asked the doctor about "brain fever," and after examining her, Doctor Adams agreed that he couldn't see any other possible cause, though he referred to it as a nervous collapse. Meanwhile, they'd set Caroline to searching the house for any sources of poisons, but nothing turned up.

"I need to speak to you alone, Cranbrook," he said, and left Caroline tending Anna, while they went downstairs to the office.

"Okay, Doc. I know you were here earlier today, and Caroline doesn't know why. She thought the attack might have been connected."

Doc Adams bowed his head. "I'm afraid so, too. Cranbrook, Miss Anna Harrison is expecting a child."

He gasped. "No! My God, Doc, you must understand what that will mean for her." If Anna were to bear a child out of wedlock, there would be a permanent reminder of her disgrace. "How long have you known? How long has she known?"

The doctor smiled in spite of himself. "For such an intelligent woman, she doesn't seem to know very much about certain aspects of a woman's life. She had no idea until I told her, this afternoon. I suspect the surprise was part of what brought on the attack. But all Anna knew until I explained it to her was that she was ill every morning, and she wasn't feeling like herself. Oh, and she had missed a couple of her monthlies, but she thought that was due to the stress she's been under. I have a suspicion that she might have had some idea deep down and she just didn't want to know. It's amazing what the human mind can choose not to know." He hesitated. "The father…?"

Jonathan wondered briefly if the doctor suspected him, because of all the time he and Anna spent together. But he must know the answer as well as Jonathan himself did, as well as everyone in town did. "It must have been that outlaw fellow, Jeremiah Brown. There hasn't been anyone else." He looked quickly away. He hated making that admission—that there had been anyone at all—that any of this was even possible. If Brown had been there at that moment, he probably would have made good on his threat to kill him. But how could he blame the man when he'd made it clear he wanted to marry Anna? She was the one who'd persisted in saying no. Her predicament now was of her own making, in good measure.

"So the gossip is true? Well, I'm sorry to hear that, but I don't think my judgment is what my patient needs right now." He turned to Jonathan, shaking his head. "The story goes no further, of course. It just shows that when a woman steps out of her proper sphere, she's liable to the same temptations as a man. I think it's safe to move her, and I think you and Melanie are the people to take care of her right now. It's not contagious, so you don't have to worry about your children."

They spent the rest of the night keeping watch, and at first light, they carried Anna to the Cranbrooks'. Later that morning, an unexpected trio arrived on their doorstep. Melanie had sent for Sarah Powell, of course. But behind her, each looking exceptionally emotionally strained, were Sarah's husband Ray, and old Nick Powell himself.

Sarah ran right to Anna's bedside, and Ray, as might have been expected, began thundering in his not-so-deep voice about infamous women and his wife being exposed to this scandalous behavior and its just rewards. But the surprise was Nick, who was on Sarah's heels the whole way. Jonathan heard the sound of masculine sobbing, and looked into the room to find old Nick, who he'd lately been thinking of as the devil himself, red-eyed and miserable and kneeling at Anna's bedside.

He saw Jonathan there, and rose to come out into the hallway. "I'm so sorry, Jonathan. This is all my fault," he said. "If only I had just kept my mouth shut about those suspicions I had, and let things be. But I just blew up at the thought that Anna had lied to me about something like this."

"Like what, Nick?" he asked, not ready to forgive the man, just because he was repentant. "The fact that she did her job and represented her clients the best that she could? The fact that she had some life outside of this little world and it didn't include you and me? The fact that she turned out to be a human being, and after all these years of being alone she made a mistake because she found a man who made her feel a little alive?"

From Nick's expression, Jonathan wondered if he'd made a hit with that last one. He wondered why he was so invested in Anna staying on her pedestal, anyway. Everybody knew that Nick was unfaithful to Cora with just about every saloon girl in town. Everybody except Cora and, until recently, Anna, that was. Jonathan himself had only been unfaithful to Melanie once. It was before he was married, but it was an experience he didn't like to remember. He could understand what Anna had done a lot better than he could about Nick and his saloon girls. At least there were real feelings involved there.

"Maybe all of those things," he said, honestly. "All I can tell you is when that outlaw walked in there bold as brass and kissed her like that and then he let on who he really was, well…I felt like she'd been putting one over on me the whole time, and it wasn't a fair fight between us, like it always has been. She'd broken the rules—*our* rules. I was mad and I wanted to get her back."

"You wanted to get her back because she fell in love?" Jonathan asked.

Nick started. He almost looked hurt by what the younger man had said, which Jonathan found peculiar, since the idea of Anna being in love was the thing that explained and maybe even excused her behavior, to his mind.

"You think she's in love with this fellow? I thought I'd heard he offered to do the right thing by her and she sent him away."

Jonathan frowned. "Guess you heard that back when your son and his wife were still speaking. Do you really think Anna would know her own mind about something like being in love? She's been all mixed up ever since she met Jeremiah Brown, and I think she's probably more afraid of caring about him than of losing him. I mean, look at who she chose."

Nick frowned. "Well, he's a good-looking man, and he certainly has a way about him. He's clearly brighter than average, and women do seem to be partial to men with something dangerous about them."

"Nick, would you have picked him for your daughter?"

"If he'd have looked twice at Lisette, I'd have locked her up until he'd been gone for a week, just so there was no chance of her tracking him down."

"Exactly. Look, Nick, it's like this. Anna waits for years after losing David, turning down proposals, or more often, keeping men at a distance so they'll never ask. She's pretty and rich, and she's been one of the prime catches in Carter's Creek for years. Only she's refused to be caught. And then she falls for a man who never stays in one place more than a week at a time, who has a shady past, who pops up unexpectedly. Nick, if he'd have been interested in Lisette, you'd have seen him as a great big threat. Anna saw things just the opposite. Jeremiah Brown is the one man she could have found who could have really cared for her, and still not posed one iota of threat to her independence. Not until you opened your big mouth, anyway."

Nick shook his head. "No wonder she keeps you around. I've been trying to figure it out for months now, and I haven't been able to make any sense of it at all. But what you say makes sense. It sounds like her, anyway."

"I never should have gotten my wife involved," he continued. "Once she had the story, it was bound to spread all over. She doesn't like Anna. She doesn't understand how things are. She just thinks that you two are out to do me and my poor clients dirt any way you can. And when Nellie, over at the saloon, got wind of it, well, I'm a good customer of hers. When she heard that the stories were coming from me, I guess she figured she'd be doing me a good turn to chime in." He paused. "But why was Anna so stupid as to let him spend the night at her house again after she must have known I was out there spreading stories about her? Didn't she know that you can't so much as sneeze in Carter's Creek without half-a-dozen people witnessing it firsthand?"

Jonathan shrugged. "Like I said, she's in love. And love is not the wisest of masters."

Nick went on, his confession not done yet. "I've made no bones about being a greedy man, all my life, but I never let my greed get in the way of a friendship. But that bounty hunter that brought in Slade and Nevada was going to give me a quarter of the reward on contingency. That's almost as much money as I see in a year. What's it the preacher says about the love of money?"

"It's the root of all evil," Jonathan confirmed. "Nick, I think there's something else you should know. Something far worse."

He started. "Worse? How can anything be worse?"

"Anna's expecting a child. That's what brought on the attack. Doc Adams told her yesterday afternoon, and she collapsed last night."

"And Jeremiah Brown is the father, of course?"

"It's the only possibility. You know better than to believe the saloon talk." He didn't bother to mention that Nick had started it.

"And he was willing to do the right thing by her, before?"

Jonathan nodded.

And then Nick Powell surprised him. "Well, then let's get after him. Do you know where he is?"

"I think the idea when she refused him a third time was that they were never going to see each other again. I don't have the slightest clue where he might be. Probably west of the Mississippi, but that's about all I know."

"What was the name of that sheriff, the one who vouched for them? You were with Anna then, weren't you?"

"I remember wiring him. I'd been her clerk for maybe a year, and I remember I was angry that I was being treated as an errand boy even after all that time. Anderson! Something Anderson, in Simpson Pass."

"Maybe he'd know?"

"Why? He was encouraging them to stay the course, to wait out the statute of limitations here and over in the Dakotas. But that's done now. Why'd they bother to keep in touch with him on a regular basis?"

"Habit," said Nick. "When you've been a lawyer as long as

me, Jonathan, you'll know all about folks and their habits. They don't have families, or regular associates, and they want someone to know where they are, you know, in case anything happens. And they're used to Anderson being that someone. I'll get to the telegraph office right now, and we'll go after Jeremiah Brown as soon as we hear back."

"He'll still be an ex-outlaw. And people will know the baby started to happen before the wedding, even if we can get him to come back with us."

Nick shot him a funny look. "Do you have any idea how many babies around these parts are born six or seven months after the wedding? Including my own high and mighty Raymond, a fact of which I'm about to remind him. You and Melanie are the exception, and I'll tell you, folks were really wondering when the baby didn't come 'til more'n a year after you were married."

"But the outlaw part?"

"Folks'll get over that. For one thing, it's pretty romantic, and they'll need a new romantic tale to get over the loss of the old one, about the Widow and her long-lost David. And for another, don't you know by now that what I say in this town goes? People around here either agree with me, or they need Anna, because she's the only one brave enough to say, 'Nick Powell's got it wrong!' If I say it's okay, folks will accept it. It may take some time, but they will." He turned down the passage, to where his son was standing.

Ray's voice was raised as his father passed by him without a word. "What are you thinkin', Pa? Are you crazy?"

Nick's disgust was evident in his tone of voice. "Get out of my way, boy. I'm beginning to wonder if you even really are my son, you disgrace to the name of Powell!"

• ❤ •

Two days later, they were on their way to Denver. It had taken a couple of telegrams before they'd convinced Sheriff Anderson they were on the level, and even then, he hadn't been able to give them an address, only a city. Nick acted peculiar the whole way, keeping very quiet, which wasn't like him in the least. Jonathan brought that book of Anna's, *The Woman in White,* to reread. He wanted to remember what had happened to that Marian, the one with the brain fever. He needed to remind himself that she came out all right.

Neither of them brought any work along. Traveling with the person who was your opponent on ninety-five percent of your caseload made that a bit uncomfortable. Jonathan read listlessly, while Nick mostly stared out of the window.

Once, though, he started to ask about Jeremiah Brown and Ed Marcus. The younger lawyer was surprised at the sorts of questions Nick asked. Did he know anything about how they'd crossed that line over to the other side of the law? Did he know what motivated them to try to cross back? How long had they tried, and how hard had it been? Had either of them ever killed anyone, and had they done a lot of killing?

They were questions Jonathan mostly couldn't answer. He spoke of what he knew of Marcus and of Brown from the time he'd spent with them when he and Anna had gone over to Greenville to help them out. Considering who they were and what they'd done, Jonathan still believed they were essentially decent men. That they'd made sacrifices to try and live as honest men, when the other way would have been so much easier for them. What he said seemed to satisfy Nick, who nodded and fell silent again.

A great deal of track and several rail lines later, they arrived in Denver. But knowing that Jeremiah Brown was in Denver was a whole different story than knowing where to find him. They figured the best bet was to find out every place in town where high stakes poker was being played, and as it turned out, they figured right.

After visiting half a dozen of Denver's finest hotels, saloons and bawdyhouses, they were resigned to a couple of dozen more before they found the right one. But, instead, on the lucky seventh, they walked in to find Jeremiah Brown. He was sitting at a large table, surrounded by cards and chips and a half-dozen men.

The players ranged from a city slicker-looking fellow in a suit so well-tailored Jonathan found himself reflexively straightening his lapels, to a mean-looking man who looked like he was a drover and probably hadn't bothered to clean up from his last drive before coming on in to gamble away whatever it was he'd just earned.

Jonathan cleared his throat, not sure whether Brown would be playing poker under his own name. "Excuse me..."

Brown looked up, clearly resentful that his concentration had been broken. "Yes? Well, if it isn't young Jonathan Cranbrook himself." He peered behind him. "And Nick Powell. Now, if that ain't like seeing Lucifer and Saint Peter sittin' down for a friendly drink together, I don't know what is. What'd you folks want that involved you coming all the way to Denver? And quickly, because I'm winning big."

"We want to talk to you. Alone."

Jonathan heard Ed Marcus's voice, cold and hard behind him. "You heard the man. He's winning big. State your mind and move on."

"Well, speakin' as the Devil himself," said Nick, "I think you may want to hear what my friend has to say." Jonathan thought he heard a hint of an Irish brogue, something he'd never detected in Nick's voice before. He looked hard as flint.

Jonathan had seen Nick mean, and seen him angry, but he'd never seen his eyes that dead-gray color. It looked as though old jovial red-faced Nick had gone for a walk, and left some stranger in possession of his corporeal self, like in one of those ghost stories.

"There's only one thing Mr. Cranbrook and I have a common interest in, and the lady has already made her position perfectly clear," said Jeremiah distinctly, before returning his attention to his cards.

"You want to hear what he has to say," repeated Nick. The brogue was more pronounced this time.

Jeremiah scrutinized Nick's face carefully for a moment, and then he looked at Jonathan. "All right," he said. "Cash me in, then." He swept his chips forward, and began to pull the pot toward himself.

"Hold on, just a minute," said one of the other players, the trail-worn drover. "You gotta give us a chance to win some of that back." Ed Marcus might have been fast, but in a moment, there were a couple of guns on Brown and only his one on the man who'd been threatening his partner.

But as fast as Ed could draw even, there was a knife at the man's throat. "I'd drop the gun if I were you," said Nick, who, to Jonathan's amazement, was holding it. "I haven't used this on a man in twenty-five years, but I haven't forgotten how. And I'm going to hell already, so I've got no reason not to do it."

Ed already had his gun out, and Jonathan was able to grab one from the suddenly nerveless fingers of the man whom Nick was threatening. In a matter of moments, the four of them, and a big portion of Jeremiah's winnings, were out the door.

"Whooee!" exclaimed Ed. "Are you sure that was legal? I

ain't had that much fun since we been honest!"

"Well, nobody got hurt, and the winnings were Brown's by right. The only one of us who actually stole anything was Cranbrook. That gun's not yours, is it, Jonathan?" Nick grinned, looking a lot more like himself. "But I think we'd still better be on the next train out of town. The sheriff won't be after us, but some of those poker players may want to get the drop on us. We left our luggage at the depot, and I assume you boys have a hotel." Nick's brogue had subsided, and he was speaking in his natural voice. Or was he?

"That *was* our hotel," said Jeremiah. "But I've got my favorite hat, and Ed's got his gun. Everything else can be replaced, especially after a big win like that. Now, why the hell did you two come all the way to Denver to find me? Did something happen to Anna? 'Cause I don't know what else we have to talk about."

"And who are you, really, Powell?" asked Ed. "Not too many small-town lawyers can handle a knife like that, or face down a man like that Sid Buford, there."

"Well, I'll tell you, but we'd better keep moving." Nick hurried them along toward the station. It wasn't until they were aboard a train a short time later that there were any explanations given.

• ♥ •

Brown and Marcus didn't question the choice of a northbound train, and Jonathan bought four tickets to Ogden, where he and Nick—and maybe the others—would change trains for Montana.

Jeremiah and Jonathan sat down, but Ed Marcus waved Nick to a different seat, not right near the other pair. Perceptive of him, Jonathan thought.

"What's the matter with Anna?" Jeremiah asked, again.

"You didn't come all the way to Denver just to pass the time of day."

"Anna's had an attack of brain fever," Jonathan said, noting the other man's sorrowful expression. "She was just starting to regain consciousness when we left, but she was still delirious mostly. Doc Adams thinks she's gonna pull through. But the shock that sent her into it...well, she's still going to have to deal with that."

Jeremiah looked at him, hard. "And that is?"

"She's expecting a child."

"My child." It was a statement, not a question. He put his head in his hands. "Then why did she send me away? I offered to do right by her."

"She didn't know about it when she sent you away—that was just a few days after it must have happened. She only found out the other day. Anna's book-smart, but there are certain things she's not real aware of. Woman things. Melanie tells me now that she'd guessed, but she was afraid to say anything."

Jeremiah was almost unnaturally pale, and his dark brown eyes were haunted. "A child. A...baby? How—"

"I expect you'd know more about that than I would," Jonathan pointed out. "Although, if you need a description of the mechanics, I'd be happy to oblige," he finished, with an edge to his voice.

Ignoring his sarcasm, Jeremiah said, "I can figure out when it happened, but it still comes as a surprise. I hadn't really gotten any farther than asking Anna to marry me—I never really thought about what would happen next. And since she kept saying no... How does she feel about it?"

"I don't think she's taking it too well, considering. She hasn't exactly been in a position to tell anyone. But I'd suggest you think about what you're intending to do. We change trains at Ogden, and you can either come with us, back to Montana, or you can get off the train somewhere between here and there and we'll pretend we never found you. Of course, I can't vouch for Nick, but then, I've never seen him the way he was back in that hotel before, either."

"That a threat?"

Jonathan shook his head. "I don't want you doing anything because somebody made you. I want you to do it, if you do it, because you know it's the right thing, and because you want to stand by her."

"I tried that already. Three times. Didn't get me far." Jeremiah Brown sounded bitter. But then he looked closely at Jonathan. "Of course, I'll come. I just can't help but wish she'd take me for myself, not just because of a child."

"I was afraid you'd be stubborn, like she is. The two of you…you are quite a pair, after all."

Brown laughed now. "I always figured life with Anna would be quite an adventure. And having a baby with her, even more so. But now you, Nick," he raised his voice, directing his attention to our companions, who were seated across the aisle and up a row. "Seems to me you've got some real explaining to do."

But just then, the conductor came through, telling them they were shortly arriving at the terminus at Ogden, where they'd change trains.

• ❤ •

They'd agreed not to break their journey, and when they'd boarded the new train, Nick made some inquiries and discovered that they could get a private first-class compartment. When they'd settled in, Jonathan looked around at his companions and thought about how much more comfortable everything seemed, now that he and Brown had begun to make their peace.

But Jeremiah Brown wasn't satisfied for long. "Okay, Powell, I think you owe us a story, don't you? What the hell was that back in Denver? You were like—"

"Like a different person," his partner finished.

Jonathan wondered if they did that to each other a lot.

Powell took a deep breath, and let it out, before he even opened his mouth to speak. "There's a big part of me that wants to make up some story, but the truth is, that it'll be a relief to tell someone, after all these years. And if anyone can understand, I guess it's you two." He looked at the ex-outlaws seated across from us. "You feel like taking a walk to the dining car, Jonathan?"

Jonathan gazed at him steadily, making no move to rise, so he sighed, and after a moment he continued. "It's like this, boys. You're not the only ones with a past. You're not the only ones who've ever called yourselves by a different name from the one you were born with, either. My real name is Nicholas Riordan, and I'm still wanted in New York. The statute doesn't ever run out on what I did." It was still Nick sitting there, red faced, heavyset, fifty-year-old Nick, but it was somebody else looking out from his eyes. He was somebody they'd met back at that hotel, and he was a lot more dangerous than Jonathan's blustery courtroom opponent.

The younger lawyer took a sudden breath, and those strange eyes met his. "So that's why you wouldn't leave your hotel room in New York City." He turned to the others. "Their ship was delayed for a day by weather at New York Harbor when he took his family to Europe. Ray complained he couldn't get his father to go sightseeing."

"It's been twenty-five years, and the law wouldn't

recognize me, but the b'hoys would. And the penalty for skipping out on the gang I used to run with is death."

"The b'hoys?" asked Jeremiah, while Ed's question was "You were in a gang?"

"I was, indeed. I won't tell you the name—I'm still a bit superstitious about that. But we ruled the Bowery, and we were making serious inroads on the waterfront. I was second lieutenant, even though I was barely older than Jonathan, here, when I left. I was known for my way with a blade. Only it's a close-up, nasty way to kill, and after awhile I couldn't take it anymore. So, I ran west until I hit what's now Montana, and by the time I hit the territory, Nick Riordan had become Nick Powell. Found me a lawyer with an eligible daughter, not too pretty, and room for an apprentice. A few years later, it was Nick Powell, Attorney-at-Law."

Jonathan began to laugh, and Nick turned to him. "You ever tell my wife anything about this, I swear I'll use that knife on one last throat." But he was smiling.

"Anna always said you had the soul of a brigand."

"If only I could tell Anna," said Nick, still smiling, "that might do me some good. It might keep her in line when she gets to threatening me in court if somebody told her that Nick Powell's more dangerous than she thinks." He sobered. "It was twenty-five years ago, but it still weighs heavy on my conscience. In the space of less than three years, I killed over thirty men for the gang."

There was a sharp intake of breath, and Ed Marcus spoke. "Thirty?" he asked. His blue eyes were steely, unreadable.

Nick was suddenly serious. "Well, you must know what it's like, being a well-known gunslinger, and all. I know I'll probably go to hell for it, and there isn't a night I don't wake up thinking about one or another of them. But, at least, I stopped, and that's my only hope of salvation." He looked at Marcus, and his expression was almost pleading. "Well, you must know what it's like."

Ed spoke softly. "Nick, I've killed three men, but only in self-defense. I can usually disarm them, or wound them in the shoulder or leg."

He looked at Jeremiah.

"I've never killed anyone, Nick."

"My God," Powell said, "I knew I was bad, but I kept telling myself that there were outlaws all over the West as bad as me."

None of them said anything.

"Who am I trying to fool?" he continued. "I've been living with this for a long time, and it never gets any better. But there's one thing I can try to make amends for, and that's what I did to Anna. I was just so angry when I started the whole town talking against her. I guess I haven't changed as much as I'd like to think I have—just my methods."

"You came all this way to find me," said Jeremiah, kindly. "That's something. So why don't you tell us about these Bowery buhoys now? We don't know much about the gangs and outlaws back East."

"B'hoys," Powell corrected. It was like a curtain had dropped, and there he was, cheerful and contentious Nick Powell. "You see, my parents and I were immigrants and..."

It was a long tale, fascinating and brutal in turn, and Jonathan thought how very thoroughly his friend and rival had been able to reinvent himself. And how Jeremiah Brown and Edward Marcus were cut from different cloth; they'd never been brutes as Nick had been in his early years, just scared, angry boys who'd become too good at what they did, and then seen how hollow it all was.

Later, when they all rose to go to the dining car, Nick signaled for Jeremiah to hold back. He fixed the younger man with a hard stare. "So, you know all about me now. You know I'm pretty dangerous, myself." He took a deep breath. "And dammit, you'd better treat her right, or so help me God, I will make it my business to turn your life into a living hell."

Jeremiah's dark eyes widened, and suddenly it all made sense. "You're in love with her, aren't you? That's why you blew up the way you did, when you found out about us."

Nick nodded. "Guilty as charged. Oh, I always knew I'd never have a chance with her, married man my age, nothing much to look at. By the time I came to town, she was already in her teens, bright as a button, but still a child. Nobody I'd ever give a second's thought to, except wishing my Lisette would grow up as clever as that. But when her father started sending her to court, for the first time I felt like I had a worthy opponent. Ben Harrison, he was a good man and a good lawyer, but he didn't have her fighting spirit."

Jeremiah laughed. "I've only seen her get that way a couple of times, but I can imagine what it'd be like, going up against her in court."

"All my life, women seemed to fall into two categories: the ones you had a good time with, and the ones who made your home and gave you children. Worthy enough, but not particularly interesting. Suddenly, with Anna, I'd found a kindred spirit. Someone who shared my interests, someone who challenged me, someone I couldn't wait to see again, just to find out what she thought about this and that. On top of that, from an awkward girl, she grew into a beautiful woman. You ask her again, Jeremiah, and when she says yes, you hang on for life. A woman like her, she could be everything to a man." He looked away, at his reflection in the window. "I know that if tomorrow I was a widower with all the world to lay at her feet, I still wouldn't have a chance. I'd still look like this, I'd still be too old for her, I'd still be the person who's done all the things I did. I've never been good enough, and she'd never love me, even if she'd never met you. But that first day or two, I wasn't thinking, I was feeling. And I'm not a good man. I never claimed to be."

"Not such a bad one, either. It means something that it wasn't the money that set you off like that."

Nick shook his head. "No. Easy come, easy go, as far as money's concerned." But then, he laughed. "So, even if I'm forced to give up on 'I can't have her, but at least no one else can, either,' at least she chose a man who reminds me a little of myself. Someone with a past. Someone who's turned his life around. But who has a chance to do it right—to marry for love, and hang onto that with all your might."

"Seems like you're assuming she'll say yes." Jeremiah shook his head. "I don't know about that. She's a stubborn lady."

"Been negotiating with her for years, and she's not stupid. She knows what's best for her client, which in this case is herself. She'll say yes." Nick rose. "Now, let's catch up with those two in the dining car, before they start to wondering what we're talking about."

• ♥ •

When they arrived at the house several days later, Anna had regained consciousness. She was sitting up in bed, being read to by Caroline, while Melanie and Sarah were fussing over little Victoria Cranbrook.

Melanie flew into Jonathan's arms, and led him to the bed, while Sarah's eyes widened as she saw who was bringing up the rear.

"Anna, honey, you've got some visitors," she said, cautiously.

Anna was obviously not entirely recovered yet, and stared blankly for a moment, her blue eyes not really focused. "Who is it, Sarah? Jonathan's not a visitor, he lives here." Her voice was weak and the rest of her seemed to match. But then she looked up, past his shoulder, and for once in her life, Anna Harrison was speechless. Jeremiah Brown walked toward her, while Sarah shooed the others out into the hallway, following them out herself, and shutting the door.

After a moment, they all looked at each other. "Here we are, six grown people, not to mention a baby, crowded into a very small hallway where two can barely pass," Jonathan observed.

"Well, are you planning to move?" asked Ed. "He's my partner, and I have no intention of going anywhere until I know what's happened."

"And she's mine," Jonathan said.

Nick and the women just looked at them. Apparently, nobody was moving.

They waited at the door for quite some time, but after awhile it opened, and Jeremiah Brown popped out his head. "The answer is yes, and will you all please go away now?"

And they did.

Chapter 19

When Anna regained consciousness, the first thing she did was ask after Jonathan. She had this peculiar sense that business must be going unattended-to, and that if something wasn't done about it, and soon, something really bad was going to happen. When Melanie told her that he and Nick Powell had gone off somewhere together, her first thought was that at least then Nick couldn't put anything over on them while Jonathan was away and she was so very ill.

She couldn't figure out why she was at Jonathan's house, except that her illness must be worse even than she could tell, or why Melanie, Sarah and Caroline seemed to be in constant attendance every waking hour. She wanted to tell them to go away, but she didn't have the energy to speak, and anyway, she was so helpless that she needed them there, at least one at a time.

Judge Clayton came by once, with flowers. He kissed her on the forehead, in a grandfatherly way, but his eyes were sad when he looked at her.

She kept hearing a loud crying noise, and then she remembered little Victoria, a few months old now. Babies, she thought. She wasn't so sure she was fond of babies. But then she remembered what she didn't want to know, that she was going to have one herself, and she wondered how on earth she would manage.

Sarah sat beside her and held her hand. "Jonathan and Nick went to find him," she whispered. "He'll come back and marry you, and then everything will be all right."

"But I didn't want to marry him. I made him go away," Anna said foggily. "Don't you remember? And now, he won't ever return to Carter's Creek. He said so."

"That was before you knew about the baby," came her soft voice. "That was before *he* knew. They'll tell him, and he'll be here in no time at all, you'll see."

But Anna knew better. He wouldn't come. Even if they found him. And she didn't want him to come back just because she was going to have a baby. She wanted him to come back because she missed him. She wanted him to come back because she loved him. Because all her fears seemed insignificant in the face of the echoing loneliness that had dogged her since she'd sent him away. That looked to stretch out for the rest of her life. The child she was carrying would only remind her of the love she'd thrown away.

So, a few days later, when he was there, she had to acknowledge that she'd been wrong. As soon as Sarah had cleared the room, he sat down next to her, on the edge of the bed. She could tell from his expression that she must look worse than she'd thought, not having been encouraged to look in any mirrors lately.

She tried to prop herself up so that she could look at him, but he had to assist her in sitting up. The look of concern on his face was almost more than she could bear. She didn't want him to see her this way, and she'd half made up her mind to ask him to leave, when he spoke.

"I hear you've been having a rough time, lately."

"Nothing I can't handle," she began, but he interrupted her by laughing.

"Anna, you don't need to pretend that everything's okay. I know what's happened."

"Yes, I do," she whispered. "I *do* need to pretend. Because if I stop pretending, then I have to admit that I'm scared, Jeremiah. I'm more scared than I've ever been of anything in my life."

He looked at her, and she'd never seen his face like that. He was pale, and his dark eyes, in stark contrast, were large and luminous. "Me, too. Look, when I asked you to marry me before, I had myself all convinced that I knew exactly what I was doing. That everything would work out just fine for us. This time, all I can say is that I'm scared, too, and that I think that marriage is gonna be hard work for both of us. I don't think either of us is what you'd call the marrying kind, not really. You might have been when you were younger, but you're not, now. And me—you know what I am, who I am. But I don't want a life without you in it, not anymore. I want to be with you when you have that baby. What do you say, Anna? I said I wouldn't ask a fourth time, but here I've come all this way from Denver, with only this one question in mind: are we gonna get married?"

"It wasn't supposed to turn out like this."

"You kiddin'? Back when I was robbing banks, and even after, if you'd have told me I was gonna be asking my lawyer to marry me, I would've told you that you were crazy. 'Course, I didn't know they made lawyers like you, then." He stroked her hair. "Pretty ones, I mean."

"I'm not very pretty right now," she said. She knew that, even without a mirror. "Are you sure about this? Because I'm fairly certain I'm going to say yes, this time."

The emotion he'd always kept hidden was on full display, at the moment, in his eyes, in the tension in his face. "Then, please say it. I need to hear the words."

Anna took a deep breath. "Jeremiah Brown, I love you, and I think I have for a long time. I *know* I have. I've just been too stubborn to admit that it should make any difference. But my life has seemed empty since you left, that day. We belong together, you and me, and the little one who's coming. I will marry you, Jeremiah. Of course I will."

He leaned over, and took her in his arms. "And we are going to have a wonderful life together, even if other folks don't quite understand us." He kissed her on the cheek. "We'll definitely have to hire a housekeeper, though. I don't think I could survive on Caroline's cooking for long. Or yours."

"I've never cooked for you," she mock-protested.

"Don't you think that's on purpose? I've heard the rumors, from those who've survived it."

She laughed, and this time, he kissed her on the lips, a long lingering kiss.

A moment later, he rose, and walked over to the door, flung it open, and said something. Then he slammed it shut again and returned to sit on the edge of the bed. "So before we have a life together, we've got this getting married thing to get through. You almost did it once before. How does it work?"

"I don't know," she said, honestly. "The last time I was planning to get married feels as though it was about a thousand years ago. I picked the man and the dress, but everything else was my mother's job. And when Sarah got married, I just tried to stay out of the way as much as I could, and no matter what she said, I agreed with it."

"All right." He leaned over and kissed her again, first on the forehead, and then again on the lips. "Guess we'll put Sarah in charge of the wedding, then." His brown eyes were serious, as he looked at her. "You were right—I have no idea what I'm going to do with my life. I don't think, living in a little town like this, I can get by just playing poker."

"The locals are likely to catch on to just how good you are pretty fast. And there aren't enough travelers coming through for you to make it your business, no. Anyway, professional gambler is not on my approved list of professions for a husband-to-be."

He nodded. "I suppose not. Anna, I'm proud of who you are and what you do, but I can't just let my wife support me."

"You'll figure it out. *We'll* figure it out. We've got time. You can start by getting the old house in shape for us to move in." She frowned. "Have you seen that big empty house on the edge of town? The white one with the wraparound porch?"

"Jonathan showed it to me, awhile back."

"Ah-ha!" she said, with a twinkle in her eye. "Marrying me for my property, eh? Which by law will belong to you, anyway."

"Not if I can help it," he responded. "Jonathan told me there's a trust or something you can set up, ways around all this."

"If we're married, shouldn't everything be ours? Not yours, not mine," she said. "Ours together. We'll draw something up, figure that out, too. Anyway, what about Ed? Will he stay? There's plenty of room in the house."

"Yeah, I expect so," he said. "There was a girl down in Arizona he had his sights on, but for some reason it just didn't take. Anyway, him and me, we do better when we're together. Always have, practically since the first day we met. You don't mind that he's part of the package, do you?"

"You have a problem with me and Jonathan?"

"Of course not."

"Well, then. We each have a partner—fair's only fair."

"You really are an unnatural woman," he said, and kissed her again. "Anyway, I'd better go fetch Sarah, so that the two of you can get this wedding thing planned. I'm not letting you stay single a moment longer than necessary."

"Agreed," she said. Without thinking, she put a hand to her midsection. "There are no secrets in a town like this one, and I suspect that everyone knows that I'm expecting already. Still, I'd just as soon get on with things before I start to get any bigger." And she took his hand in hers, and held it there for a moment.

There was a Russian novel that she'd been reading before she fell ill, one that had recently been translated into English. The author began it by saying that happy families were all alike, but unhappy ones were each unhappy in their own way. *But we,* she thought, *are going to be happy in a way all our own.*

And so, as it turned out, they were.

Epilogue

Two years later…

"Have you got the papers drawn up on the Hawthorne matter, yet?" Anna turned to face her partner, at his desk across the room.

"Yes. We're filing them tomorrow, in Helena. Sorry you can't be there."

Anna glanced down, somewhat ruefully, at her distended belly, covered in what felt like acres of dark calico. "It wouldn't be wise to travel when I'm this far along. Anyhow, it seems that some folks think it's not quite decent for me to be seen in public, when my indelicate condition is so obvious."

"People are funny, that's for sure," Jonathan agreed. "Where do they think they came from?"

There was a clattering on the staircase from the rooms upstairs. Shortly after their marriage, she and Jeremiah had moved into the big white house on the edge of town, taking Caroline and Ed along with them. The rooms upstairs from the office, where Anna had lived, had been turned into a day nursery, so that mother and child could always be close together, even when her hours at work were long. A little girl with golden curls made her way down the stairs, with slightly unsteady steps. Caroline was close behind her.

Having successfully navigated the stairs, Alice sped up, and flung herself at her mother, whispering a greeting to the soon-to-be sister or brother inside her mother's tummy.

"Hello, my brave girl," said Anna, stroking her daughter's hair. "Are you ready for our afternoon walk?"

"Yes!" said the child. "See Daddy?"

"Of course, sweetheart."

Caroline settled down at Anna's desk with a book, waving at Alice as she walked out the door. The child held her mother's hand, and waved back with the other. "Bye, Caro!" she called. "Bye, Jon'than!"

They walked down the street slowly, nearly everyone in town stopping to speak with the little girl and her mother as they passed, ranging from the sheriff to the shopkeepers, even to an overly rouged young lady from the saloon. They reached the livery stable, which Ed Marcus had taken over from its former owner the winter before last, and went inside to say hello.

"You'll be home for dinner tonight, won't you, Ed?" Anna asked, as Alice uttered a cry of delight, and ran to Ed's dog, Blue. "Sarah's making something really special."

The former outlaw looked a little sheepish, his blue eyes not quite meeting hers. "Guess I can arrange that. I'll get Bob to work this evening." He'd always had an easy way with women, flirting and romancing and breaking hearts, but where Sarah was concerned, he was a whole different man, hesitant and sincere.

Anna shook her head. "She asked specially if you'd be home. Ed, her divorce has been final for nearly a year. If you don't start courting her soon, someone else is going to close the deal before you've even let her know you're interested."

It was not easy to have a divorce granted, but after the last, and worst of the beatings, the one she couldn't hide, even Ray Powell's own father had taken Sarah's part. He'd worked alongside Anna to make sure the young woman regained her freedom, and Sarah, too, had moved into the big white house on the edge of town. Ray had moved to Chicago, to take a position with the Cattlemen's Association, shortly afterward; he and Nick no longer spoke.

Ed gave her a look, and turned away to look at the little girl romping with the dog. "The question is whether *she's* interested, after everything she's been through."

"She asked especially if you'd be home. She's been doing that a lot, lately. I know business has been booming, but you've really got to step up, Ed. That is, if you're sure how you feel about her."

He nodded. "Never surer of anything in my life. See you this evening, then."

Alice reluctantly pulled herself away from her canine friend and took her mother's hand once more. "Bye-bye, Blue!"

But they turned a corner, and a few doors down, they reached their final goal, the offices of the *Carter's Creek Chronicle.* Jeremiah Brown was setting type when they arrived, but he quickly put down the tray of letters, and hurried toward his wife and daughter. "How are my best girls?" He kissed Anna, and took Alice up in his arms.

"The size of a whale," complained Anna, "and unable to join my partner in court in Helena tomorrow. Both of which are entirely your fault, directly or indirectly, and I find myself having great difficulty forgiving you." But she gave the lie to her words, by slipping her arm around her husband's waist, and snuggling up to him. "What do you think, Jeremiah? I can say without a doubt that I am the happiest, luckiest pregnant lawyer in all of Montana."

Jeremiah resisted pointing out the extreme unlikelihood

that she had any competition in that category, and instead, he kissed his wife again. "Guess I'm pretty lucky, too. For a no-account outlaw, that is." And he looked at her, and smiled one of those brilliant smiles of his, and though she was tempted to respond, she decided to let him have the last word, after all.

About the Author

Cate Simon is a former lawyer who discovered she enjoyed storytelling far more than litigation and went back to graduate school for Victorian literature. Although she loves her current job, teaching writing and speculative fiction to STEM students, she really missed the 19th century. Having discovered, doing her dissertation research, that there were women lawyers in the United States as early as 1869, she realized she had found the perfect subject to combine her interests, and now writes historical fiction. She lives in Manhattan's East Village with her partner and perhaps too many cats.

She can be found at the following:

Website: www.catesimon.com

Facebook: www.facebook.com/catesimonbooks

Instagram: www.instagram.com/cate_simon_books/

Made in United States
North Haven, CT
11 February 2023

32424447R00153